TRAITOR WITCH

THE BONEGATES SERIES

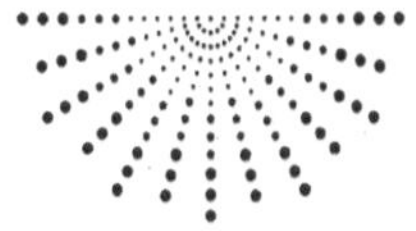

ASHLEY MCLEO

MERAKI PRESS

For Flicka, my Naela.

CHAPTER ONE

LANA

A shock of energy zapped my arm the instant I extended it out the window. I yanked it back, a stream of swear words leaving my lips. Tears stung my eyes, but they weren't from the pain.

I was bloody furious.

Spinning away from the window, I threw myself on the bed. The cup and saucer atop the bedside table shook from the impact. I rolled over to look at the ceiling, papered in a gold design, and scowled. This room was a far nicer prison than the dungeon Pari locked us inside before, but it was a prison all the same.

The morning soldiers relocated us to our new, posh room. Queen Pari claimed she wished to speak with Crystal and me. However, days had passed and the meeting had yet to take place. She'd disappeared.

No one knew where she was, or what she was doing. Or at least, they wouldn't tell me.

Yet, I thought I knew what the Queen of Buyan was planning. As always, Queen Pari was playing mind games—her specialty. I hadn't been in Buyan long, but I was dead tired of such games already. I almost wished she'd get on with it and torture me for information.

A shriek pierced the walls.

"Not again." I rolled my eyes.

Crystal demanded answers from whoever was unfortunate enough to walk into her room. She'd been acting that way for days, questioning the servants who brought us our meals or drew our baths. While I related to her anger, even I was sick of my sister's tantrums.

Most likely, the servants didn't know a damn thing, so yelling at them was a waste of time. Pari would keep us here for weeks. Perhaps months. She would bore us to tears and hope to break us, so we'd share our father's secrets. She wanted to see the annihilation of Lyonesse and everyone we cared for in Faerie.

Too bad for her, I would not break.

Crystal's door slammed shut, and as if someone had flipped a light switch, the shrieking ceased. I knew what came next, so I counted down—three, two, one.

Thunk! The door adjoining our rooms flung open,

hitting the back wall. My half-sister stormed in, her face as red as her hair. Her impressive muscles, courtesy of her mother's dwarf blood and years of elite-level gymnastics training, popped with every tense step.

"I swear if they don't let me out soon, I'll—"

"Scream your head off? That's really shown them so far." My eyebrows arched in challenge, and she glowered back at me, her light brown eyes blazing. "There's a line of guards outside and we're only two people."

She didn't look convinced, so I added. "Two people locked in spaces specifically warded against our magic."

Crystal's growling grated my ears as she tipped her chin to the ceiling.

"Might as well make yourself comfortable." I patted my bed. "Perhaps we should play cards again? Until Queen Pari calls for us, we're not going anywhere."

My sister's shoulders slumped. Unlike me, she wasn't accustomed to people ignoring her. Crystal was tops at everything, so she was used to being seen, heard and respected.

I, on the other hand, had been a wallflower most of my life. Living in obscurity was my wheelhouse. I used to like it, to thrive there. Not so much anymore, but the practice helped in a situation such as this one.

"I know," Crystal sank into my bed, her fists

clenched in her lap. "I just want some damn answers. And to leave my freaking room."

Clearly, she wasn't up for cards. I turned to face her, wanting to listen and make her feel better.

"Why did Pari move us out of the dungeons?" Crystal continued. "If we're her prisoners, which we *totally* are, it makes no sense. I'm more likely to talk freezing my ass off in a cell, than I am under a comfy blanket with a full belly."

"Mind games." I tapped my temple.

"How do you mean?"

I wanted to laugh. As far as I was concerned Crystal was aces at mind games, but I supposed this was a new level of manipulation, even for her.

"She might be using reverse psychology on us," I said. "Or maybe she's taking her cues from history. In the Old Land, people used to keep wards or hostages, as part of their courts. The hosts treated their wards well enough, sometimes like family. At least, they treated them well until their bloodline misbehaved or the ward acted out. They were like a bargaining chip."

History had never been my passion, but my child-hood bestie, Finn, loved to tell tales about wronged youths seeking revenge. Most often he'd spin his yarn over a pint and earn himself another from a charmed tourist visiting Dublin. They couldn't resist him.

I used to roll my eyes when he got to putting on a

show. Now I'd do anything to hear one of his stories again. To know he was safe and unharmed.

"In the books I read about Faerie, they did that too." Crystal's eyebrows furrowed together so tightly that they resembled a red caterpillar. "But I don't know . . . this feels different. Don't you think?"

My shoulders lifted and fell. "Feels like we're being manipulated."

I rose from the bed and walked to the window once more. Fae courtiers strolled below me, dressed in bright, cheerful colors. Children played among them, their laughter tinkling up to my window.

Beyond the wall surrounding the castle, stalls peppered the way and merchants' voices roared. The scent of roasted nuts filled my nostrils. While we were hostages, everyday fae went about their business, buying food, goods and whatever else they needed for their family. It was undeniable that the fae here held themselves differently than those in Lyonesse. In my home kingdom, fae were often hunched over from years of backbreaking work and lack of magic. They were starving, shrunken and weak. A pang of sadness cut through me. Their situation—at least as it stood now—reflected my failure.

Those in Lyonesse would remain downtrodden, all because we cocked up our mission. Had my siblings and I succeeded, Queen Pari would be dead and my father's ancestral bonegate would no longer be in the hands of a thief and a liar. The portal would belong to Lyonesse. Magic would flow freely from the Old Land over the barren, bleak kingdom of Lyonesse, transforming it and filling it with life.

My throat tightened as I gripped the windowsill, anger rising in me again. I'd failed many times in my life, but failing to execute my mission was the most devastating of them all.

The hollow sound of a knock at my door made me whirl about, and my eyes connected with Crystal's. I nodded to her, and she returned the gesture. We were ready, united.

"Enter," I called.

When the door opened, the funniest sensation came over me. My stupid heart sank to find it wasn't Garret standing there, waiting for me and telling me that I was running behind.

Of all the irrational things to think! Why would he be here? In fact, as much as I wished to see him, I was glad he wasn't here. If he were, that would mean he'd been captured in the battle for the bonegate. I highly doubted Pari would allow him a plush room and three square meals a day. I hoped he was home, safe; I had to believe it was true.

"Is there a problem?" the soldier asked. I must have been staring at him strangely.

Straightening to my full height, more like a princess should, I stared the new guard right in the eye. "You're the one who knocked on my door. What do you want?"

"Queen Pari requests your presence." He stepped to the side so we could exit. A contingent of ten other armed soldiers stood behind him.

Crystal hopped off my bed. "About flipping time."

Once we exited my room, the guards closed in around us. Subtly, I tried calling on my power and frowned. It was no use. My gaze shifted to my sister to find her staring at her hands, scowling. Clearly, she'd discovered the same thing.

Pari had the entire castle warded against Crystal and me. Father warned me that the queen's ward-maker was extremely powerful and skilled, and now I was experiencing those qualities firsthand.

"Move!" My steps faltered when a guard shoved me from behind. I tossed him my fiercest glare before continuing my way.

Clad in borrowed satin slippers, my feet made almost no sound on the polished floors as we walked the corridors. One thing was for certain, Pari knew how to keep her hostages comfortable. Between the shoes and the light linen pants and tunic I wore, I felt like a wealthy person on a tropical holiday.

The hallways unraveled before us; endless tunnels of gray stone veined with colorful gems. Rivers of sapphires, amethysts and diamonds wound their way through the stone, coming close to one another on occasion and then veering off into swirls and lines. The beauty of the display mesmerized me.

Had the giants handled the artistry as well as the construction of this fortress? Could their massive hands, each the size of dining room tables, perform such delicate work? It didn't seem likely. I suspected a fae had woven the gems through the stone. Perhaps one gifted in the earth element? Whether it be a giant or fae artist, the effect was gorgeous and it elevated Castle Dalir to rival my father's palace—crafted largely of elegant white marble and gold.

A shriek, followed by a wave of giggles, tore me from my thoughts when a pack of children kicked a ball right into our lead guard's shins.

The soldier, who had been nothing but stern with us, laughed. "This wing is closed." He pointed back the way they came. "Take your game that way."

Small sets of sparkling eyes peered around him and widened as they caught sight of us, the notorious Fullfeather heirs. The monsters who tried to kill their queen. Without a word, the children scurried away.

While I would normally delight in the kids having fun, being little and free-spirited, I couldn't. Their appearance only brought to mind that I'd never seen a single child around that age, eight or so, playing in Lyonesse.

By that age, the children in my kingdom were already working hard to help support their families. If they were lucky, they lived in Castle Phoenix and trained to become guards, or the next generation of

Feathered Fae. Their childhood was yet another thing Queen Pari stole from them.

My fists clenched, but before I could get too wound up, the head guard ground to a stop in front of a beautiful doorway made of solid turquoise and threaded with gold. His calloused hand fell upon the heavy stone three times. A shiver tried to dart down my spine, but I repressed it. The Queen of Buyan would not see a sliver of anxiety from me.

Crystal's sharp eyes met mine, and she, too, looked ready to go to war.

We ride together, I thought, standing taller, prepared to face Queen Pari yet again.

CHAPTER TWO

FINN

I collapsed on my bed, exhausted. Barely a second passed when a splash sounded from the other room. Another followed, more exuberant than the first, and a faint chuckle parted my lips, even as my eyes fell closed.

Kane had wasted no time in returning to his specialized mew and washing the barren wasteland of Lyonesse from his feathers. He'd never liked getting mucked up, not even during a hunt. From the sound of it, he was having a whale of a time too. There would probably be a lake to clean up later.

As suddenly as it started, the splashing stopped and a familiar screeching hit my ear. The pitch was telling. Bloody bird had a bottomless pit of a stomach, much like his handler.

"Someone will be by with your meat soon," I assured him, without opening my eyes.

After the grueling four-day ride to Lyonesse, I needed a bit of time to collect my thoughts. Just a moment to rest before I had to . . . unleash myself.

A groan escaped me. I'd been dreading this moment, but it was inevitable. The darkness, my demon born magic, had been building for days, insisting I let it out. I wouldn't be able to hold it back for much longer and didn't want to discover what would happen if I ignored my new-found magic.

The power that had slain a dozen guards and saved my life.

I swallowed thickly, recalling the night my demon gift had appeared. The blood that had spattered my face. The terror in the soldiers' eyes. I wasn't even sure how I'd let my dark power out the night of our failed assassination attempt. All I knew was that since they appeared, my shadows would not be ignored.

As we neared Castle Phoenix, my siblings started to comment on changes in my appearance. They knew something had happened in Buyan, though not exactly what. I wasn't about to tell them, either. Not yet, anyway. First, I needed to come to terms with it myself.

Opening my eyes, I took in my room—all the reds, whites, and golds. Colors of royalty and my secret family. After losing Lana and Crystal, those colors meant more to me than they ever had.

History books told us that war changed a man. It was true.

A huffed breath left my lungs, and I perched on my elbows, knowing I was out of time. Upon our arrival, a servant told me father was waiting. He expected someone, *me*, to debrief him soon and I had procrastinated long enough. I needed to man up and get this done.

Rising to my feet, I lifted my hands. Fire begged to burst from the fingertips. It was my strongest element, born of my elven blood. I shoved it away, needing another type of release. A darker, demonic one.

Memories of the night in Queen Pari's castle flashed before my eyes. What had happened when I released the shadows that ripped the breath right out of the Buyan soldiers, and tore out others' throats? What had I thought? Felt?

One word sprang to mind…

Fear.

From what Lana had told me over the years, demons were the lowest of the magical low. They possessed ultimate power, but no humanity. They thrived on negative emotions, like fear, jealousy, hate and rage. It was really no wonder my demon gift appeared in Buyan. I'd never experienced fear like that before; not even during the Successional.

On the flip side, I'd also never felt so powerful. That scared the hell out of me, but I knew it was better to conquer the power than to let it command me.

So, what was I missing?

Another memory slipped into my head. The feeling of my sword running through a Buyan guard, who had nearly sliced Gio's head off, made my hand tingle. I'd killed him, but I'd also been too careless in the execution, and somehow cut myself open too. As my blood spilled, the shadows poured forth alongside it.

That was it. The precise moment.

My demon gift required blood, my blood and some type of negative emotion. Blood and fear.

"Bloody demons," I muttered.

I had yet to change out of my traveling clothes, so my dagger still hung from my hip. Yanking it out of the scabbard, I pressed the blade into my palm. Blood welled, beading red against my dirt-caked skin. I closed my eyes and dragged up memories that would elicit emotion.

The first moment guards ambushed us inside Castle Dalir. The instant I realized that two of our siblings were missing, one of whom was my best friend since boyhood. And then, finally, the sheer grief, rage and horror I felt when I understood I wouldn't be able to turn around for my sisters. That I couldn't save them.

A lump rose in my throat, and I swallowed it down, but my emotion was not about to be buried. Tears fell from my eyes to streak down my face.

As if I'd called it, a dark wisp of smoke curled

from my blood. Terror trickled through me like ink in water, but I couldn't tear my eyes away. The smoke grew and stretched, and another sensation came over me. Relief—like I'd been under pressure and was now letting off some internal steam.

The smoke continued to expand, twisting and turning until it took on the shape of a small, horned person—an actual demon. It hovered before me, waiting for my say. Curious.

The first time I'd seen the shadows, they had requested no permission to act. They'd moved on instinct, slaughtering the opposing guards in my proximity. They'd acted on *my* instinct. Hating the idea that I could desire such violence subconsciously, I shuddered. I'd always fancied myself more of a scholar than a warrior.

"Climb the walls," I ordered, needing to test the amount of control I had over the dark form in front of me.

The shadow darted across the room. Its feet rushed up the pure white wall, making not a sound and leaving not a mark. After it got to the top, it returned to hover before me. I drew in a deep breath and glanced down at the blood still beading against my skin.

"Another, emerge."

From my blood, another creature bloomed. Even though the pit in my stomach deepened, there was also something in me that rejoiced. My demon born side relished in using this power. I stared at the new creature.

"Fetch me a book from my library."

The younger shadow darted under the door of my personal library. Rustling sounds reached me, as if it was trying to figure out what type of tome I would want. Once the door opened, the creature flew back out, extending the book to me—head bowed. The paperback was one from the Old Land. Smoke curled and twisted around the item, but the hand that held it appeared solid. Disconcerting.

"Thank you. I'd like to be alone now. Can both of you leave?" The question was tentative, laced with fear. Would they leave? I wasn't sure what happened to the original shadows I'd conjured. Were these the same? How many were there? Could they split into more? I hadn't been in a good place to count that night, and since then I hadn't wanted to consider what had happened too hard.

My worries were quelled a second later, when the shadows vanished as if they never existed. My hand swept through the space they'd occupied, but nothing remained. Stunned, I shook my head. What should I do with this newfound power? Clearly, it could be used for good as well as bad. One of them had fetched me a book. There was nothing evil about that.

For some reason, I didn't believe myself.

A knock came at the door, and I groaned softly as

I went to answer—knowing what it would be regarding.

I opened the door to find a goblin. He bowed. "Prince Finn, we've been looking for Lana, but can't find her so your father wishes to see you."

"She's not back yet." The words stuck in my throat. "Tell him that I'll be right there."

Nodding, the goblin darted away. Quickly, I washed my hands and face, in a small effort to be presentable, before leaving my chambers.

As I made my way through the castle, no one approached me. No one dared to ask me questions. Or even wonder if I was all right. Did those in Castle Phoenix already know what had happened? Ryker might have told them. The fae was known for his big mouth.

Usually, I enjoyed Ryker's fun, loquacious nature, but with all the pitying looks being thrown in my direction, I wished that he, or whoever had spoken out of turn, had kept their trap shut.

I rounded the final corner to my father's chambers to find that a petite figure stood at the end. Her piercing green eyes shot through my heart.

Ebba . . . My pace quickened, and I walked toward the soldier until we stood face to face.

"What are you doing here?" Emotion thickened my voice. Since I had learned that many died at the battle for the bonegate, I'd been trying my best not to think my friends were among the slain. Seeing

Ebba made me realize that I'd feared the worst for her.

Every time I looked at Ebba, I yearned to stroke her hair, to run my finger across her plump bottom lip, to kiss her senseless. This woman was something special, and I wanted her, but she did not seem to return my affections. Or if she did, she kept her feelings well hidden.

As if she could hear my thoughts, her cheeks grew pink, and she looked away briefly. "I heard you had finally arrived, and the king was calling for the highest-ranking official. Rather than run all around the castle searching, I figured I'd wait for you here."

"I'm glad you did." I nodded. "Are Sai and Garret back too?"

"Yes. We're all fine. Garret is distraught over Lana, but he's alive." Her gorgeous eyes became doleful, an expression I'd rarely seen on her face, which I'd studied as often as possible. "I'm so sorry about Lana and Crystal."

A deep breath made its way into my lungs. "Thank you . . . I shouldn't keep Father waiting any longer."

With a small nod, Ebba reached for my hands, awkwardly patting them. "Good luck. I'm sure His Majesty will come up with a plan to get them back."

"I'm sure too." I offered her what I hoped was a reassuring smile.

My gaze followed her retreating steps, before I

knocked on the white door with a gold feather etched into its surface.

"Enter!"

Taking a steeling breath, I let myself into the king's private chambers. My father sat in a high-backed red chair. His eyes, the same golden shade as Lana's, bored through me.

"Join me, Son."

I sat across from him and immediately began to squirm. It wasn't often I felt uncomfortable around others, but unease hung heavy in the air of the king's private chamber. Without me telling him, he knew something had happened. Something horrible.

After an age, he cleared his throat and laid his hands flat on the table. Rings of gold glinted on his thin fingers. One held a moonstone the size of a quarter, the other showcased a phoenix etched into the metal. The bird's ruby eyes winked up at me.

"I take it that my forces retreated in waves." The tone of his voice, calm and understanding, pulled my gaze away from the jewelry. "I informed my servants to send the highest ranked heir to my chambers when my forces returned. Since you're here, I can only deduce that Lana shall arrive with the second wave leaving Buyan?"

The pit in my stomach deepened. Father had rationalized my appearance, but now I would have to smash his reasoning to bits.

Hoping my proximity might somehow make

things easier, I leaned forward. "Unfortunately, Father, that is not the case." Muscles popped in the king's neck, but I barreled on, unable to take the anxiety mounting in his eyes. "Our mission did not go as planned. Most of our group is safe and back home, but they captured Lana and Crystal."

A lump formed in my throat, forcing me to stop. I gulped it down, trying to remain strong. The most important thing now was to relay the information he needed so that we could make a plan to save Lana and Crystal.

"They were captured, but Pari—?" His voice cracked.

Feeling uncomfortable, I cringed. I'd never been good at breaking bad news. Normally, I was the guy people sought to share a pint and a laugh. The fun guy.

"We infiltrated her castle successfully. Dak and Himari, who were on Lana's team, claim they made it to Queen Pari's rooms . . . but somehow, she knew we were coming. We believe Lana took it upon herself to attack. Victoria says Crystal barreled up the stairs to save her, but neither made it out." I paused, squirmed. The last bit would be what drove the point home for him. "Once we reached a safe distance from the castle, I sent Arlo back to check. He sighted Lana and Crystal being led to the dungeons. Naela was flying around the castle as we left too, calling to Lana."

The intention had been for Kane to return with Lana's familiar, but it hadn't worked. I should have known Naela would never leave my sister and best friend. I shouldn't have done so either. A bloody bird was more heroic than I.

My father's lips pressed together in worry. "A familiar calling for her master." Rising to his feet, he went to the tapestry depicting a map of Faerie. His bone white hands ran over the colorful weaving. "Come here."

When I joined him, my father's eyes shifted to me. He looked like he'd aged a decade since I entered his private chambers.

"This news is unexpected and unfortunate." Father's hand grasped mine tightly—one of the few moments of contact we'd had. Something inside me cracked open as tears filled my eyes. "But I am glad that most of you returned safely." Once again, his golden gaze sought the tapestry. "Certainly, we will find them. Although it might take some time and securing of additional allies. Now that Queen Pari knows of your existence—"

"She'll strengthen the wards. We won't be able to sneak in again." I'd already worked it out on my return journey south. "To get them back, we'll have to infiltrate the city with a larger force. One with no intention of hiding. Or by a different means entirely."

His jaw tightened as he studied the map. "It

appears that I have planning to do. Let me consider our next moves."

A part of me wished we would discuss it sooner, but as an academic, I understood the value of careful thought. Acting on your impulses often got people into trouble. I'd learned that firsthand.

"Yes, Father." Walking to the door, I opened it to exit.

"Finn?"

I turned to see he had moved to the firlon. The enchanted object was alive with flames. In it, I saw the familiar walls of Buyan. The hairs on the back of my neck lifted. "Yes?"

"Is Queen Pari dead?"

My lips pressed together, and I shook my head. "It was all for nothing."

His shoulders, usually straight and proud, slumped. Several long breaths passed before he glanced at me again. "We'll make it right."

His reassurance vibrating through me, I slipped into the hallway with one thing on my mind. I needed to send a message to Lana.

CHAPTER THREE

LANA

A ferocious-looking blonde guard opened the turquoise door. She met my stare, aquamarine eyes flashing, before shifting and allowing us a peek inside the room.

Queen Pari sat at the head of a long table, swathed in white with hints of purple at her wrists and ankles. Upon seeing us, she stood and walked closer.

As she had each time I'd seen her, the queen looked annoyingly gorgeous. The embellished loose tunic she wore hinted at her curves. A gold necklace dipped into her cleavage, and a gold stud nose ring complemented the amethyst touches in her outfit. Her brown skin glowed in the morning light.

Yet, as she drew closer to hover between the door and the table, I noticed dark circles weighed down her eyes. Pari, it seemed, had been losing sleep. Good. She deserved those hideous bags.

"Welcome, ladies. Please, have a seat." Pari motioned at the chairs flanking the table's head. An assortment of foods already dotted the table, mostly pastries and fruit. "Guards, my ladies will take care of the room. Remain outside until we finish our meal."

The door to the breakfast room shut, and a disconcerting *swish* whispered through the stone as a dozen blades hissed out of their scabbards. The blonde guard herded Crystal and me to our seats—one hand clenching the hilt of a broadsword while the other stayed palm up, ready to spew magic should she need to do so. Two other female guards stood against the far wall of the breakfast room, their eyes tracking our every move.

Queen Pari followed my gaze, and her lips turned up at the corners. "At ease, ladies. As you well know, they are weaponless."

The ladies didn't relax in the slightest. One of them, a brunette guard who reminded me a bit of Sai —with her striking violet eyes and dusky complexion —clenched the hilt of her dagger until her knuckles whitened.

Queen Pari sighed as the three of us took our seats. "I'm serious, Bellona. Stand down. In fact, all of you, *sit down*."

My eyes widened as Pari's guards grumbled but obeyed, sliding into seats just a few places down from our own. Her invitation was odd. My father never let servants sit with him.

"Perhaps introductions will ease the tension?" Pari pointed to the tall blonde whose eyes blazed down the table at us. "This is Buyan's Head Lady in Waiting, Isis."

She moved on to Violet Eyes. The woman scowled menacingly. I was pretty sure that she was still clutching her dagger beneath the table.

"Bellona is also a lady in waiting and my Master of Weapons. And last but certainly not least," Pari's long finger floated to the final woman at the table, "Armina, my third lady doubles as Master Wardmaker of Buyan."

A sneer lifted the right corner of Armina's ruby red lips to reveal a hint of gold. So this was Pari's legendary wardmaker. I tilted my head, studying the fae.

"Make no mistake," Armina growled. "Now that your father has played his hand, I have strengthened my wards to include sensitivity to those with human blood too."

"Ladies in waiting, huh?" Crystal leaned back in her chair, her arms crossed over her chest. "I'd always pictured those to be a bit more *fluffy*. You know, wearing ribbons and feathers in their hair and stuff."

Pari laughed. The sound was annoyingly musical. "I'm not surprised. Queens in your world used to choose the most ridiculous women for their court. No talent whatsoever. Here in Buyan, it is common practice for a queen or king to choose the fiercest warriors to be their protectors and closest confidants. These women will rip your head off as easily as they would help me undress."

Pari's words were light, but the warning in them was clear. Isis, Bellona, and Armina took no shit.

Cool as a cucumber, Crystal helped herself to a cup of tea.

"I hope you're finding your new accommodations comfortable?" Pari plucked a strange pastry from a platter and placed it on an amethyst-ringed plate. The sweet scent of it filled my nose, threatening to distract me.

"Besides the whole being locked in my room for four days thing, yes," Crystal answered.

"Ah, well, that was merely a precaution. Now that I have returned, I've seen to it the entire castle is open to you. Warded, of course, but still open for you to explore. If you're to stay here, I'd prefer that you are comfortable."

"Then why lock us in the dungeon in the first place?" I challenged, meeting her stare.

Pari shivered, making me frown.

"Excuse me," she said. "But you look so very much like your father. Especially in the eyes. It's disconcerting." She shook her head. "And to answer your question, it would be foolish of me *not* to place you in the dungeons temporarily. Who would allow two would-be assassins to run amok in their castle before it was properly warded? A dead monarch, that's who."

Crystal snorted, and Pari's lips lifted slightly at the sound.

"I never intended to keep you there, but the dungeons are null magical zones. I needed time to discern your powers."

"Which you got from the blood you took," I quipped. "How barbaric."

Pari sipped her tea. "Yes, we tested your blood. And for good measure we asked the fae we captured at the bonegate about your powers. They all agreed that Lana possesses only light magic, whereas Crystal has enhanced strength from her dwarf lineage as well as air from the Fullfeather line. So far, that seems true."

The fae we captured. My heart fell into my stomach. Did that include Garret? Ebba? Sai? And where were they now?

"You went to the front lines to check out what happened?" Crystal asked. "That's not something queens usually do. Why did you?"

It was a good question. Our father had a pack of advisors he sent to do his bidding. However, on two occasions, he had sent his heirs on missions. The only time I'd seen him leave the castle was during Ration Day. Then again, no one had recently attacked his land. The situation wasn't exactly apples to apples.

"I had people stationed at the bonegate. I needed to be sure that healers were seeing to them. And as their queen, it is my duty to bless the dead." Pari's eyelids lowered, and a fierce queen, the one I'd seen the night of our failed assassination, appeared.

"How were things?" Crystal's tone remained casual, as if she couldn't care less about what happened. Or the dead. Her feigned nonchalance couldn't be further from the truth. We both cared deeply about the outcome of the attack.

Leaning forward in her chair, Pari placed her elbows on the table and tented her fingers. "The death toll was in the hundreds. Your father's fallen have been buried with respect next to the bonegate. Other than a monumental loss of life, the circumstances of our kingdoms have not changed. If it had, I would not be here."

My heart broke. So many had died for nothing. Though I figured Pari still held our father's ancestral bonegate, I'd hoped to be wrong. Even after we failed, I'd hoped that my father's army had gotten away unscathed. But no, the mission and diversion my father had painstakingly orchestrated had all been wasted.

Servants filed into the room, carrying more platters of food—savory by the smell. I was thankful for their interruption. I needed time to think, to soak in what the queen said. Platters landed on the table, and Pari helped herself.

Mindful of the possibility of poison, I waited until the queen chose what she fancied and selected the same food as her. Once everyone had a full plate, Pari cleared her throat, breaking the thick tension. "If you are open to it, I'd like to tell you something about your father and me?"

My eyes flew across the table to meet Crystal's gaze. Was it wise to listen to what Queen Pari had to say? Surely it would be manipulation. She'd seen what Crystal and I could do, and probably wanted us on her side. Then again . . . my attention shifted to Armina, Isis, and Bellona, all hunkered down over full plates and watching us like Naela watched her prey. Isis, in particular, looked as though she may tear my head off if I refused to listen.

"As if we have much of a choice." I gestured to Pari's ladies in waiting.

The queen's lips lifted into a small smile. "You'll have to excuse them. We've been together a long time, and they're quite protective of me. But you *do* have a choice. Leave now, if you don't want to hear what I have to say. I won't stop you. Neither will they."

How foolish did she think I was? It was better to know what the enemy was thinking. We had to level the playing field before we made any rash decisions. I took a bite of a delectable, buttery pastry and leaned back in my chair.

"I'll listen."

"Then I'll get to it." Pari's hand trembled as she

pulled an aged Polaroid from her pocket and laid it on the table.

My gaze latched onto the photo, so out of place in Faerie. A flash of white caught my attention first, then long white-blond hair.

In the photo, a younger version of Pari and my father beamed at the camera. She was perched on his lap, all dressed in white, much as she was now. Strangely, my father was not wearing white, which he, too, favored. He wore pants and a loose top of brilliant blue. He smiled for the photo, but his eyes were locked on Pari. It was clear that in that long-ago moment the couple was deeply in love.

Mind games, I reminded myself. No doubt Pari had been planning this moment since she locked us up. She'd probably been banking on the idea that we knew nothing about their engagement. Unfortunately for her, I'd learned that the royals were childhood friends months ago. Additionally, Ebba had told us about their romance on the way to Buyan.

And yet, the evidence was still hard to swallow.

"What is this?" Pushing her plate to the side, Crystal snatched the Polaroid.

Armina thrust back her chair, a sharp blade in her hand and her lips bared to reveal a full mouth of pointed golden teeth.

I gulped. That wasn't creepy at all.

"Sit, Armina," Pari commanded, and the black-haired fae lowered herself, her inky eyes never leaving Crystal.

"That is a photo of your father and me on the day of our official betrothal," Pari answered.

"It's a Polaroid!" Crystal hissed. "I haven't seen one of those in Faerie."

"We had taken a clandestine trip to the human world, where he proposed," the queen replied. "This photo was our way of documenting the moment. Soon after, we returned home and announced our engagement. We were one of the lucky few from the royal couples allowed to choose who we wished to spend our lives with. Our parents could not have been happier when we chose each other, as our kingdoms had always been close." When Pari gazed at the picture again, her hand lifted to wipe away the tears forming in her eyes.

Shite, she was an excellent actress.

"He never mentioned this," Crystal murmured.

Her words made my stomach churn. Crystal hadn't known? I tried to remember. She hadn't been close to Ebba during the march to Buyan, and I supposed no one had brought it up to her before, like Garret had to me.

"Which doesn't make sense," my sister continued. "Why wouldn't he say something about it? Especially since we were to . . ."

Pari raised an eyebrow. "Kill me?"

Crystal turned to me. "And why don't you seem

surprised? Did he tell you? Because there's no way in hell you'd figure this out on your own if I didn't."

The insult made me bristle. It was no secret that Crystal was more intelligent than me, but why did she have to point it out in front of the enemy like that?

"Ebba told me on our way here," I replied. "Father broke off his engagement because of something his fiancée did. He went into a long depression afterward."

Again, the musical tinkle of Pari's laughter filled the room. "I have to say, this role reversal thing is getting rather old."

"Don't listen to her, Crystal," I pressed. "She plans to infiltrate our minds and turn us away from what is good and right."

"Pardon me for saying this, my dear, but I believe that gryphon has already taken flight." Pari leaned back in her seat. "Now, if you don't mind, I'd like to get on with my tale?"

"No one's stopping you from telling your *tale*." I snorted.

Crystal jerked her head in a tight nod.

"After our engagement we spent many months together, each living in the other's castle to ensure we were compatible. Our kingdoms were happy to see us together." A sad smile crossed Pari's face.

I rolled my eyes. Bloody hell, she was really playing this up.

"We were a month away from our wedding day,

when your father approached me with an idea that would alter the course of our kingdoms. In Faerie, each ruler retains primary rights to their inherited kingdom. So, although Oberon's title would be the King of Buyan, in Buyan, I would still outrank him. Meaning, I would retain control over my people and army. My say would be final, just as his would be in Lyonesse. Therefore, when he came to me with the question, it was because he needed to be sure I'd comply with his plan."

"Can you spit it out?" I snapped. "What's this so-called plan?" My fingers did air quotes around my words.

Pari's gaze bored into mine. "Oberon wished to use the bonegates to infiltrate the Old Land and conquer your world."

CHAPTER FOUR

Glinting swords pointed at me as I burst out of the breakfast room. A guard grabbed me by the shoulders, and my magic flared to life, only to fizzle a second later. Fecking wards!

Falling back on more mundane defenses, I shoved the guard away, but before I took two more steps other wankers fell upon me.

"Release her."

Every head turned to find the queen of lies herself standing in the breakfast room's doorway.

"Are you sure, My Queen?" A guard asked, his grip tight on my arm.

"Captain." Once Pari's dark gaze leveled the guard, he released me, taking a step backward.

Right behind Pari, Bellona jostled to the side. A flash of red appeared as Crystal shoved her way through the line of ladies in waiting.

"Don't touch my sister," she hissed. Though she wasn't able to use magic, the venom in her tone could curl hairs. The guards shuffled, unsure what to do about two aggressive adversaries being allowed to walk free.

"Show Lana and Crystal back to their rooms," Pari commanded. "Armina, go with them."

Not about to wait for anyone, I took off, stomping down the hallway and praying that I remembered the way to our quarters. Luckily, Crystal and the same guard who'd led us to breakfast jogged to join me, but sharp, clipped footsteps told me Armina hung behind us.

My cheeks scorched as we moved through the halls of the castle, but before I could work myself into a frenzy, a whiff of myrrh filled my nostrils. My magic pulled deeper inside me as if it were constricting into a small ball. The wardmaker was at work.

I glanced over my shoulder and repressed a shudder as Armina's black eyes locked with mine. Her lips curved into a spiky-toothed smile.

Shifting my attention to Crystal, I noted the indent in her cheek as she gnawed at it from the inside. What was going through that meticulous brain of hers? My pace quickened, desperate to reach our rooms and discuss what we'd heard.

Lies. Lies. Lies. It would take more than a sappy photo and a story to fool me.

Our escort halted in front of our doors, and I

waited for him to unlock mine before yanking Crystal inside.

"The nerve of Pari!" I hissed after slamming the door shut. "How dare she think we're going to roll over and fall in line with her story! Doesn't she realize everyone in Lyonesse told us all about the horrific things she's done! She's mental!"

Crystal said nothing, choosing instead to walk straight past me and jump on my freshly made bed.

My gaze inspected the place. Someone had tidied my room. The nightgown I'd worn last night had been replaced with a new one, alongside new clothing. The garments lay folded on the bench at the foot of my bed, ready for me to wear tomorrow. As expected, the outfit I wore upon arriving in Buyan was still absent. Although the bones of Kate and Kumar, circular and shining, were on the bench. They might have taken my clothes but they had not taken the tokens given to me after the Successional. The tokens that, theoretically, gave me access to my deceased siblings' power, though I'd never use them for that purpose. I just liked to keep the memory of them close. I missed them terribly and their bones had traveled with me to Zatus and now Buyan. I was grateful the servants who cleaned the room hadn't taken a part of my past.

My gaze landed on the fresh clothing, annoyance at what had happened rising within me again. Nor would I let them shape my future. I picked up the clothing, stomped over to my window, and hurled them outside. Great satisfaction coursed through me, as the wards didn't stop them from dropping to the ground.

When I turned around, Crystal shook her head as if I'd chucked a million euro out the window.

"She can't buy me. I'm only keeping this on because I *need* something to wear." I gestured at the loose trousers and a tunic I wore. "When they return my normal clothes, these will meet the same fate."

"Normal clothes? You mean our armor? The filth we traveled here in?" She rolled her eyes. "You've got to be kidding. You'd rather be dirty? Even I'm not that ridiculous, and *believe me* chic, I can hold a grudge with the best of them."

I blinked at her brashness, but brushed off the comment. "Whatever. Why am I the only one freaking out here?"

Crystal's eyebrows threatened to disappear into her hairline. "Is that an actual question? You're the only one freaking out because you never *take a pause* before you make a move."

"Says the girl screaming at servants to give her information whenever they bring her tea."

"A calculated choice," Crystal assured me. "Although they piss me off pretty often, that's another matter. Who in the world wants their milk warm?"

"Back to the topic," I pressed, not caring about warm milk or anything other than what we'd just heard. "Or I'm going to try and bust down the ward outside my window and run to Lyonesse."

She rose to her feet and began pacing my room. "Jesus, Lana. You're smart, but your emotions get out of control. When something affects you, it *really* affects you. Your actions become reactive."

"Excuse me?" Why were we still talking about me?

"It was one of the first things I noticed about you when you were training for the Successional. If things don't work out your way, you flail and often explode. You don't take time to consider *all the options*."

My hands landed on my hips. "Funnily enough, I still beat you in the tournament."

Crystal scoffed. "And that still amazes the crap out of me! The way you were running about saving everyone. Crashing through the jungle like no one could hear you? If Pari is playing mind games with us, shouldn't we play them right back?"

"We haven't had the chance."

"Also, I have a question for you." Crystal's eyes blazed into me. "Why didn't you tell me about their relationship? I understand why you didn't before the assassination attempt. Who cared when we were supposed to kill her?" She halted her pacing and leaned against the bedpost. "You can't tell me it didn't cross your mind since we've been holed up in these rooms? You've had nothing but time. Strategically, me knowing about their past would have been beneficial to both of us."

Shite. Heat moved up my neck, creating the unattractive red blotches that dotted my face whenever I felt humiliated. After what seemed like an incredibly long time, but couldn't have been over thirty seconds, Crystal loosed a huff.

"Imagine how that exchange could have gone had you filled me in ahead of time? Pari would be stupid not to bring something like that up." Crystal strode up to me, a vein in her neck throbbing. "If we want to get out of here, we *have* to work together. That being said, is there anything else that you've kept to yourself in a pathetic attempt to feel in control?"

She was right. I'd buggered it up. How many times was that? Too many to count. It couldn't happen again.

"No more surprises."

Her shoulders eased a smidge. "Good. Then, if you don't mind, I'm going to go to my room and consider how best to proceed. I suggest you do the same." Turning on her heel, Crystal left my chambers.

After she disappeared, I fell back on the bed to think, which I did, tirelessly, endlessly, for hours. It wasn't until a servant brought in a late lunch—caj, a salad, and a side of bread—that I did something other than consider how best to beat Pari. And that was only because I was famished.

The servant set down my tray with trembling hands. She reminded me of Tess, my goblin maid at Castle Phoenix. Despite my attempts at trying to befriend Tess, she remained wary of me. This fae seemed anxious in my presence, too. Once done, she stood there, watching me.

A sigh gusted out of me. "Can I help you with something?"

"Queen Pari," the queen's name was but a squeak coming out of the fae's mouth, "would very much like it if you came to the dinner feast tonight."

I shot out of my chair. "Is she serious? I'm never sitting at the same table as that liar ever again!"

The servant's eyes narrowed. My slight on her precious queen had strengthened her resolve. "With all due respect, Princess Lana, you shall not be sitting with My Queen. Only her ladies and invited guests sit with her. She's only asked that you leave your room. Everyone else enjoys our meals together."

My spine straightened. "Oh."

I supposed I should have expected that. In Lyonesse I'd also sat among the guards, nobles, and people invited to supper at the castle. My father and my brother, Casimir, Crown Prince of Lyonesse, always sat at the head table. Sometimes they shared it with guests, but they were often alone.

Mulling over the idea of eating in the great hall, I quickly concluded that sitting among Pari's people might be a gift. No doubt the queen was good at maintaining and covering up her lies, but she couldn't expect her *entire* kingdom to be so secretive. Or even believe her. Perhaps I'd find allies amongst the common people.

"Fine. I accept. What time is dinner?"

The servant nodded, pleased I'd come to my senses. "When the sixth bell tolls. A guard will show you the way."

"Thank you."

She inclined her head. "Additionally, My Queen reiterates that the castle grounds are open to you. As long as a guard is with you at all times, you may roam."

That gave me an idea. "Can you send a guard in a half an hour? I'd like to get some air after I eat lunch."

"As you wish, princess," the servant said and left my room.

Half an hour later, a smiling and jovial guard who introduced himself as Tau arrived at my door. He claimed he was to be my regular escort during the day.

At first, I didn't like the idea of having one person watching over me. They would notice too much. After considering it a bit more, however, I decided that if I had to have a shadow following me around, he would be ideal.

Tau was young, about twenty, with a shock of blue hair that made him stand out in a crowd. His lanky limbs and thin frame gave the impression that I could overpower him, even without my magic. He smiled easily and even tried to joke with me. Sometimes he pointed out areas of interest in the castle.

His cheerfulness was annoying, but I let him ramble. If I wanted to escape, I needed to gather information.

We had finished a tour of the gardens, a riot of green and tropical flora, when I requested to return to my room. Tau agreed it was time, and to my surprise, he turned in the opposite direction I would have gone.

"Isn't my room that way?" I gestured the way we'd come.

"Yes, but you can also go this way. It's quicker."

I followed him, figuring it was better to know more of the castle than not. It was during the detour that I happened upon the most stunning part of the structure yet.

The rest of Castle Dalir's walls were rich in gemstones, and very luxurious looking, but the gorgeous corridor I spotted took luxury to a new level. The entire length of it was plated with solid gold that was dotted with amethyst, diamond and sapphire stones.

"What's down there?"

"That's the queen's wing. Nice, isn't it?"

No, it wasn't the queen's wing. That was one floor above us, as I'd seen in the firlon. My eyebrows furrowed. For the first time since I'd opened the door to my room and commanded him to show me around, Tau recoiled slightly.

"Ah, that's right. You know where our queen sleeps."

"So why are you telling me something different?"

"Our queen requires more than one set of rooms. She may sleep on the floor above yours, but her favorite personal chamber, a study of sorts, is down this hall. I've heard it's the same with your father, though never having been to Lyonesse, I cannot say for sure."

Pari had a private study, too. I should have expected that. What was the point of being a royal if you didn't have a room for every purpose? What did her study have in it? A firlon like my father's chambers? What other sort of magical items might be inside?

My silence set Tau on edge, and he fidgeted. "Her ladies reside down here as well. Close enough to defend the queen on a moment's notice, with the stairways connecting her bedroom suite to theirs, but far enough away to ensure privacy."

"What else is down there?"

"Nothing. Or if there is, I can't tell you. It's forbidden to anyone but the queen and her ladies to enter those rooms. Unless invited, of course."

Forbidden. People hid things in forbidden rooms. Maybe in there I'd find morsels of the truth? Proof that the queen was a monster? If I could do so and get a few guards on my side, Crystal and I might be able to escape.

Tau cleared his throat. "I've heard your father requires an entire wing to himself. Is it as large? I find it hard to believe anyone would need so much space, but what do I know? My family shares one cottage. I plan to move out as soon as I earn enough to buy a place of my own."

"That's nice," I murmured. Clearly my staring at the queen's private wing was freaking him out, but I didn't care. I just knew that if there was something that incriminated Pari, she would keep it down there.

Yet, her ladies slept down the gilded hall . . . . I shuddered at the thought of trying to investigate and running into Armina. Or worse, choosing the wrong door and walking into her room. What would I say? What would she do?

"Princess? We really must get on if you want to be on time for dinner."

"Right. We should get moving. I'll change quickly." I threw one last glance down the glittering hallway before making my way back to my room to prepare for the feast.

An hour later, after cleaning up, I entered the great hall. My eyes widened, taking in the scenery.

Color was everywhere, a visual feast. Live music played in the corner of the room, a mix of harp and an unidentifiable horn. The most striking of all, were the dancers who moved gracefully between tables.

Was Pari putting on a show for Crystal and me? Or was this a normal meal at Dalir? I glanced at Tau, my escort, finding no sign of shock. Normal then.

My neck craned, searching for Crystal's bright red head. We hadn't seen each other since that morning, and I had a lot to talk about with her. A minute later, I found her at a table by herself. As I approached, a troop of servants practically assaulted me, each asking my preference on a specific course. I mumbled a reply and pressed forward.

"Can we talk?" I asked, sitting down across from her. Right away, a bowl of soup and plate of bread landed in front of me.

"Wait until you get your main course, though. Fewer ears." She nodded to my right.

My gaze followed hers to find three of the servants who'd taken my order behind me, waiting for me to finish the soup to retrieve my next course. The service was a bit over the top.

Filling the minutes with small talk, I ate my way through the menu. As soon as I took the last bite of my main course—a leg of cooked bird with bright purple and pink turnip looking things—I turned again. Only one servant waited behind me now. That was as good as it would get.

I leaned closer to my sister. "I spent the day wandering and came across a hallway I want to explore. It looks like a place where Pari would hide evidence of her misdeeds. A study, perhaps. Problem is that her ladies in waiting also sleep in the hallway."

Crystal set her fork down and shook her head disappointedly. "That's what you did all day? Did you put any thought into what we learned this morning?"

My mouth fell open. "Course, I did. It's obvious what's happening. As soon as we get enough evidence, we can convince a guard to help us, or at least allow us to slip out of here." I paused. "Why, what did you do all day then?"

"Fell back on my training."

"What?"

"In med school, we're told patients will lie. They're embarrassed. Or they want something badly —like drugs. You have to think 'what's the motive here'."

"So, you . . . looked for Queen Pari's motive? More power, right?"

Crystal glanced around before returning her gaze to me. "I don't think so."

My lips pressed together, but I said nothing, waiting for her to finish.

"I went over what Pari said in minute detail. Then I tried to piece together everything I've learned since coming here. It's been a rough few hours, but very eye opening. And not in a way you're going to like."

"How do you mean?"

She inhaled deeply and placed her hands on the table. "Lana, I think I believe Pari."

Every muscle in my body stiffened. Of all the things she could have said, that was the most unexpected. "What?"

"I believe Queen Pari."

My teeth gnashed together. "Why? You've only known her a day, yet you've known our father for—"

"Four months," Crystal hissed. "And consider all that we've been through! No, never mind, don't do that yet. First, listen." She leaned in so close our noses were practically touching. "It all comes down to incentive. What motive did Pari have to steal Oberon's bonegate? Especially when they were in love, and she'd lose everything?"

As much as I wanted to deny that they looked like lovers in the photo, I couldn't. And not only because of the pictures. Father had told me they were together, in love. I'd seen the pain on his face, too.

"A person willing to give up a love like that," Crystal continued, her tone low, "to betray their other half, would only do so for some higher duty, like her calling as a queen." She gestured behind her to the fae in the hall. "Have you noticed how happy her people are here? The guards smile all the damn time. Children run and play. People love their lives."

Frustrated, I dragged my fingers down my face. "The fae in Lyonesse are happy too! It's like you don't have eyes."

"They're not happy." Crystal's lips flattened. "They're *hopeful*. Hopeful our father will change things and make their lives better. And maybe he will, but at what cost?"

"I . . ." I trailed off, unsure.

"I just think that he's hidden one thing too many, and his *motives* don't line up."

I shot out of my chair, at my limit. All around, fae stiffened. Magic crackled inside me, but Armina's wards proved strong and sturdy.

"What do you know about the motives of a king?"

Crystal's eyes narrowed slightly before she caught herself. "Not much, I guess. But I know lots of fathers. He doesn't act like any of them."

"We're not in the Old Land. This is a whole new world. One where our father is responsible for thousands of people." I needed to make her see sense. Crystal and I had just become friends. She was my only ally in this place.

"Still . . . I just have a gut feeling, Lana. He's up to something and Queen Pari is telling the truth."

"A gut feeling!" I hissed. Where was the coldly calculating woman I'd fought in the Successional? "Are you bloody serious right now?"

"I am. I believe the queen. Our father is not acting right. From the day he knocked up Mom something has been off about this." When she included her other parent, a switch flipped. Memories of our conversations in the dungeons rolled through my mind.

I shook my head "I should have known. You spoke so poorly of your own Mam earlier. Why not spread a little disappointment around to the other parent who failed you? No one is ever good enough for you to *really* connect yourself to, are they?"

Crystal rose, her hands pressing into the table. "I may have said a few things about my mom, but you have no right to judge me on that. If she was here, she'd—"

"She'd what? Say you're being a fool? That's what my mam would say. Sinkers, I *wish* Mam was part fae. Then she could cross into Faerie and knock some sense into you."

My wish to see Mam increased tenfold. It was a selfish desire, but I couldn't help it. I missed her. Thankfully, Mam didn't have a drop of fae blood to see her through the bonegates. She was safe and far away from Queen Pari, who might use her against me.

Crystal opened her mouth to argue further, but I'd said my piece. Turning on my heel, I marched out of the great hall.

CHAPTER FIVE

FINN

I gripped the glass container full of salve as I strode away from the healers' tower. The cuts I'd made along my arms and palms to release my shadows were adding up fast. I hoped the balm would minimize the scarring.

If not, I would have to figure out a different way to relieve myself, because one thing was becoming clear: my shadows needed to be let out at least once a day or they terrorized my insides.

Just as I was about to turn back toward my rooms, a roar hit my ear, and my spine straightened. Not that I'd forgotten about the dragon living at Castle Phoenix, more like I didn't have time to go see her. During my time here, I'd only popped by twice to check out the mythical beast. One of those times, I had been on my way back from the healers like I was now.

However, today we didn't have mandatory training. Of course, some of my siblings were sparring for fun, but I wasn't feeling up to it. Although, since I still hadn't heard word from my father about another mission to Buyan, now seemed like a great time to do some dragon-watching.

I crossed the wide hallway to the windows, which were glassless and always open. Wards stabilized the castle's temperature, so you only felt the winter chill when you stood close to the window, like I was now. The big black dragon lay down, spiked tail curling around her body. Guards surrounded her, but they seemed unfazed.

I supposed that if you lived in a world where dragons were normal, you might be that way, but I wasn't. Not yet. Despite living in Faerie for months, I was thankful not to have lost that sense of wonder.

Placing the salve on the windowsill, I opened it, and began applying the balm to my cuts on my forearm as the beast stretched out her legs, grumbling at a guard that got too close.

She looked as ill as she did when we arrived. I knew that Casimir and the king had found her while on a diplomatic mission, but beyond that, I didn't know how the dragon got to Lyonesse. I often wondered why my father kept her here, too. Maybe the next time I saw him, I would ask. Hopefully, that would happen soon. I was dying to know when we'd move to rescue Lana and Crystal, but I also under-stood that well-constructed plans took time.

My fingers dipped into the glass jar, and I applied more balm, trying not to notice how black the veins on my forearm had become. The color always intensi-fied when the shadows wanted to appear, and although they were quiet now, the darkness lingered. I hated it, but as far as I could tell, there was nothing to be done. With a huff, I continued to watch the dragon.

"What are you doing here?"

Startled, I jumped and turned, container still in hand, to find Victoria and Wikolia headed my way. Victoria held her arm awkwardly. She must've injured herself while training with Wikolia.

I pulled down my sleeves swiftly, but it was too late.

Victoria's dark blue eyes had zeroed in on my forearms, her eyebrows raised.

"Why do your veins look black? And what are those cuts from? Are you okay?"

"They're not black. It's nothing. Must have caught the light strangely."

"Don't lie to me. Let me see your arm," Victoria ordered.

I pressed up against the window, and at that exact moment, the dragon roared again, the force of it raising the hairs on the back of my neck.

Wik and Victoria sucked in breaths and raced forward.

"She's awake!" Wikolia squealed.

"Do you come here often to gawk at her?" I teased. Not only was it a change of subject from my strange inky veins and cuts, but I was curious.

"About once a week. More since we returned from Buyan, and we don't have as much to do. She's the ultimate predator."

That I understood. Watching the predator, perhaps even worshiping it, would appeal to the wolf in Wik. In our world, she loomed near to the top of the food chain, but here there was something bigger, stronger, more dangerous than her.

"I haven't been back often," I admitted. "But she is a sight, isn't she?"

"I wonder why they keep her chained up," Victoria mused, the same thing that I had just been questioning. "She hasn't gotten better. They should just let her free. She'll fly to wherever the other dragons are."

"Do you know where that is?" Wik asked me.

When I wasn't training, or at the tavern with the boys, I was usually in the library picking up bits and pieces of information. So, I had acquired a reputation as the scholar among my siblings.

"There's an island off the eastern coast of Faerie. That's where dragons live," I informed her. "It's quite far away. She must have gotten blown off course in the storm or something, and ended up here."

Victoria's lips pursed. "It's so wrong. Dragons can live for a long time. Who would want to spend their time trapped like she is?"

"It would be a shitty way to spend a couple hundred years," Wik quipped.

Frowning, I nodded; I hadn't considered that. I was about to ask if she knew more about dragons in general, when I spotted something odd. Casimir, and an older, bald man wearing red robes, strode through the courtyard—toward the mythical creature.

"What's he up to?" I mused as our white-haired brother marched past the guards, right up to the dragon. When he raised his hands, the beast stood. I blinked.

She studied the crown prince. It almost seemed as if she listened to him, which from what I'd seen was an oddity. Then again, Casimir did have a presence about him. Did the beast recognize it? Did she know that Casimir, to a large extent, was in charge?

The crown prince waved the bald man to his side, and only then did I notice the flask in the man's hand. The pair approached slowly, Casimir never taking his eyes off the creature. If I hadn't been watching so closely, I wouldn't have caught the glint of the blade, nor the dragon's wince.

"That guy is cutting her!" Wik growled, incensed.

"He seems to be taking blood. Weird that the

dragon is okay with it." My lips twisted. The dragon was acting completely unnaturally. Not even Kane would be so docile should I want to take his blood, and he was not of the alpha persuasion.

"Maybe that robed man feeds her?" Wik suggested, though she didn't sound so sure.

The bald fae tipped the flask toward the dragon, filling it with dark red blood. Once he pulled it back, he nodded to Casimir, who snapped his fingers at the surrounding guards. The shimmer of a ward falling back into place appeared the instant they took a step back. Once again, the dragon was trapped.

"Or maybe they're running tests on her blood to see if they can make her better?" Victoria offered.

"Both options seem valid," I agreed. "It makes me wonder if this is part of the plan to get our sisters back." I suspected that dragon blood had to have magical properties, otherwise why take it?

"What is the word on getting them back, anyway?" Wik asked once Casimir and the other fae were gone. "Crystal and Lana have got to be terrified."

Rarely did our wolfish sister show concern for others. She possessed a stern exterior, but Crystal had been one of her best friends, and Lana had earned her trust.

"Still waiting." I wished I could tell her otherwise.

"It's taking too long," Wikolia lamented.

"Totally agree," Victoria added, opening her

mouth to continue, when a streak of fire blazed across the sky.

I pointed. "You don't see that often! Xerxes is usually in Father's chambers."

The phoenix gleamed black as night, but behind him flames danced in the sky. The bird seemed to be having a good time. I wished I could share his joyful mood.

"Do familiars share emotions with their people?" Victoria asked. "Do you and Kane? I often wondered about that. I don't understand the whole familiar thing."

"Kane and I don't. Nor do Lana and Naela. We can sense what the familiars are feeling a wee bit, and them us, but not strongly. It's more like a hint." My eyes drifted up again. Xerxes made his way toward the castle, rounding toward father's tower. "I'm not sure about that one, though. Naela and Kane are more than regular hawks, but nothing like a phoenix."

Nodding, Victoria pushed away from the window and winced. "Right, well, it's been fun, but I gotta go take care of this disaster." She pointed to her other hand. "I'm pretty sure I dislocated a finger. I'm hoping the healers will get it taken care of quickly."

My gaze fell to her hand. Her pinky had twisted oddly, painfully. I cringed. How had she just been standing there with that pain, taking in the scene?

"I've always had a high pain tolerance," she

quipped, noticing my expression. "Fear is hard for me, but pain I can handle."

"I can see that." A breath of relief left me when my sisters disappeared down the hall, on their way to the healer's tower. I'd dodged a bullet with them, not prying further about my veins, or why I needed medicine. Still, I would have to be more careful with exposing my arms until I was ready to tell everybody about my demon gift.

Trying to get out, the shadows pressed against my skin.

Inopportune as ever; I snorted at their timing. "Not now."

They pressed harder, more insistent, desperate to fly free.

Huffing, I rolled my eyes. "Just wait until we get to my room. Then you can go wild."

I grabbed the salve and made my way back to my quarters, wondering if perhaps Victoria was right, and Xerxes' good mood would be reflected in Father. Honestly, I hoped so, just as I hoped that soon we'd set plans in motion to get Lana and Crystal back.

CHAPTER SIX

LANA

Days passed and my emotions were still on the fritz.

Since our fight, Crystal spent her days at the queen's side—walking the gardens with Pari, laughing with Pari, and taking breakfast with Pari. Just as she was at that very moment. My fist clenched around my hairbrush at the idea of her fraternizing with the enemy.

Don't get mad at her, I told myself. It wasn't worth it. I should be thankful Crystal was providing a distraction for me to find proof against Pari's misdeeds.

Sighing at the mirror, I finished brushing my hair. I looked a mess. Once sleek, my hair had grown wild in Buyan's humidity. The brush helped a little, but the frizz wouldn't entirely go away. It was a battle that I lost daily, one of the many, it seemed.

When done, I laid my fingers on the bones of Kate and Kumar, set in a place of reverence on my vanity. They were all I had left of home. Supposedly, the bones could bring me power or enhance my magic, though I didn't know how. Nor was I sure I wanted to use them. Just having them here was powerful enough. They gave me strength.

"See you two later. Wish me luck in finding what I need to bring Crystal back to our side."

The bones gleamed, promising some sort of magic that the fae insisted they possessed. One day, when time permitted, perhaps I'd learn more about their hidden qualities.

When I emerged from my room, Tau beamed at me. He remained on permanent guard rotation outside my door, though, for the life of me, I still couldn't figure out why they'd chosen him to watch me. The young fae looked as if he may blow over in a stiff wind.

"Good morning, Tau." I smiled at him, trying my best to channel the Trinners girls who others liked. The women who always got what they wanted. "I'd like to walk around town today, if you wouldn't mind?"

If I couldn't explore the forbidden hallway, then I would cast my net wider.

Tau's eyebrows furrowed at my shift to a sunny demeanor, but he fell into step at my side, and we continued down the corridor. "I'll have to request my leave from the queen."

"Let's do that now," I suggested. "If you want, we can request that another guard come, too. Although, you're more than enough to keep me under control."

That I would surround myself with more guards had to hint that I wasn't attempting to escape, which was true. I wouldn't get far, anyway. So far, I had had zero luck snooping around the castle, so today, I wanted to get out among the people. Maybe I'd hear or see something of interest.

Tau shot me a stunned look. First cheery Lana, and now a compliment? He didn't know how to handle this new princess. "Sure. We shall ask Queen Pari."

As usual, guards waited outside the door of Pari's breakfast room. Their eyes narrowed at my approach, but they stepped aside so that I could enter. The doors were already thrown open, so we walked right into the space. Pari saw me first, and surprise rippled across her fine features.

Mid-story, Crystal turned to see what had distracted her audience. Her smile bloomed, wide and welcoming. Perhaps she believed that I'd changed my mind.

Not happening, I thought, stepping up to the table with my hands clasped behind my back.

Before a single word left my lips, Bellona

whooshed over to my side, prepared to retaliate should I lay a finger on her queen.

"Down girl." I arched an eyebrow at the brunette guard. "I'm here to ask a favor of your queen."

"And what's that, Princess Lana?" Pari rested her hands in her lap.

I focused on the queen's nose ring, not able to bring myself to look her in the eye and ask for a favor. "I'd like a tour of Buyan. To see more than what's behind these castle walls. You can even bind me magically to Tau if you'd like assurances I won't escape. If there ever was an excellent guard, it's him."

A gulping sound came from behind me, and I imagined Tau's cheeks turning pink.

"Interesting . . ." Pari stood. "Armina, can you bind her to Tau?" Seeing her lady nod, the queen's attention returned to us. "And Tau, are you willing?"

Tau's shoulders straightened. "Yes, My Queen. I am able and willing. However, the princess offered to be under the watch of numerous guards, too. I mention it in case you don't believe I can do the job alone."

Pari cocked her head, clearly surprised I'd suggested such a thing. I inwardly fist pumped. Who was the master manipulator now?

"I see no issue with you being Princess Lana's escort. However, I will send word to the city guard and the gate of Buyan too." Pari leveled her dark eyes at me.

"I promise to return to the castle by this afternoon."

"Very well, then. Armina, perform the binding so that our guest may leave at her leisure."

Once the binding, which was painless and fast, was complete, Bellona escorted us to the castle gate. Although she was less creepy than Armina, Bellona wasn't a party to be around either. She was cold and harsh. Even as we faded into the bustling streets, I swore her gaze kept pummeling my back like icy balls of hail. Pari may give me a little freedom, but if it were up to her ladies, my head would have been on the chopping block days ago.

I made it only a couple of blocks away from the palace, and already I could tell that the entire town was on alert. The eyes of common fae widened as we passed, and people took to the sides of the streets, clearing the way for us.

For once, my companion appeared less than jovial, but I understood why. Tau was a likable guy and quick to laugh, so he probably wasn't used to being the social pariah. I didn't mind. It wasn't uncommon for people to pretend I didn't exist at Trinity. That was especially true with certain types of ladies after I refused to set them up with Finn.

Finn. My heart cracked a little. Had he made it home okay? Had the others?

I hoped the rest of my siblings were alive—that they hadn't acquired lethal injuries during our attack, or after. Even if they'd left the castle unscathed, there were many deadly creatures in the jungle surrounding Buyan. Not to mention the dangers on the road from North Faerie to South Faerie. The flock of harpies we'd passed on the way north crept into my mind. One of the guards had called them scavengers. If one of our own was bleeding, would the smell attract them?

Bile rose in my throat, and I pushed the questions bubbling in my mind away. There was nothing I could do about them right now. I had to stay focused and find proof that Queen Pari had tricked Crystal. I needed my sister on my side again. Needed her companionship, support, and her sharp brain for when we escaped.

"Where would you like to go, Princess Lana?" Tau asked, his face taut, and I suspected he wanted to talk to distract himself from all the staring. "I can show you around the historic market if you like?"

Tau reminded me so much of Finn. Everyone seemed to like him. He was knowledgeable, able to give me information on many things in the castle and presumably out here, too. Yet, what reminded me most about Finn was that Tau truly seemed to like me. That parallel made it even harder to deceive him.

Sinkers, I couldn't stop thinking about my siblings! Tears pricked in my eyes, but I wiped them away before Tau noticed. Yeesh, what an emotional morning.

"Perhaps not the historic market then," Tau mumbled when I didn't answer fast enough. "What about—"

"No. The market is good. Perfect even." The market meant crowds, and the stall keepers wouldn't be able to dodge me if they wanted to monitor their wares. "Sorry, I spaced."

"Spaced?"

"I was thinking. This is all overwhelming after being in the castle. When I arrived, the city wasn't like this."

We'd breached the city wall near nightfall. While the city was busy then, it was *nothing* to the hustle and bustle before me.

Throngs of people streamed along the sides of the road, maintaining their distance from me. Not one person made eye contact, but I sensed their burning desire to say something. I could practically hear the taunts being held in the backs of their throats until I had passed. Fury simmered at the tips of their fingers, and fear radiated from them. They were not only curious about me, but angry that I'd tried to kill their queen.

The prevalence of magic in the area threw me off, too. It simmered in everything. Even the babies, who weren't able to walk, had more power than an adult fae in Lyonesse—clear evidence why bonegate portals were so valuable. They provided vitality to the fae of Buyan by allowing magic to drift from the Old Land.

The fae in Zatus had not been so strong, at least not the part that I'd visited, but I suspected that was because Pari had two bonegates. That meant two times the chances for power to be exchanged between Faerie and the Old Land.

After turning the corner, we stopped before the twisted market maze. The paths were narrow there, so the people doing their shopping had no choice but to walk closer to us.

Stallkeeps grilled up fat legs of gryphon. Others sold charms and potions and small magical objects. Handmade maps of Faerie were open for display, and even a few I recognized as low quality, grade school world maps depicting the human realm lined the walls of one stall. None of the vendors tried to get my attention. In fact, they flatly ignored me.

Only one stallkeep—a young, petite woman with light pink hair and umber skin, who sold wooden carvings—met my eyes. Seizing that moment of connection, I stopped before her stand.

She winced and took a step back.

"Good morning, Petal." Tau stepped forward to assure her with his presence. "How's business been of late?"

The girl, Petal, dragged her gaze up and smiled at Tau. His cheeks dusted with pink as his lips curled up, too.

I quirked an eyebrow. It seemed that Tau had a

thing for Petal. I couldn't blame him. The fae was absolutely lovely.

"Well enough," Petal answered, her pastel pink eyes sliding to me warily.

"Don't worry," Tau assured. "Princess Lana has promised not to use magic, and she's bound to me. But even if she wasn't, so far, she has been the perfect guest at the castle."

Perfect guest, my butt, I thought, though I didn't contradict him.

"Is Petal your real name?" I asked, wanting to start collecting information. "It's unique."

"Not for a dryad. My kind prefers names that revere nature." She met my gaze and gulped.

The Fullfeather eyes got them every time.

"What are these?" I pressed. Trying to move past the cloud of discomfort hanging around, I pointed to the carved wooden figurines on her table. "Do they do anything special?"

"I craft them from the sacred rowan trees that grow in the Alatry Wood. Once crafted, I imbue them with the power to help you out of the woods or jungle, should you find yourself lost."

"How?" I picked one that resembled a goblin before noticing the one next to it was in the image of Queen Pari.

"How?" Petal echoed my question and shot an uncertain glance at Tau. "They walk before you and show you out of the woods. Is there another way?"

Not as good as that one. These little figurines put a compass to shame.

"Interesting. Why would you make that one in the queen's image?" I pointed to the one on the table, not about to touch it.

"Our queen is reliable and always sees us through anything."

"So, she has never led anyone astray?"

Petal's eyebrows knitted together. "Never. Our queen always has our best interests at heart."

I sighed, already sensing that Petal was a bit too much of a loyalist to gossip about the queen. She and Tau were perfect for each other. After asking a few more questions that led absolutely nowhere, I inquired how much it would be for the figurine.

Petal gave it to me for free. Though, I figured she didn't want it back after the notorious illuminator witch who threatened her beloved queen had touched it, so I accepted. She'd likely burn it if I didn't. No need to waste good craftsmanship.

"Come on, Tau, let's explore," I urged, walking away so my guard had no choice but to follow me deeper into the market.

Speaking with Petal hadn't panned out, but somewhere in the vast market, there had to be *someone* willing to dish the dirt on the queen.

CHAPTER SEVEN

Sunlight streamed through my open window, hitting my face, so I pulled the pillow over my head and groaned. I was still in Buyan, *still* captive, and I hadn't gotten close to the gilded hallway. Worst of all, I was failing to dig up dirt on Queen Pari.

For days I'd scouted the city, and always returned to Castle Dalir empty-handed. Not a single person had been willing to call Pari so much as mediocre. It was maddening.

The most frustrating part was that I believed their fervor. She'd brainwashed them all.

As I lay in bed, I didn't have the heart to try again, but I couldn't sit around either. I needed to extradite Crystal and myself as soon as possible. We had to get back home, to safety, and to our loved ones.

Not that Crystal wanted to leave. If I'd thought that she and Queen Pari had been friendly days ago, it was nothing to how they acted now. I'd actually spotted them walking together, arms linked as they whispered secrets in each other's ears and laughed.

"Nauseating," I muttered, throwing my pillow on the floor and lifting myself out of bed to plant my feet on the ground.

My knees popped as they took my weight, and my ankles creaked. During my months in Lyonesse, my body had become used to hard-core training every day, but I'd been sedentary since arriving here. My most strenuous activity was strolling the city with Tau. I craved more. To sweat and work my muscles. It would be nice to use magic too . . .

Would Pari allow me to train without magic? Reasoning that the worst she could say was no, I figured I might as well try. In fact, I'd ask about my magic too. I had nothing to lose.

I put on my tunic and loose pants. After nearly two weeks of captivity, I'd changed my mind about my wardrobe. Even if someone returned my old clothes, I wouldn't want to wear them in Buyan's intense humid heat. I'd sweat through them in an hour, maybe less.

"Where are we going today, princess?" Tau grinned as I opened the door to my room. He'd come to look forward to our daily outings. Especially when they took him by Petal's stall in the market.

"Nowhere." I stepped into the hall. "I'm going to ask Pari to lift the wards against my magic so I can train. I need to exercise, and it's inhumane not to allow me to use my body to its full potential."

Tau sighed, probably lamenting not being able to see his crush, but I ignored it and strode down the corridor—toward the throne room. He fell into place a half step behind me.

Like most of Castle Dalir, the throne room was stunning. Not as amazing as the pure gold hallway I'd glimpsed, but close. Gemstones ran through the walls, representing all four elements in their design. Closer to the throne, blue sapphires and amethyst stones became more prominent—Pari's house colors.

I'd timed my arrival well. None of Pari's subjects had shown up to seek an audience with her, at least not yet. Then again, it was still early.

Only Bellona, Armina and Isis stood with the queen. All three placed their hands on their swords as I strode up to the throne—an imposing chair made of pure gold. The familiar threat proved easy to ignore. As long as Pari wanted me alive, they wouldn't touch me.

"Princess Lana, it's good to see you again. You've been enjoying speaking with the locals?" Pari spoke sweetly, although her knowing smile convinced me someone, *Tau*, had told her I was attempting to dig up dirt on her.

It took everything I had not to look behind me and scowl at him. That smiling, friendly, charming little sneak!

"I've been enjoying myself." It wasn't a total lie. There were a few pleasant moments here and there between my utter failures. "Though wandering about your city, and savoring the culinary delights these past few days, has me feeling sluggish. I'd like to request to train with my magic."

"Surely not!" Isis interjected. "She—"

The queen raised a hand, and the blonde guard's mouth snapped shut. "That is not an issue. It's natural to need to expel your magic from time to time. I wouldn't want you to have adverse effects from it being bottled up inside you."

My lips parted. I hadn't even known that could happen. Then again, before I was held here, no one had ever forced me to keep my power at bay.

"I've already set up a training room for your sister," Pari continued. "She's there presently. If you wish, you may spar together. Armina did not ward the room itself against your magics, though the walls and windows are protected so your power will remain contained. Use the space whenever you like."

Could it really be that easy?

"As it is, I have a favor to ask of you too, Princess Lana," the queen continued when I said nothing.

Ah, now her quick agreement made more sense. "Which is?"

"Today is our Sinker's birthday. It's a monumental holiday in Buyan and a large portion of my kingdom will come to celebrate this evening. I would like for you to attend the feast."

My lips compressed. Normally, I took meals in my room. Alone. I didn't see why my presence would be desired, and as much as I didn't really feel like joining all of Buyan to celebrate one of Pari's long dead relatives, I also didn't want her to take away my chance to train and use magic. I needed this more than I needed to stoke my pride.

"Consider it done. What time?"

Queen Pari smiled. "At the sixth evening bell. Tau will escort you, so you don't miss it. I believe it could be something you enjoy."

Not bloody likely.

The queen's dark gaze snapped behind me. "Now, Tau, will you show Princess Lana to the training facilities? The Fullfeather-approved chambers are at the end."

"Thank you. I will make good use of it," I said, my tone cool, revealing none of the surprise surging through me as I bowed and left the throne room.

THREE HOURS LATER, MY MUSCLES ACHED AND SWEAT dripped off my face as Crystal and I circled one another. I blasted light at her, and she darted away, her gaze slipping to the floor for a heartbeat. A single moment was all that I needed. My body spun into a roundhouse kick, and I grunted as the hit landed on Crystal's shoulder. She spewed out a stream of curse words.

My lips curled up. Despite the soreness, I felt more alive than I had in days. I could barely comprehend the idea that using my power made me feel better, but it had to be true because the longer I trained, the more energy I possessed. In the Old Land I'd regularly gone weeks without performing a speck of magic. Now that I was acclimated to using my magic daily, I eventually suffered adverse effects if I failed to do so. It was so wild.

Crystal must have felt the relief too, and wanted more, because the moment I'd arrived in the training facility, we'd gravitated toward each other—falling into our familiar sparring stances.

After days filled with pastries and caj—the fae's answer to tea—and laughing with the queen, Crystal was as rusty as I was. Neither of us had a leg up on the other. We did, however, have an audience from the start. Guards lined the balcony above, watching us fight. There were gasps and murmurs each time I called forth my infrared sword.

It made me roll my eyes. If the fae of Buyan could only see what Prince Casimir was capable of, they wouldn't be impressed with me. My magic was nothing compared to his.

Using my sword, I slashed at Crystal as she lunged in my direction, tornadoes tearing from both her hands. I flung myself to the ground in time for the air to soar over me. Not wasting a second, I leapt, but Crystal was ready for me. A poof of air pummeled me in the gut.

"Ouch!" My body doubled over, but thanks to my training, I recovered quickly. Fast enough to stop her when she came closer. Again, I dropped and kicked her legs out from underneath her. This time, Crystal wasn't prepared.

She fell as I rose. Her body thunked to the ground —a satisfying sound, since she was normally so poised and balanced.

Light collected around me as she was about to bounce back. It materialized into a sword and extended to within inches of her neck.

"Not base spectrum. It'll cut," I warned as a challenge glinted in her eyes.

I wanted to win, but not at the cost of my sister lunging forward and cutting her throat open because she thought I was using visible light, not a more detrimental sliver of the spectrum.

"Damn you," Crystal growled.

A comment about how she must have meant 'I surrender' grazed the tip of my tongue, but a voice from the sidelines called out Crystal's name. Releasing my power, the sword retracted, and I turned to find Bellona standing at the entrance to the sparring room.

"The queen requires your presence in the throne

room," the lady in waiting announced, violet eyes flashing.

"I'll be right there." Crystal hauled herself up off the ground. "Good practice today," she paused for a heartbeat, uncharacteristically hesitant. "Do you want to come with me?"

"Rather not." I wiped sweat from my forehead. Did she think a friendly sparring match would change things between us? Definitely not. We'd had no choice but to practice together. It wasn't like the guards wanted to fight us. "Same time, same place tomorrow?"

Nodding, she made her way to where Bellona waited. After spending months disliking one another, it was strange to miss Crystal's companionship, but I did. Being the only one to see the truth was lonely. If only I could get her to recognize how Pari had manipulated her.

As I no longer had anyone to spar with, I requested that Tau escort me back to my room. Now that I'd worked out some of the energy, I wanted nothing more than a hot bath, followed by a massive dinner. When I slipped inside my chambers, locked myself in, and turned, my heart nearly leapt out of my chest.

Naela perched on my windowsill. Her head tilted to one side as she keened softly, waiting for me to acknowledge her.

"Boss," I whispered, not wanting Tau to hear.

Willing my bird to stay quiet, I pressed a finger to my lips and rushed across the room. She did, and a second later, I gathered her in my arms and hugged her.

It was a testament to how much she'd missed me that she allowed the embrace. Despite being a familiar, Naela did not appreciate coddling. Tears filled my eyes as I ran my hands over her feathers. "I missed you, girl."

She'd been missing since the night of the assassination attempt. While I'd known she'd survived the fighting, Pari had claimed to hear Naela screeching that night, I'd worried that a dragon or some other colossal beast had gotten to her. The best-case scenario was that my hawk had trouble getting through the most external layer of wards Armina had reinforced around the city. Buyan now resembled an onion with so many varied layers of protection it was maddening. The ones specific to my magic were the most infuriating, but I was pleased that apparently those restrictions did not extend to Naela.

The instant her cuddle meter maxed out, Naela squirmed.

"Where have you been, Boss?" I set her down.

In answer, Naela quirked her head to the side again, and shuffled onto one leg.

My heart clenched for a second, thinking someone injured her, until I caught sight of the small tube tied to her leg.

"Sinkers!" I untied it and rushed to unscrew the tube's top, finding a tiny scroll rolled inside. A smile bloomed on my face when I unfurled it, glancing at the familiar, cramped scrawl.

Lana,
The rest of us are safe. And as I write this Ebba, Sai, Ryker, and Garret are all present and accounted for, too.

I gasped, my gaze lifting from the paper for a moment. The guards I knew best were fine. Garret was safe. My heart fluttered as I thought of his sparkling gray eyes, but I ignored the reaction and resumed reading.

Whatever you do, don't lose hope. I spoke to Father, and he will send a rescue team for you and Crystal. Keep your eyes and ears open, but don't do anything mental. Kane will act as an envoy to let you know when we're close. If you need to contact me with any information, send Naela back. She seemed to know I wanted to talk to you and popped up at Castle Phoenix at just the right time.
Our familiars are bloody geniuses, aren't they?
We miss you,
Finn
P.S. No mental business, Lan. I mean it.

My heart nearly exploded. Finn and Father were

going to rescue us! This nightmare would be over soon, and Finn had signed off with 'we miss you.'

That hinted that someone else was missing me. While I missed all of my siblings and friends, I couldn't help but hope that Garret was among the people thinking about me. I'd give anything to see his mercurial gray eyes, or hear him tell me I was late again.

Emotions welling up, I brought the scroll to my heart and flopped on the bed with a sigh. "They'll come. Soon, this will all be over."

CHAPTER EIGHT

LANA

It did not take me long to realize that Naela's return, combined with a kingdom-wide holiday in Buyan, afforded me an opportunity to snoop a little more thoroughly.

During the feast, the great hall would be the place to see and be seen. Pari had said the servants would be there and Tau informed me that most guards would be, too. The few on duty would be stationed near where the festivities took place, to protect the queen, so that meant fewer soldiers would make the rounds.

I considered it the perfect time to explore a part of the castle that had caught my attention, but was restricted—the gilded corridor. With Naela's help, I was sure I could make it work.

If I'd told any falconer in the Old Land my plan, they'd have called me crazy. Hawks, with the exception of Harris Hawks, like Kane, did not hunt or gather in groups. They were solitary creatures. However, those falconers didn't know my Naela. Unlike most goshawks, she did okay with other birds. In fact, every time we'd visited the Ireland School of Falconry, birds of all sorts flocked to her.

I suspected that was because Naela was no ordinary hawk. She was a beacon of power—a familiar. Animal senses were usually better than a human's, and I bet they could sense that. So, tonight, I hoped Naela charmed the birds of Faerie into following her like the winged creatures of the Old Land did.

"Alright, Boss. Bring some new friends to the great hall and make sure you arrive when it's bursting with fae." I flung Naela out the window, and because she wasn't me or Crystal, the ward confining me did not affect her. She disappeared around the corner. I rolled my shoulders back, ignoring the lingering ache from training that day. "Showtime."

"Princess!" Tau jumped up from where he sat on the ground as I stepped out of my room, dressed for the feast.

I arched an eyebrow at him. "You're comfortable."

"I apologize." Pink splotches stained his cheeks.

"You get a pass. It's a holiday and I'm a little late." Actually, I was so late he probably thought I'd changed my mind, but I wasn't about to apologize for my tardiness. I started down the corridor, my loose tunic flapping in Buyan's muggy air.

Footsteps followed. When Tau reached my side, he was beaming like a loon.

"What are you smiling about?"

"I'm pleased you're attending the Sinker's birthday celebration. You won't be disappointed. It's a feast unlike any you have ever seen!"

Tau's happiness likely hinged more on the food he was about to shove down his gullet and the people he was about to see, rather than my willingness to eat among the fae of Buyan. The guy had been putting up with a lot. People dodged me all the time, and he'd missed out on countless castle meals because I refused to attend. He'd also been very lonely, sitting outside my room by himself for hours, eating his meals and trying not to fall asleep. The least I could do was let him have this moment.

Fae already packed the great hall when we arrived. My eager eyes scanned the tables, of which there had to be at least a hundred. There were so many people, and yet, I still found Crystal's bright red head quickly. I veered in the opposite direction. I didn't want to be around when she spotted Naela. She'd recognize my familiar straight away.

A table near the back was almost empty, and I claimed my spot there. Tau gazed at a group of fae, his friends, a few places away.

"Go on. Sit with them." I grasped at my chance to

remove an obstacle. "Face me, and I'll wave when I'm ready to leave."

"You're my ward."

"What, you think I'm going to try something with all these people around?" I arched an eyebrow. "You deserve to spend the Sinker's birthday fete with your friends. If the queen notices, I'll tell her it was my idea."

Queen Pari sat at the head table, surrounded by dozens of fae vying for her attention. Some of them were groupies I'd seen hanging around the castle. Others were new to me, but they all carried themselves in a refined, confident manner natural to those flush with money and power.

When I shoved Tau toward his friends, he shot me a guilty grin before mouthing 'thank you', and scampering away. He did as I suggested, requesting one of his friends move so he could watch me. I waved, and in response, Tau beamed before inserting himself into the conversation.

Mentally, I brushed off my shoulders. Once my distraction arrived, everything else would fall into place.

I just had to be patient.

A SERVANT PLACED A BOWL OF FRUIT IN FRONT OF ME. "To cleanse your palate, Princess Lana."

"Thanks," I replied, swiveling the bowl around, and studying it. The fruit was odd, reminding me of watermelon, but bright purple. I sighed and pushed it away. The celebratory meal was drawn out with way too much food. We finished the third course, and yet I hadn't spotted Naela.

What was taking her so long? At this rate, the celebration would be over by the time she returned with her flock of chaos.

Picking at my plate, I tried to appear like I was eating. Tau checked in on me for the millionth time, and my lips lifted into a huge, fake smile. He waved and fell back into a natural dynamic with his friends.

Queen Pari milled around the room, having a few words with her citizens. I hoped Naela would return before the queen got to me.

Suddenly, my plan seemed to have too many holes in it, and my palms slicked with sweat. Many things could go wrong. After all, my only break—Tau leaving me alone—had been sheer luck.

What if he came back? What if Crystal stopped by for a chat? What if Pari stood right next to me when Naela arrived? How would I run out and into the gilded hallway then?

As if she had felt me thinking about her, Queen Pari glanced up and focused on me. Her lips tugged up slightly, and she took a step in my direction.

The small muscles in my back stiffened. No. No.

No. My heart raced, and I pushed back my chair. It would be best to leave and bag my plan.

My movements halted when a servant swept in and questioned the queen. There was a brief conversation, a flutter of the servant's hands, and a reassuring nod from the queen. Then Pari shot a look in my direction, waved, and turned to walk back to the head table.

A relieved sigh left me, and I collapsed into my seat. It must be time for a speech, which in Lyonesse was always orated before the second to last course. I had time.

Come on, Naela . . .

Pari made her way to her spot on the dais when a blast of trumpets sounded from the side of the room. Queen Pari beamed at the crowd and lifted her arms, asking for silence. Her drapey white sleeves exposed well-muscled arms.

"Citizens, I thank you for coming to celebrate our dear Sinker's day of birth," she began, white teeth gleaming. "My great-grandfather would be proud to see you all here. Proud to know you. To shake your hands."

I zoned out as she droned on and on about Buyan. How great it was. How the people were model citizens. The improvements she had planned in the city square. Blah, blah, blah, whatever.

Naela's delayed arrival was making me antsy when I noticed a part of the crowd was no longer paying attention only to the queen. A few people whispered to one another. Two tables in front of me, a grouping of young girls—all with shocks of bright green hair—pointed above the head table.

My eyes snapped upward just as the beautiful stained glass above exploded inward. Shards of glass flew forward, and Isis darted to her queen, throwing her body over Pari.

Fae shrieked, and an assortment of wild sounds filled the air, raising the hairs on the back of my neck. Flocks of birds filled the great hall, cawing, trilling and screeching as their wings flapped frantically.

A smile bloomed on my face. Naela hadn't just brought a distraction. She'd assembled a proper fleet. Brilliant girl!

Pandemonium reigned as hundreds of birds dive-bombed diners. Larger birds of prey stole whole pastries, while tiny sparrows claimed the crumbs. Naela was a sight to behold, circling above her army like a general.

Some guests hid under tables. Others stood and stared as a bird devoured their meal. Many ran for the door, eager to put space between themselves and the winged barbarians ruining the celebration.

The door! Shite!

Tau was among the fae staring up at the birds—except, instead of freaking out, he was smiling and whooping. It figured. The guy was lovable, but a real weirdo. I scanned the head table next. Only Queen

Pari remained standing, her hands on her hips as she gazed at the ceiling in disdain. Seizing my moment, I bolted out of there.

My heart thundered as I sprinted through the corridors. As I'd hoped, dozens of soldiers raced toward the great hall. Fae had fled the hall in droves, but thankfully, no one was going in the same direction as me. My breath was tight in my chest as I rounded the last corner and exhaled in relief.

The two guards who patrolled the mouth of the hallway had abandoned their post. Knowing my distraction wouldn't last forever, I moved toward the queen's wing, but stopped short of entering. No guards meant there was a high likelihood the hallway was warded. Especially, seeing as Armina was the master wardmaker.

I took one cautious step into the corridor. Then another. When nothing zapped me, I hastened my pace. There was no map telling which door led to Pari's study versus her ladies' rooms, but luckily for me, the layout of the hallway made that pretty obvious. It was short, with four doors on one side and only one on the other. A space fit for a queen, with her ladies in waiting right across the hall. Part of me wondered what could be behind the fourth door.

My hand landed on the knob, and as I twisted it, it met no resistance. My eyes widened as I pushed the door open, bracing myself. Would this be the moment that I turned into a frog, or some odd Faerie creature? A harpy?

Once again, nothing came. No blade thrust at my heart. Not even a tingle of magic trickled through me. Perhaps Queen Pari thought her castle so secure, her servants and guards so loyal, that she'd never considered warding her private chambers? Or perhaps the threat of Bellona, Armina and Isis looming across the hallway was enough to keep sensible fae away?

Unfortunately for Pari, I was not at all sensible. I'd been a captive too long, and was desperate for proof that she was lying to get Crystal on her side.

My breath slowed while I took in the expansive room. I had been correct in my assumption that this half of the hallway suited the queen's personal needs. The room was as large as the public chamber of the Old Trinity Library and had nearly as many books lining its walls. A variety of contraptions I'd never seen, but knew had to be magical, dotted the dark stone floors. One device looked much like my father's firlon.

I approached it, yearning to use the instrument to look upon Lyonesse. Perhaps even speak to Father. No! I shook my head. There was no time for that! I needed to find proof to convince Crystal I was right. Then we would devise an escape plan together. Perhaps we'd even do so tonight. A pang of hope cut through me. I needed my sister back because there was no way in hell I was leaving her here.

A desk stood at one end of the room, with a high-back chair swathed in imperial purple velvet behind it. Four other chairs faced the desk. It was easy to imagine Isis, Bellona, and Armina sitting with Pari, discussing the matters of Buyan, watching their queen, maybe even laughing at a shared joke. Yet, who sat in the fourth chair? The same person who stayed in the fourth room?

Blinking, I once again pulled myself to the mission. Why was I getting caught on such stupid minutiae? I needed to seize the moment.

My gaze flew from the chairs back to the desk. It was an obvious place to look. As Pari seemed to trust everyone here, the obvious choice didn't seem like such a terrible one. I threw open all the drawers and rummaged, but the usual things filled them—papers, cards, a journal, which I skimmed only to find that it was an heirloom from her father. Not her own diary.

There was also a book of magic. Within its pages, the section on illuminator witches had been marked.

The queen had been studying up on me.

Amused, I arched an eyebrow before moving on. My hand landed on the last drawer when a powerful screech blasted through my heart. I whipped around to find Naela hovering outside the study's window, gray wings flapping frantically.

The distraction had bought me less time than I'd hoped.

Yanking open the last drawer, I bit back a wail of frustration. The bloody thing was empty.

Desperation mounting, I scanned the rest of the room. Hundreds of hiding places stared back at me. Far too many to search. I should have gone for a bigger distraction—a stampede of elephants or something!

When I shoved the drawer shut, a strange sound caught my ears. Brows furrowed, I opened the drawer again. This time, a crumpled-up ball of paper sat at the front of the drawer. Curious fingers wrapped around it to find a torn corner. Bending down, I peered into the back of the drawer and saw a scrap of paper stuck out from where the wooden slats joined. The paper had gotten caught and ripped when I slammed the drawer closed.

Taking it as a sign, I opened the message. Bits of debris from within the drawer fluttered off it as I straightened out the paper against the desk, and blew on it, only to have dust litter Pari's immaculate desk. Cursing under my breath, I wiped it.

Naela screeched again.

I waved at her. "Yes, yes, I know! I'll hurry! Dammit, if only I could use an illusion right now!"

Once the paper was unwrinkled, I read it hungrily. When I finished, I couldn't breathe, nor hear anything beyond the pounding of blood in my ears. The signature at the bottom suggested the letter was from my father, but the contents made no sense.

Shocked, I read it again, my lips tightening, my blood pressure rising with every word.

No fecking way.

As Naela's screech became louder, I knew I'd run out of time. I could practically feel her little heart beating, threatening to burst from her chest. Keeping the letter, I slammed the drawer shut and scampered out of the room.

Miraculously, no guards had returned to the gilded corridor, so I made it to my room with no one seeing me. When I arrived, Naela waited for me on the windowsill.

"Well done, Boss. Amazing diversion." I threw myself on the bed and unfurled the paper again when someone pounded on my door. Adrenaline spiked within me again.

"Hide, Boss!" I whispered and shooed Naela outside. I managed to shove the piece of paper under my pillow milliseconds before Tau entered, his eyes wide, his blue hair askew.

"Thank the Sinkers you're in here, Princess Lana!" Tau looked so relieved that guilt sliced through me.

"Sorry I didn't wait. I ran out as soon as the birds appeared . . . didn't want to get pooped on."

Tau's eyes widened further, and a strangled laugh escaped him. "Well, yes. Although, I was thinking of more serious attacks. A vicious gray hawk dive-bombed one of my dearest friends!"

My teeth dug into my bottom lip. Naela had taken her job very seriously.

The young guard glanced down the hall as if to make sure no one was coming. "But now that you mention it, a dropping landed on Bellona. It didn't go over well."

A snort of laughter escaped me, and Tau grinned, having achieved his desired effect.

"Thanks for checking on me. Please let—whoever you need to inform—know that I'm here. In fact, all the activity wore me out. I think I'll turn in for the night."

"I shall do that. Rest well, princess." He shut the door as he exited.

A sigh of relief sunk my chest, and I pulled the paper from its hiding spot. It was an elaborate hoax. A fabricated letter from Father to Pari, informing her of my father's plan to use the bonegates to take over the human realm.

The tone was boastful, crass, so unlike anything I'd ever heard from my father's mouth. There was no way he'd said those things. Still, how would Pari know to plant it there? Had I been so obvious in my desire to study the gilded hallway? I didn't think so . . . . I'd really only been near it once. My obsession had been purely in my head.

Naela's wings fluttered, and I turned around to find her returning to the windowsill. She stretched her leg to me, as if trying to tell me something.

"What is it, girl?"

Her leg stretched a little farther before settling on the sill, steadying her. An image of the last time she'd done that, when she showed Finn's letter to me, barreled into my mind, and I straightened. Naela was right! I needed to write to Finn and Father to tell them of the lies Pari was spreading.

I ran to where I'd stored Finn's letter and wrote a note on the back, explaining everything. How I'd gotten captured, how Pari was treating us, and as a result, how she had convinced Crystal of her purity. I assured him that once I had proof, I'd help Crystal see the light again.

"I know you just got here, but are you up for another trip, Boss?" My fingers swiftly rolled up the scroll, placing it in the tube.

Naela lifted her leg again, and I thanked the Sinkers for giving me such an amazing familiar.

"Take this to Father. If you can't find him, then get it to Finn. He'll make sure father gets it. Sound good?" I ran a finger along the top of Naela's head, which she bobbed up and down.

"Fly safe and be quick."

With that, my hawk took off, back to Lyonesse.

CHAPTER NINE

FINN

Two seemingly endless weeks had passed, but I'd barely seen Father since our first meeting, let alone spoken to him about his plans to save Crystal and Lana. The delay made me nervous, but I tried to keep calm and carry on as my stuffy, but reliable, stepfather would tell me to do.

Perhaps the king had already sent someone on the mission? Would they be talented enough to save two princesses held hostage? If they were, why had he sent us to Buyan at all? Perhaps he didn't want to risk the lives of his other children? Still, he wouldn't have sent someone without telling me, right?

I didn't understand why our father would keep me in the dark. Before the mission, he met with Lana frequently, and now I was in her position. Worry gnawed at me, and while I didn't want to push him, I also wanted action, motion. I needed to *do* something.

It was the reason Kane and I decided to tramp around in the barren woods, braving the blistering cold wind that whipped through the dead trees. The wilds of Lyonesse were bloody depressing. The palace was far more comfortable, and yet, for both Kane and me, it was better to be outside—more soothing.

My hands rubbed together for warmth, and my breath plumed from my mouth. I needed all the soothing I could get. If it came with a few chills, then so be it.

Each passing day, my shadows grew stronger. I still hadn't told anyone else about them, and only released them when I was alone. Although my control over the shadows increased every time I used them, they still terrified me.

Kane's screech echoed through the forest, ripping me from the churning ocean of my thoughts. He soared above, peering down.

"Come on then." I extended my gloved arm for him to land.

Kane, usually very chill, approached warily, his talons digging into the thick leather when he landed. His grip was lighter than normal, probably suspecting he might have to take off at any second.

As if sensing someone to bully, my shadows surged, and Kane launched himself back into the air. A sigh gusted out of me.

Since my magic was first coaxed out of me by the Feathered Fae, my body looked different to me. It glowed, perhaps in a way that only I noticed. The glow became especially noticeable when I used fire magic—my preferred element. Yet, the look of my skin had changed even more since I began releasing my shadows routinely.

An eerie darkness swam through my veins, turning the blue in them gray. The sight repulsed me. Thankfully, it was winter, so I could hide the ink swirling through me fairly well, but only one thing got rid of it. That was, of course, releasing the shadows.

The darkness inside pressed harder, insisting that I take notice. With a resigned breath, I glanced around. No one else roamed the woods. We hadn't seen a soul, and we'd been out here for at least an hour. Not surprising, considering the cold. Once I was positive that no one was nearby, I took my dagger and reopened an old wound.

Blood welled and a sense of euphoria overcame me; two shadows emerged and bloomed into a human form. My body loved using the shadows, even if I found them appalling. They were like a drug I couldn't quit.

Waiting for a command, the inky creatures hovered in front of me. My gaze swept the area once more, wondering if I should ask them to build me a fire or something. Felt a bit senseless though, seeing as I could ignite fire with a flick of my fingers.

I was still wondering what I should have them do when a screech cut through the silence of the woods.

Head snapping up, I saw Kane soar unencumbered, pointedly ignoring the creatures that lived in my blood. The sound hadn't come from him.

A moment later, an enormous harpy eagle torpedoed out of the castle. Meegra!

"Hide," I ordered the shadows, and they immediately flattened against the ground—effectively disappearing into the black earth. Sure she wouldn't see them, I watched the Master Feathered Fae head west. Where was she going?

"False Realm, Beast Realm, and the Free Realm are to the west," I muttered, staring into the distance, watching the harpy eagle grow smaller. Meegra eventually veered south, which showed she was not heading for the home of the giants or that of the chimeras. She was going to the Free Realm.

My eyebrows furrowed. "Is Father reaching out to the Masters of Swords in Zatus again? Why wouldn't he tell me?"

Frustration rose. Were things moving ahead without my knowledge? That pissed me right off. My sisters' lives were on the line, and I wished to be in the know. I wanted to call Meegra back to demand that she tell me what was happening, and if they had a plan for rescuing Lana and Crystal.

Trying to get my attention, one of the shadows surged upward, a thin stream of ink trailing Meegra's path. I drew in a sharp breath, understanding what it was telling me. Perhaps there was a way to learn what was happening and not piss off my father.

"Can you follow her?" I asked. "Tell me where she goes."

Both shadows took bodily form and nodded their heads. Amused, rather than repulsed for once, I snorted. I didn't understand how the shadows would transfer information to me after they got it, but at least that was some sort of action. Action *and* relief. If they soared about Faerie, doing my bidding, they couldn't be inside me. Or at the very least, there would be fewer of them. How many I could create was still unknown, and I wasn't about to push that measure. Two was enough for now.

"Follow Meegra. I want to learn what she's doing and why. Don't let her see you."

The twin shadows launched into the air and soared away. As soon as they left, Kane dove toward me, wanting to perch. A second later, he landed, but he wasn't alone. I blinked as another hawk swooped from behind him to land on my arm too.

"Naela! Where were you hiding, girl? Did my shadows scare you too?"

Lana's familiar puffed up her feathers, letting me know nothing frightened her. She always had been a brave wee thing. Braver than Kane, though I liked to think of my hawk was more thoughtful and scholarly, like me.

Naela held out her leg, exposing the tube tied to it.

"A letter! Lana got my other one?"

Naela bobbed her head in confirmation.

"Good girl, Boss." Using Lana's nickname for her familiar, I pulled out the small scroll and unfurled it.

The message was for father, but now that I'd already opened it, I couldn't stop myself from devouring the note. With each word, my heart rate sped up. Lana and Crystal were alright, but things seemed tense between them. Crystal had fallen for Queen Pari's deceit. But why? By all accounts, she was horrible.

"We have to give this to Father." I looked at the birds. "Kane, wait in my room for me, will you? Naela, come with me. We might need you to send something back to Lan."

Agreeing, Kane soared away, while Naela inched into a better position on my falconer's glove. I marched into the castle, hoping Father would be in his chambers. I was nearly there when someone called my name. Twisting, I found Dak and Gio strolling the halls.

"We're heading into town for an ale. Want to come?" Gio's smile was wide with the promise of mischief. "Ryker and Ronan are joining."

"Can't right now," I replied.

Dak's eyebrows pulled together. "Isn't that Naela?"

"It is. She arrived with a message. I'm taking it to Father."

"What's it say?" Gio looked intrigued.

While I was glad to see the diviner witch return to his usual boisterous self after being injured during the mission, I wished he wouldn't pry. No one should learn about this before Father. After all, Lana meant it for him. Guilt niggled at me for opening it, even though Naela had brought it to me, and I couldn't have known it was addressed to Father from the outside.

"I don't know," I lied. "Perhaps he'll tell me. I better get moving."

"Meet us at The Wilted Wing later!" Gio called after me.

I threw him a non-committal wave and left. When I reached the king's chambers, a vast suite of rooms I'd always thought of as a den, I knocked. The sound of stone grating on stone hit my ears. Where the sound came from remained a mystery, although it wasn't the first time I'd heard it. The next second, the door swung open.

"Finn. Is everything okay?" My father inclined his head.

"Word from Buyan," I said, extending the letter to him.

Gold eyes widened as he took the parchment. "From Lana or Crystal?"

"Lana. It's for you but didn't say that on the outside, so I read it. Sorry 'bout that."

His lips tightened, but the annoyance vanished quickly. "No matter. It was natural. Come in."

I eased the heavy door shut. Naela launched off my arm, fluttering to the perch normally reserved for the king's phoenix, Xerxes, at the back of the room.

Father swept past the firlon, following her to the rear of the chamber. Sitting at his long table, he spread out the paper to read. When he finished, he looked up at me.

"Has anyone else read this?" Sorrow brimmed in his gaze, and I suspected it was because Crystal no longer believed in him. That had to hurt.

"No. Naela brought it to me, and I came straight here."

Father's eyes shifted to Lana's familiar. She puffed out her feathers a bit, as if trying to impress the king.

"Good. Tell no one about this letter. I do not want your sister's reputation tarnished."

I hadn't even considered that, but it made sense. The fae of Lyonesse loved their king. That Crystal had doubts might cast her in a different, negative light.

"Lana says they're safe, but who knows how long that will last?" Historically, sometimes hostages lived for years as bargaining chips. Sometimes not. "When will we ride to retrieve them?"

Father's gaze lowered to the letter again, exhaling

a burdened breath. "I must consider these recent revelations. I know I am not moving as quickly as you'd like, but we no longer hold the element of surprise. When we make a move on Buyan, it has to be perfectly timed and planned."

"So, there's not a timeline?" My gut clenched.

"Not yet. You'll be the first to know when things change." Father stared into my eyes. "I know this is as difficult for you as it is for me, but I give you my word. I will inform you when we're ready to journey north."

Part of me wanted to ask about Meegra, but I held my tongue. It seemed a long shot, but perhaps she wasn't sent west for anything having to do with Buyan. Plus, my shadows would learn what she was doing and report back. No need to annoy the king.

"Finn, do you understand?"

"I do. As you said, I would like to move faster, but I understand."

"I too wish to move faster, but our forces are greatly diminished. Once we move, we cannot fail again."

"Is that all, sire? I should send Naela back."

Again, his golden gaze flashed to the hawk. "Leave her. But yes, you may go."

What use did he have for Naela? I wanted to ask, but didn't press. Father was not one to give more information than he was ready to divulge, and I recognized a dismissal when I heard one. So I merely left the room with my head still filled with questions.

Gio and Dak appeared again when I was halfway to my quarters. Gio's arm hooked mine, redirecting me. I should have known he wouldn't give up so easily.

"It's time for some brotherly bonding," he announced, though I could tell he wanted to hear all about the meeting.

"I'm not sure—"

"Nonsense! You're coming."

Dak snorted. "He won't take no for an answer."

"Fine," I huffed. "*One* drink." One wouldn't hurt, and Gio wouldn't be able to wheedle the truth from me after a wee pint, so knowing the distraction would help, I allowed the guys to escort me into the heart of the city.

Three hours and four pints later, my head spun, but I had maintained my silence against my silver-tongued devil of a brother. He'd persisted in asking questions and handing me pints for nearly two hours, when finally, an attractive fae approached Gio. A few bats of her long lashes, and he decided that dancing was more interesting than interrogating me.

The tavern was busy and just the kind of distraction I needed, but in the rare lulls of conversation or music, I couldn't help but think of Lana and Crystal. How had I left them to their fate? What kind of person did that?

A person who valued the lives of those who made it out of the castle, I told myself once again. Others had insisted this was true, and yet, I still found it so difficult to believe.

"I'm going to head back. Gio's going to be busy for a while." Dak set his empty cup of ale down on the bar top. His pale cheeks were ruddy, and I suspected mine looked much the same. "Want to come? He won't even notice that we're gone."

Dak was right, and while I'd been reluctant to join their outing, I no longer wanted to leave. The moment I stepped foot in my quarters, I'd be alone with my thoughts. "I'll stay a bit."

"Suit yourself." Dak waved to Ronan, who along with Ryker milled across the room, talking to a crowd.

The guard joined Dak. "Time to go?"

"If I have another ale, you'll be carrying me home."

"We don't want that." Ronan grinned and glanced at me. "You'll leave with Ryker and Gio?"

"Sure." Technically, we no longer had guards escorting us around, but since the failed mission Father had been extra cautious about our safety. Any time we stepped outside the castle, escorts joined.

The pair left, and I twisted to face the room. The bar burst with pretty fae, but none caught my fancy. The woman I couldn't stop thinking about wasn't here, but I supposed flirting for a wee bit of fun couldn't hurt. At the very least, it would distract me, and the fae might enjoy it too. Lana had always called me a bit of a ham around the ladies. She wasn't wrong, but I liked to think the women had fun chatting with me, too.

Shoving off the stool, I groaned as my full bladder became apparent. The ladies would have to wait for a mo'. The loo called.

I lumbered toward the facilities. On the way, Ryker caught my eye, so I gestured to the back of the tavern. With a nod, he returned to his conversation. There was no line, so I entered.

The moment the door shut, a nebulous inky cloud materialized in front of me. A shadow.

"Bloody hell!" I jumped back against the door.

My shadow darted back too, as if apologizing. Should I have sensed its presence? It was a part of me, after all.

"Sorry, I wasn't expecting you." Quickly, I locked the door so no one else would enter. "Where's the other one?"

The shadow pulsed. Maybe they could combine? I supposed it wasn't out of the question. They all lived inside me as one, so why not separate and join at will?

"You already journeyed to Zatus and returned?"

The shadow took human form and nodded. Handy, that.

"Did you follow Meegra?"

Another nod.

It didn't seem right. Meegra might have flown to Zatus in a few hours, but there was no way she could have returned by now.

"When you returned, did you fly? Or . . . poof?" I raised a fist and opened it, fingers splayed.

The shadow pointed to the hand.

My eyes widened. "Ah, well that's—"

My words faltered when it came closer, and a black, smokey arm reached out to caress my temple. It wanted inside my head.

"You'll tell me what you saw?"

A nod.

"Err, okay." What could it do? As much as I didn't like to think about it, the shadow came from me. It was a part of me, and unless I wanted it floating around my person, it would return to my body, anyway. "Go on, then."

It entered my body painlessly, and images flashed through my mind. In them, Meegra landed in Zatus and stormed down a hallway—one I'd seen, too.

A fae answered the door and showed her down the hall to Gory's lair. She was almost to the chambers where we'd asked the spriggan for help, when the vision went black.

I blinked. "Wait, what else is there?"

Again, blackness took over my mind.

"You couldn't get in?"

Inside me, it felt like the smoke shook its head. Weird, but effective.

"Gory's headquarters must have wards up." I frowned as I tried to work it out. "But why? I didn't sense any when we—"

Bang! Bang!

"Finn? Are you in there?" Ryker's voice boomed.

"Yeah! Hold on!"

The guard was not keen on me being out of his line of sight for too long. After I did my business, I found Ryker waiting for me in the hall.

"You okay?" he asked. "You look spooked."

"I've been thinking about Lana and Crystal a lot lately."

"Me too. You received word from them today?"

Damn Gio.

"I did. It was for Father, but Naela found me first."

"What did it say?"

He sounded interested, but then he would be, wouldn't he? Ryker and Crystal had had a thing going on before she got captured. What would he think about Crystal if I told him what the letter said?

"I didn't read it," I lied. "I saw Meegra flying west today. Toward Zatus. You wouldn't know why, would you?" I asked, wanting to turn the tables.

Ryker's eyebrows arched. "Master Meegra journeyed to the Free Realm?"

"I think so." I studied him. Was that a hint of understanding I saw cross his face?

For a moment, Ryker remained quiet, but then he

shrugged. "No idea why she'd be going there." He turned. "I can't leave Gio alone for too long, or he'll leave with someone and I'll have to turn the city upside-down to find him."

Without another word, I followed the guard. Something told me he knew more than he was telling me. But what?

CHAPTER TEN

LANA

Days flew by and yet no one questioned me about the fiasco in the great hall. Did they not suspect me? I couldn't imagine they would be that dense. Crystal had to know, but she'd fallen radio silent.

Why?

Even before I had unleashed my flock of chaos, I figured I would be a prime suspect. Yet, as long as I got what I wanted, I hadn't cared. It was a calculated risk to find the dirt on the queen. One that would bring Crystal back to me. A risk that hadn't panned out.

At the very least, the queen should have been upset, but the guards told me she had left the castle. Where was she? What had she gone there for?

The waiting made me tense. So when a knock

came at my door on the morning of the fourth day, it was almost a relief. Finally, *something* was happening.

Dropping the pastry I'd been eating, I crossed the room. I knew it wasn't my guard. Tau never knocked unless the queen ordered him to interrupt me, and my maid religiously waited two bells after breakfast before collecting my tray. If it was her, she was early.

It had to be the queen coming to question me. My hand landed on the knob, and I inhaled, steeling myself for confrontation. When I opened the door, a woman with dark hair and gray eyes stood before me.

"Mam?" I took a step back, heart stopping. Was this real?

Her eyes filled with tears. "It's me, love."

"Mam!" I threw myself at her.

My mother wrapped her arms around me. Tears pricked my eyes and streamed down my cheeks. Since I'd been a captive, I tried not to consider how much I'd missed her.

Wait a minute . . . how was she here? And why?

I jerked back from the embrace to study my mother. "What are you doing here? When did you arrive? What did they do to bring you here? Are you hurt?"

The questions gushed out of me, nearly unintelligible. Days ago, I'd interrupted a kingdom-wide holiday and disrespected a founding fae of Faerie. No one had reprimanded me for those actions, but now my mother was in this realm? A place she should not be able to cross into because she did not possess a single drop of fae blood. It didn't make sense.

"I'm fine, darling." Mam's hand cupped my cheek. "I arrived at the bonegate late last night and rode back with Pari and her ladies. You'll never believe where the bonegate is, either! It—"

"But *how* did she do it, Mam?"

I didn't mean to sound like a disrespectful shit, but at that moment I didn't give a damn where the opening of Buyan's bonegate was in the Old Land. I was more concerned about Mam being here when it should be impossible. Father had told me that only those with fae blood could enter Faerie. Mam was pure witch.

Had Pari learned how to charm her bonegates to allow those without fae blood through? Or did she do something to Mam to make it possible? My heart rate spiked.

"What do you mean?" Mam asked. "We simply walked into a portal. The queen had horses waiting on the other side, and we rode to the castle."

My lips pressed into a thin line. No, that couldn't be all of it. Somehow, Pari had tricked my mother.

Mam didn't seem to notice my hesitancy though.

"The moment we arrived a guard showed me to your room," she continued.

Behind her, Tau shuffled. In all the excitement, I'd almost forgotten that he was there—forgotten to keep my emotions in check. I cursed myself. Would he report what he'd heard to the queen? Of course, he would. Why would I think otherwise? Tau might be friendly toward me, but his loyalties lay with the crown of Buyan.

Mam noticed me looking at my guard and turned to Tau. "Young man, would you mind if I had a moment alone with my daughter, please?"

"As you wish, Ms. Shea." Tau shut the door.

As soon as we were alone, I sprang into action, examining every inch of my mother and pushing her to the bed to sit down.

"Lana! What's going on?"

"You can tell me the truth now that no one is listening. Are you sure you're not hurt?"

Mam smacked my hands away. "I'm fine! Don't you think I would know if I was injured? Darling, you're acting crazy." She righted her shirt. "Two nights ago, Queen Pari came to the house and explained who she was and that you were in her kingdom. She offered for me to visit, and I jumped at the chance to see you. It's been weeks since I've had any updates."

"I'm fine, Mam." Well, if you counted being a captive as fine. At any rate, I was not physically injured. "It's *you* I worry about. She might have drugged you in your sleep. Did you let her stay at the house before coming here?"

"Excuse me?" Mam's tone rose, disbelieving.

"That might explain how you got through. You

don't have fae blood, so you shouldn't have been able to travel through a bonegate. And I'm certain Pari only brought you here to use against me."

Turning, I began to pace the room, wishing I hadn't sent Naela to Lyonesse. Father would want to learn about these recent developments. If he knew Pari was threatening innocent people from the Old Land, he would act right away. When would my familiar return? It had taken us days to march across Sinkers Realm, but we'd traveled with a whole army, and my hawk flew there directly. I expected it would take her a day, two at most.

"I'm afraid, you have it all wrong." My mother's words stopped me in my tracks.

"How would you know?" I shot back, strangely defensive. Oh hell, now I sounded like a child, but I couldn't help it. My heart was beating far too fast from being so worried about her. Having Mam here meant she was vulnerable, and I couldn't live with myself if someone hurt her.

Mam came closer, her gray eyes softer than her tone. "Lana, honey, what are you doing here? Pari didn't tell me much, but she insinuated you may have come here with ill intentions. And you admitted you think Pari is using my presence here against you. Why would she do that?"

I froze. "That woman is a liar."

Glancing at me like I'd gone mental, my mother shook her head. "I haven't known her long, but she doesn't seem that way. I like Queen Pari very much. At least she let me come see my daughter."

Ha!

I exhaled a patience-filled breath. "You don't understand what's going on here. That's my fault. I should have told you."

"Well, I'm here now, and I'm all ears."

As much as I didn't want to admit all the sins I'd committed, I had to. Mam was in danger and had proven herself far too trusting. If telling her the truth of why I was here would open her eyes and make her more careful, then I had to confess.

Determined, I launched into the story of my time in Faerie. Everything I had done. Everything I'd learned. To my surprise, Mam stayed strangely calm. Even as I divulged the part about me killing Nigel in the Successional, and my mission in coming to Buyan. When I finished, Mam stared at me as if I'd told the tallest tale she'd ever heard.

Heart pounding, I waited for her to say something. I needed her to understand the urgency so we could get her out of Faerie, or at the very least see her to Lyonesse, somehow . . .

"Mam? Do you need me to explain anything else? Are you okay?"

"I'm trying to work out how I raised a daughter who allows herself to be manipulated so easily."

My mouth opened and closed like a fish gulping

for water in the desert. A response tipped my tongue, but Mam continued.

"I mean, really? Who makes their own children fight to the death? Or fight at all?" Tears sprang into Mam's eyes. "Then again, Oberon hid his true nature from me too, so maybe I'm the original fool. Perhaps it runs in the family."

"That's not fair!" I hissed. "The Successional is a fae royal ritual! It's cultural." As I said it, my stomach churned. A glance at my vanity, where the bones of Kumar and Kate sat told me why.

I had mixed feelings about the Successional, always had. It reminded me of gladiatorial combat in ancient Rome, which reflected fae culture better than human culture. Although I didn't like the violence, I saw that there was a purpose for it. Mostly, I tried not to think about the Successional too much and respect fae culture. Still, people had died. I couldn't deny that no matter how many warnings we'd received, I hadn't been ready for that. Not really.

"How politically correct of you, darling. I suppose I should expect more of that? After all, I hear you're a princess now . . . Won first rank and all." She rubbed her temples. "I'm to blame for all this. Perhaps if I'd been keener on telling you about your father, this would never have happened. You were always asking where your father was. Who he was. I always hoped if I brushed it off, you'd grow out of it, but now I see that my method didn't work."

Her statement made me bristle. Why couldn't she see she was in danger? I was about to press the matter of her safety again, when a rustling of wings hit my ears. A soft click of a beak followed, and I turned. Naela perched on the window sill, her eyes trained on me.

"Boss!" My heart leapt. "You're back!"

I darted across the room, and after a quick examination to check that no one attacked her, I stroked her head. "I worried about you."

"Where did you send her?" Mam asked, coming closer.

Wanting to read the letter my familiar carried first, I remained silent. As if she knew what I was thinking, Naela held out her foot, and I untied the ratty string that connected the cylinder to her leg, taking out a new scroll.

The scroll unfurled between my fingers, and I smiled at the old-fashioned way the "L" of my name was written—how it smeared slightly because Father was left-handed, before devouring the words.

Lana,

It causes me great suffering to know that you are now under the watchful eye of Queen Pari. That we shall never again have the relationship we were developing, Father and Daughter, King and Princess-General. For I know, now that you are there and Pari has spoken with you, you have been compromised. There is nothing to undo the poison she has poured into your ears.

I can no longer trust you.

My heart stopped as a shocked gasp ripped from me. What had I read?

"Lana? Are you okay?" Mam took a step closer.

I didn't reply. Couldn't. What did this mean?

I suggest, should you want to leave Faerie, you find your way back to the Old Land. Queen Pari has two bonegates under her control. Surely, with your magic, you can find your way to one. Should you wish to stay, know that you are not welcome in Lyonesse. Nor is your familiar. Do not send her back to speak with anyone. She will be killed on sight.

My breath grew thin. No signature. No, nothing. My legs shook, forcing me to rest my weight against the stone wall, but it couldn't hold me. I slid down to the floor. Once more, my eyes ran over the letters my father had written.

I can no longer trust you.

You are not welcome in Lyonesse.

Why? My hands shook so badly I couldn't read the paper again if I tried. Was that a code? Reverse psychology in case this note fell into the wrong hands? Or was it something else?

My throat tightened as doubt spread through me like ink through water.

I glanced up at Mam, who watched me with careful interest. According to my father, she shouldn't be here. It shouldn't be possible, and yet, here she stood.

Pari had brought her here. The same woman who claimed to have stolen Father's bonegate for the good of the Old Land. The letter I'd found in her study, crumpled and forgotten in a drawer, burned in my mind. Had that been a fabrication or was it real?

Glancing down at the parchment in my hand, I leapt to my feet. I was across the room and snatching the letter out from under my pillow in a second. The paper remained crunched into a tight ball—better for hiding it. With less care than I had the day before, I opened it hastily, then I flattened both sheets side by side.

Behind me, Mam inched closer. She probably thought I was crazy, but an explanation would have to wait. Only the letters mattered. As I focused on them, obvious differences stuck out.

The aged brown ink on the older letter, versus the fresh black on the recent one.

Its tone.

The texture of the paper differed too.

Yet, the handwriting was spot on.

When he called Queen Pari 'His Love', the "L" was *exactly* the same as the "L" in my name. The smear was there too, taunting me, squeezing all the air from my lungs.

"It was from him." I took a step back as the fantasy I'd built in my mind shattered. "He wrote this."

He lied.

I, not *they*, had been brainwashed. Queen Pari's story was true, and I was the fool.

My hand flew to cup my mouth, holding back a sob. A worthless attempt since it escaped through the cracks between my fingers, anyway. The guttural noise forced its way from me and once it started, I couldn't stop. My chest heaved as tears fell from my eyes freely, sliding faster and faster down my cheeks.

Mam's hand landed on my shoulder, her touch soft, warm. "What happened, Lana?"

With trembling fingers, I pointed to the letters on the bed. Mam shot me a perplexed look but eased around me to read them. Her eyes scanned the pages and confusion morphed into understanding and then, sorrow.

My father was a horrible man. He'd left Mam, and then tricked his most vulnerable children into coming to Faerie, knowing we were the ones who wished to know him most deeply. He'd been willing to put the Old Land, my old world, at risk as long as he got what he wanted. Resting my head on my arms, I let the pain flow through me.

How had I been so stupid? How had he tricked us all?

"I'm so sorry, my darling." Mam snaked an arm around me.

I was hyperventilating in agony. Gulping, racking sobs that shook me to the tips of my toes. My father hadn't loved me. Ever. None of us. The king had used us expertly, secretly, to gain an empire.

An image of Casimir, high above me in the stands, looking down during the Successional crystalized in my mind. I shuddered.

Perhaps, and that was a big *perhaps*, based on the stories of Casimir's childhood neglect, Father loved his natural born fae son, but he certainly didn't love those from the Old Land. He'd only needed us to serve a purpose. One he'd been planning for years.

Turning, I looked Mam straight in the eye. "You were right about him all along. Crystal knew it as soon as she heard the truth too. How was I too stupid not to see it?" My face scrunched up again.

"Shhh, honey. You're not stupid," she reassured, soothingly. "We all want love. From our parents most of all. Crystal seems like she has a questioning mind. Maybe she never was quite sure about him."

That stopped me. "Wait, you met her?"

"She came with Pari to the bonegate. Her mother is here too."

"Oh . . ." Her room had been strangely silent, but after my stunt in the great hall, I hadn't wanted to face my sister, anyway. No wonder she hadn't confronted me.

So much had happened while I hid away in my room, weak and stupid.

Mam smiled and stroked my hair like she had when I was a girl. "I'm so glad you came around. I didn't want you to try and assassinate Pari again. Though, how you would get past Bellona, Isis, and Armina, I have no idea. They're quite intimidating-looking."

At the mention of what I'd done, shame surged through me so strongly that I feared I might shatter. God, I'd been such a fool. Why was I so desperate for love and attention? What was wrong with me?

Mam's gray eyes sought mine unflinchingly, but I could no longer meet her gaze. I was too ashamed.

"You've changed since being here, Lan. And while the healer inside me does not love you being in the military, I think it may have been what you were born to do."

"What do you mean?" My lips shook as I spoke. Who in their right mind would follow me now? I'd been a total idiot.

"I've never seen you so fired up, honey. You did what you did for him, yes, but I think you also thought you'd be helping people. The fae of Lyonesse." A soft smile curved her lips. "Traveling here might have helped you to find your purpose."

I sucked in a breath. She was right. People I loved

were still in Lyonesse, and they had people they loved there too. I couldn't leave them to that horrible fate. The fate my Father had instigated and blamed on another.

However, to save them, I'd have to confront the person responsible for hurting them. For tricking us all —King Oberon.

CHAPTER ELEVEN

LANA

Once the initial flood of emotions passed, I could see with frightening clarity all the awful things my father had done.

While the old me might have holed up in her room to heal before tackling other matters, I couldn't do that here. There was too much at stake. My other siblings and friends were still with that monster—unknowing pawns in his plan. I had to seek an audience with the queen, beg her forgiveness, and ask for her help.

Sinkers, I hoped she would oblige.

"Are you sure you don't want me to go, darling?" Mam asked as I knocked on Crystal's bedroom door.

"Positive." The letter my father had sent trembled in my hand like a leaf blowing about in the wind. The one I'd taken from Queen Pari's study rested in my pocket, balled up tight. "I need to do this alone."

When the door opened, Crystal's eyes widened as they latched on to me. Past her, another woman, tall and poised, waited by the window.

"Hey," Crystal greeted, prying my attention back to her. "What's up?"

She was trying to be nonchalant, but hope brimmed in her expression. Like me, she'd been told that non-fae people could not cross into Faerie. Her own mother was part dwarf and qualified, but Mam was all witch, so she did not. My sister would have known that about family. I suspected she had hoped that Mam being here would help me see the light. Perhaps she'd even suggested it to the queen.

While it hadn't been enough on its own to reveal the truth, when one part of my father's house of cards buckled, it didn't take long for the rest to come crashing down. His letter, delivered by my own trusted familiar, was irrefutable proof. I was so stubborn, I literally needed to see it spelled out in front of me.

"I received this." I held out the letter from Lyonesse.

Crystal took it, her analytical eyes still on me. Assessing. Wondering.

"It's important," I urged. The moment she stopped trying to read me, she'd understand.

Her gaze lowered to the paper, taking in the words. With each line, the muscle in her jaw fluttered a little harder. Once she got to the end, Crystal sucked in a shallow breath and lifted her gaze. Tears shone in her eyes.

"You were right."

"For once, I didn't want to be."

My lips twitched in an almost smile that felt odd on my face after all my time crying and moaning. Mam's hand landed on my shoulder, gentle as a feather.

"I need to speak to Pari. Show her this." I held my hand out for the letter, which Crystal returned. "Can Mam stay with you two? Perhaps someone can show her around?"

"Oh, darling, I'm fine in your room."

"Mam, I want you to meet my sister properly. Share a glass of caj and get some fae culture," I replied, smiling at her. I knew how much she loved immersing herself in other cultures. "Perhaps she can tell you more about Lyonesse. Or give you a tour of the gardens. She knows Buyan better than me."

"We'd love the company." Crystal threw her door open wider. "Actually, you should meet my mother, too." She twisted to where her mother still watched out the window. "Mom? Can you come here?"

The other woman approached, a tight smile on her face. I was about to learn where Crystal got her rough exterior from, I suspected.

"Mom, this is Lana."

"I'm Celine," the other woman greeted. "You and

my daughter have been through a lot. I'm still trying to take it all in."

"You and me both," I assured her before turning to Mam. "Can you have a chat with them, and I'll see you later?"

"Sure, darling."

"Yes, please, come in. The ride was long, and we didn't get to speak as much as I would have liked." Celine waved Mam in as if it were her room, not Crystal's. From the way my sister's lips tightened, her mother's attitude might be a normal thing.

"Thank you," Mam replied, and the two older women walked back to the window, conversing in low tones.

Slight relief coursed through me. Mam would have been fine in my room, but I'd been anxious over what she'd think of me if I left her alone. Probably that I'd been a bloody idiot. That time would come, of course, but I didn't need to be bogged down with it now. Not when I had another anxiety-inducing task on my plate.

"Do you want me to join you?" Crystal asked. "I've told my mother everything, and as you can see, she's not shy." She gestured back to where the older women sat in chairs facing one another. Celine was chatting up a storm.

"No thanks. This is something I need to do on my own."

"Good luck." She began to shut the door, so I turned and took a few steps. "Lana?"

I pivoted on my heel. "Yeah?"

"I'm glad we're on the same page now. There will be no hard feelings from me. It was a shitty thing to discover and come to terms with. I can understand why you wanted to believe. I did too."

"Thanks." I gave her a small smile. "See you soon."

I left with Tau at my side, but before we even exited the hallway that Crystal and I stayed in, he cleared his throat.

"Yes, Tau?"

"I'm happy you're doing what you're doing."

I was too, but it also terrified me. What if the queen did not accept my apology?

"Do you know where she is?" I asked.

"In her study."

Ah, the gilded hallway. I should have guessed. We walked the rest of the way there in silence. When we arrived, the guards stopped us.

"What's your business here, illuminator?" one asked, his tone gruff.

"I wish to speak with the queen."

"About what?"

"She may speak to me," a voice called from behind me.

I twisted to find the queen walking toward us. In her hand, she held a steaming cup of caj. How she could drink a hot beverage in this humidity was beyond me. In Buyan, I preferred my caj cold.

"My queen," the guard bowed. Even though it would be appropriate for me to follow the gesture, I didn't. I met Pari's gaze, ready to eat my frog.

"Thank you, Queen Pari. Actually, I hoped that we might have a word alone?"

Pari's eyebrows lifted. "Very well. Please, remain here, Tau."

She led me down the exquisite hallway, and I allowed myself to wonder where Bellona, Isis and Armina were. Why would a queen, who'd been so worried about me attacking her again, allow herself to be trapped in her study with me without really questioning me? I had my answer as soon as she pushed open the door to her study.

Armina stared at the door, waiting for her queen. Her full lips cracked into a golden sneer of nightmares.

A shiver ran down my spine.

"What is she doing here?" Armina asked, her tone gritty, harsh.

"She asked to speak with me. Alone, but my ladies should be here too. Is that a problem?"

I shook my head. I was not about to tell Armina to leave and have her hate me more. She'd probably murder me in my sleep.

"Good. Take a seat, Lana."

I stared at the chairs before Pari's desk. As before,

there were four, like the rooms on the other side of the hall. Then, remembering I should act a bit more astounded by the queen's private chambers, I widened my eyes.

"This room is amazing." Instantly, I sensed the overkill of wonder in my tone.

Armina shook her head and looked away.

"Please don't insult me by acting as if you've never seen this room before." Pari pointed to the seat next to Armina, and sat in the great chair behind the desk. "You may take that chair."

Armina's face tightened. She was Queen Pari's Naela, and would watch over her no matter what. Anyone foolish enough to take violent action on Queen Pari, with her ladies in waiting around, was as good as dead.

The door opened and the other two ladies strode inside too. Isis ground to a halt, her crystalline blue eyes widening when she took in my presence. Bellona, still pulling her hair into a loose ponytail, collided with her fellow lady in waiting.

"What the heck, Isis . . . ?" Bellona's question trailed off once her eyes met mine. Hers narrowed.

"My queen?" Isis inquired, shoulders thrown back, her hand inches above her dagger.

Once again, Pari waved toward chairs. It was about to be a party in here.

"Sit, my ladies. Lana has something she wanted to speak to me about in private. Of course, in private means with you as my witnesses." Pari's dark eyes leveled me.

I shrugged. I really didn't care if they listened. It was time to rip off the bandage and move on.

Once the guards settled in, all eyes fell on me.

The burden of what I was about to do weighed on my shoulders. I had made my decision and nothing could change my mind, and yet, I was letting go of a lifelong dream. Letting go of the idea of a relationship with my father. The father I had dreamt about meeting since I was very young.

That dream had all been a lie, but that did not mean it didn't hurt all the same. The pain awoke, making eyes sting.

"How can the Fullfeather cry after what she did?" Bellona sneered. "After you tried to slaughter my queen."

Her words cut deep, but my spine straightened. Time to get this done.

"I've come to say that I believe you." My eyes sought Queen Pari's in time to see hope flashed across her face.

"Explain why you changed your mind." Ice shot through me as Isis spoke. Her hand rested near her dagger. Ever so ready to take me out should I make one false move.

"Yes, explain." Compared to Isis, the queen's tone was calm, warm. "I need to understand everything that he told you. Everything you've done while you have been here."

Steeling myself, I told her everything. I admitted to sneaking about her castle, to interrogating her subjects, and to sending Naela back to Lyonesse.

"Naela returned today with this. Once I read the letter, and compared it to the other, I knew." I unfurled the scroll I'd received and handed it to Pari. Then I gave her the one I'd stolen too. "There was no way it was a fraud. Those were his words. But why would I believe you, a woman I'd heard such terrible things about and trained to kill, unless what you said was *true*? The handwriting being identical helped a lot too." I gulped. "As did the fact that you went looking for my mother and brought her to me."

"What do you mean?" the queen asked, confused.

So it had been Crystal's idea. No surprise there.

"King Oberon told me that only fae could cross through the bonegates. It was another lie. Probably everything he said was false. Maybe even that barbaric Successional." I stopped, catching myself. "I mean no disrespect if you perform the Successional, or something like it, here."

The exotic nature of the ritual was a distant memory, but I still thought of the event every time I looked at the bones on my vanity, all that remained of Kate and Kumar. Before we took part in the Successional we'd all assumed it would be fine. We believed that no one would die. We'd been wrong, of course.

No one could have expected one of our siblings would be a psychopath.

Now that I knew it had all been part of a plan for our father to manipulate us, the Successional felt even more barbaric and horrible.

Pari set the letters down before leaning back in her cushioned chair. "You are right, it is crude, and I take no offense. Although I cannot say Buyan never participated. It truly is a fae royal rite. We used to have a Successional in Buyan, but my father did away with it. Though, I will admit ours was never of the sort Oberon put you through. There were never other creatures used, nor weapons allowed."

"Did people die?" As I asked, images of Kate and Kumar flashing in my mind's eye. Even Nigel appeared, and I tried not to think about him too much.

The queen shook her head. "Ours was a fight to surrender. Instead, my father devised a series of tests to sort my siblings and me for the crown. Very similar to the ones I've heard Oberon puts his Feathered Fae and guards through when they are children. He learned many things in Buyan and turned them all to evil purposes."

"Do you believe me?" I asked.

The queen's eyes softened. "Yes. More so than your sister, who for the record, I believe in, but I was not sure of right away. When someone comes to your side too quickly, you learn to be wary. But you were different. It took weeks of searching for you to learn the truth, and I can see the change in you now. In how you hold yourself and speak. It wasn't easy to believe something so vile about a person you loved. I can respect that. I feel your pain for what you have lost."

"Thank you," I whispered and stared down at my hands.

"Release her wards, Armina."

My head snapped up. "What?"

I'd come here to apologize, and hoped that the queen would forgive me. That, though, I had not expected.

"I must agree with the Fullfeather princess, Your Majesty," Armina added. "Why?"

"There's no longer a reason to hold Lana or her sister bound."

"Are you sure?"

"Certain."

Armina did not look so convinced, but she followed orders, performing a complicated hand gesture—all without taking her narrowed gaze off of me.

Something dammed up inside me exploded, and my magic flowed freely once again, and I gasped. Weirdly, my skin began to glow.

"Her eyes are glowing," Isis pointed out, a hand still on her dagger.

"Yes," Pari replied. "She's an illuminator witch.

Those powers will be helpful in the days and weeks, perhaps even months to come." Standing, she extended her hand. "Thank you for coming to me, Princess Lana. You have no idea how much I needed this news. I knew your father well when we were young, and you know him well now."

"I wouldn't be so sure about that."

"Well, I am," the queen assured. "Oberon had to have shown you some truths to get you to trust him. Together, we shall be an unstoppable force when we liberate the fae of Lyonesse."

"What?!"

"Did you believe I liked imagining those fae being poor and magicless? According to my sources, Lyonesse is in dire straits. I could do nothing while Oberon sat on the throne, and his people believed him. *Loved* him. But they know you too, and you can change things." She extended her ringed hand to me again.

I took it, lips parted in shock. Pari's magic brushed mine as it ran through her, as wild and free as mine did. It felt amazing to have my magic back.

We let go and my hand fell to my side. "Thank you. I—"

The door to Pari's chambers flew open. The ladies in waiting leapt to their feet, weapons at the ready.

"Your Majesty!" A guard burst in, his emerald eyes wide and wild. "I'm sorry for the intrusion but there's urgent news!"

"What is it, Captain?"

"Hired swords attacked our bonegate. There have been casualties. They damaged the magic on the portal, too."

Queen Pari's face fell as dread pooled in my stomach.

"We need to go," Armina spat. "I must check the wards."

"Yes," the queen replied. Her gaze snapped to me. "Lana, get your sister. You two are coming with me."

CHAPTER TWELVE

LANA

I clung to Crystal as the gryphon plunged.

"Can't breathe!" My sister squirmed to loosen my vice-like grip.

Hell, me neither. I was too terrified I might fall off the beast to take a proper breath. Since Pari informed us we'd be flying north to her bonegate, rather than riding, my bones had been mush. No matter how sure Crystal was that she could maintain control over the gryphon, I couldn't stop picturing it bucking us off and sending us plummeting to our deaths.

The wall of trees came closer and closer and unable to stop myself, I squeezed my eyes shut. It would only take slamming into a single tree to end it all. How did the beast know where the break in the branches was, anyway?

We were going to die.

My stomach dipped as a flutter of leaves brushed

against my skin. Crystal let out a strangled sound, and my arms wound tighter around her torso.

"Dude, seriously! Loosen up!" Crystal gasped. "It was a branch!"

A response tipped my tongue, when the rush of air around us ceased and the gryphon touched down. I exhaled. We'd survived.

Moisture hung heavy in the air, making my breath strain, as I opened my eyes to find a jungle rising on all sides. The foliage crowded overhead so thick I only got peeks of blue sky. How many strange fae animals nested above, watching us with interest? Naela would have a grand time hunting here.

Crystal dismounted with a huff and scanned the area. I got off too, my legs wobbling when my boots hit the dirt. Just when you had horses mastered, they threw a bloody gryphon at you! Unbelievable!

"Your bonegate is around here?" Crystal asked. "It's so hidden."

"Much unlike Lyonesse's portal." Pari wiped stray feathers off her pants. Her ladies joined her one by one, all looking a million times more put together than I felt. "My ancestors put it here for that reason. My people are experts at jungle navigation. No other kingdom in Faerie can say such a thing. The terrain makes foreign attacks more difficult, though not impossible. Obviously."

"How did they do it?" Crystal asked.

"We're about to find out." Isis' voice was clipped. "Follow me."

She led the way through the woods, and the other two ladies flanked their queen, leaving only her back exposed. It took me a few minutes to realize that Crystal and I trailed Pari, and that was a show of confidence. The ladies in waiting would never have positioned themselves in that way if they did not trust us.

I hadn't gotten that impression from them when we spoke in Pari's study. I wondered what had changed since then. Had Pari spoken to them while the gryphon master gave me and my sister a brief riding lesson?

All my questions halted when we stepped through what felt like an invisible curtain of water, a ward, and a small civilization appeared before my eyes. "Whoa! Cool."

"Totally cool." Crystal agreed, pointing upward. "The six-year-old in me is so jealous."

Because the vegetation was so thick on the ground, Pari's people had built tree houses as their homes. The few structures on the jungle floor were very small. None could hold over three people. I suspected they were restrooms or huts to wait in while guards held watch.

Pari and her ladies kept walking, addressing fae as they moved through the camp. I followed, silent, admiring the village before me. As I did, my keen eyes searched for the portal, but found nothing that my brain correlated to a magical door to the Old Land.

"Queen Pari, welcome," a man approached, his eyes weary.

"General Fylson, it appears our worries have come true."

"Yes, My Queen. The portal is malfunctioning. I'm sorry that despite all your precautions, I let you down."

"You didn't. This is why you're here. After the last attack on our bonegate I figured Oberon would try again, and I wanted someone I trusted implicitly to be here and manage things. His first coup didn't work, nor the second. He's getting desperate." Despite the serious situation, a small smile curled her lips.

"There have been *two* attempts?" Crystal voiced the question budding in my mind.

"One before you arrived in Buyan," Queen Pari replied. "That one was initiated in the Old Land by those working with Oberon in your world."

"What? How?" I didn't realize that my father had contacts in the Old Land.

"Demi-fae relations to the nobles of Lyonesse speak to the Feathered Fae when they're in the Old Land," General Fylson explained. "They laid siege to the bonegates earlier this year. The attacks were debilitating, but they did not produce the results Oberon wished."

"Which were?" Crystal pressed.

"An infiltration of vampires to take down the kingdom of Sinkers Realm."

"Vampires? Why would they come here?" I questioned, shocked.

"Vampires love nothing more than fae blood," the queen answered. "And if they turn us, we become a powerful creature called nosferatu. Such creatures, they would love to control. For your father, it was an easy bargain to make, as the vampire Oberon allied with was desperate too. Luckily for us, the newly crowned queen of Ys was strong enough to take Oberon's partner down. Without that alliance, his plans failed." She turned her attention back to the general.

"I presume you caught the culprits from today's attack?"

"There were about a dozen. All bearing the tattoos of the Zatus mafia. Most perished when we opened fire," General Fylson cleared his throat. "Two, however, escaped."

Pari's calm façade hardened. "You have soldiers searching the area for them?"

"Of course."

She sighed. "Very well. Keep me updated. And send word to Ys, too. Their new queen will want to hear of this. Tampering with bonegates is becoming too common. Let's proceed."

The general bowed. "Very well, My Queen."

As we continued, I caught Crystal's eyes. She

shrugged. There had been even more drama in Faerie than we'd known, and a new queen in Ys had something to do with it. I wanted to hear more, but now was not the time to pry, so I tucked my questions away for later.

We trekked deeper into the camp before the queen stopped again, this time in front of a large tree. She pressed her hand to it, and the trunk trembled as if it were a person.

"What's going on?" I whispered.

"She is testing the bonegate," Bellona replied as if I were stupid. "Trying to discern the basis of the malfunctioning magic."

Pari threw her lady a chastising look, but I ignored the tone. There were more important matters on my mind.

My lips parted in surprise. "This tree is the bonegate?"

"They don't all look the same," Bellona added, her tone slightly softer. "The Lyonesse one resembles a grave of sorts. Morbid, if you ask me."

"Well, it is where the first fae buried the Fullfeather's Sinker's bones," Crystal replied, nonplussed. "Why wouldn't it resemble a grave?"

"How did they get your Sinker's bones in a tree?" I asked. Other than the fact that they were valuable portals, and magic flowed through them, I knew little about bonegates.

"Magic. The tree enveloped him." Bellona answered.

An image of a man being swallowed up alive by a tree came to mind and I pressed my lips together. I hoped it wasn't like that—maybe he'd already been dead—but I wasn't going to ask.

"Stop talking," Pari hissed. "I'm concentrating."

We fell quiet for another minute, before she turned to face us, seeming troubled.

"Someone powerful led this attack. It feels like they might have inserted a ward in there, to make it unsafe. Or perhaps even impossible to use. Maybe they were also a wardmaker. I'm afraid it will take multiple rounds to fix the magic." Her gaze sought Armina. "You're the best wardmaker in Faerie. Will you start?"

"Of course, My Queen," she replied, bowing her head. "Would you like me to do so now?"

"We're not leaving until it's functional."

"Do you think hired swords did this?" Crystal asked, shooting me a glance. "Are they normally that skilled?"

I understood her reservations. The hired swords we'd seen in Zatus looked like they'd only be good at one thing—fighting with muscles, rather than magic.

Queen Pari turned her dark gaze upon us. "I do. I—"

A small, winged man dropped from the trees to hover right in front of me. Caught unaware, I gasped, and was about to conjure my infrared sword when he thrust his blade into my chest.

"Argh!" I collapsed, blood gushing from the wound. My hand pressed desperately against my chest to staunch the flow, but the blood kept pouring out— pain searing through me. A whine left my lips, high and terrified.

"Lana!" A gale of wind blew the fae away from me before he could lift his dagger again. A second later, Crystal was on her knees, cradling my head. "It's okay. Isis is on him. He . . . oh shit."

Her tone dropped and although the stab wound was agony, my gaze snapped up in time to see another fae drop from the trees. He shot a round of arrows at Queen Pari, and then twisted to loose more on us.

Crystal's air magic came to the rescue once more, hurling the arrows into the woods. Yet, the fae was not to be deterred. He fought the gale and swooped upward, pointing another arrow at us.

I called light, and it blazed forth, blinding him. Crystal did the rest, redirecting her blast at the attacker and slamming him into a tree. The fae's head hit the wood, and he fell to the ground with a hard *thunk*.

A moment later Isis was next to the fae, kicking the weapon away and binding his hands and wings. The second they bound him; she lifted the man over her shoulder. He looked like a child next to her

Amazonian frame. "Do I Interrogate him, My Queen?"

"Ask Fylson to use their offices. Post guards around him."

"Can I come?" I asked, woozy. My shirt clung to me, warm with blood that wouldn't dry in the humid jungle. The wound had to be bad, but I couldn't think about it. If I did, I'd lose it.

"Don't you worry about that." Pari knelt next to us. "The other one is dead. Bellona ran for a healer. Stay still."

"They were waiting for us, weren't they?" Crystal whispered, hands trembling.

"Why?" I asked. Stars swam in my vision and against my better judgment, I glanced down. Bile rose in my throat at the sight. Blood coated my front, so much blood.

"Lana, relax. Close your eyes," Crystal guided, her tone soft. It was the first time I could actually picture her as a doctor, easing the pain of the sick.

"I-I . . ." I twisted, so I wasn't pointed straight at her and retched.

"Oh crap! She's puking blood!"

"Stay calm. Bellona will return momentarily."

Queen Pari continued to assure Crystal, but I didn't take in a word as darkness encroached on my vision. My heart rate sped up, intent on getting in a few last good beats. I was dying. There was so much I hadn't done with my life.

I hadn't saved my siblings.

Or the fae of Lyonesse from my lying scumbag of a father.

Or told Garret how I really felt.

Again, vomit climbed up my throat. This time, I noticed the tang of metal that coated my tongue. Tears tore down my cheeks and after I emptied my stomach, I began to hyperventilate.

"I think I'm dying," I whispered before everything went black.

CHAPTER THIRTEEN

FINN

Meegra had returned yesterday, and since then, she'd been in my father's private chambers. It was late morning, and yet, no one had called me to discuss plans to extract Lana and Crystal from the clutches of Queen Pari.

Furious I punched my pillow. Didn't Father realize how dire this situation was? Throughout history, people killed their hostages all the time! Sometimes just to prove a point, but in this case, Queen Pari would be rightfully angry. Lana and Crystal might be slated for execution at this very moment.

No. I refused to believe the deed had already come to pass. I couldn't think that way. Knowing they were out there, in need of help, was the only thing driving me forward.

The delay confused my siblings too, though none of us spoke of it. I suspected they, like me, felt guilty for leaving our sisters. The guards closest to us were troubled too.

But our Father?

He almost seemed to be avoiding rescuing his daughters.

The familiar debate of whether I should approach him played in my head as I paced my room. When I reached the window, I pressed my hands onto the stone sill and gazed outside. Spring was slowly encroaching on winter, but the air remained cold. It seeped through the glass, and I pressed my cheek to it, needing to cool down, to douse my inner fire.

That was when I saw him.

"What the bloody hell?" I muttered as Father rode through the castle gates, a handful of the Feathered Fae as his escorts. The king had been cooped up in his chambers for days. He hadn't even attended meals in the great hall.

Yet, Meegra returned, and he took to the town? Where was he going? And why?

If I left my window, I'd never catch him, but from here I could see into the greater city. I watched my Father travel down the main street and then turn west, on the road leading to the homes of the few wealthy Lyonesse residents. Noble fae who, because they had strong earth magic in their family lines, grew most of the food for the kingdom on small plots of land around their manors.

"Why is he speaking with them and not me?" My

tone was tense as my jaw ground down. Deep inside, my shadows surged. In the safety of my rooms, I'd been letting them out daily, and yet, they weren't appeased. They only grew more insistent to be free.

I tried to ignore them, but they surged up again, painting the veins of my hands a deep navy, almost black.

"I can't have you follow him." Following Meegra hadn't been smart, but at the time, I'd been too curious to stop myself.

Following Father would be even more dangerous. He would know the shadows were my demon gift, and he'd be furious I used them against him. I wanted information, not to piss him off.

Once more, the shadows surged, this time so strongly they erupted from my fingers like flames. I drew in a sharp breath. So far, they hadn't been able to leave me without blood being spilled from my veins. That appearance was a new development. They disappeared back into my skin, reminding me of the way my fire magic vanished after I used it.

Fire . . . I looked into the town and sucked in a breath.

"Could you get me into my father's chambers?" I spoke to my shadows. They'd know the question was for them. "He'll have wards up. Think you can get through them?"

The strange sensation of my shadows nodding

stirred inside me, but I was getting used to it. At least, that's what I told myself.

"And we can have a lookout?"

Another nod.

They didn't seem at all worried about wards like the ones that had stopped them at Gory's place. I didn't know why that was. Perhaps not all wards were the same? I had no idea, and really it didn't matter. If it didn't work, I was just back where I started. There was no loss.

My lips pressed together. Did I dare?

Father and his line of Feathered Fae trailed farther away when I glanced out the window again. My anger at being kept in the dark rushed through me and I spun on my heel. Hell yes, I dared.

Whirling around, I stormed through the halls. I'd been in such a piss poor mood lately that no one stopped me to talk. At the moment, that suited me. I was on a mission and needed no distractions. When I reached the hallway where Father's private chambers were located, I peered down the corridor. No one milled around the area.

"I need a lookout to stay here. If someone tries to come down the hall, stop them. I don't care what you must do, short of killing."

I pulled my blade from its scabbard and pressed the metal into the skin of my arm, right next to an old cut. Soon, I'd have so many that people would start asking questions. I might have to start opening up scabs.

Blood welled, and a shadow slipped out of me. It floated upward to hide in a crevice where no one would see it. Sure that it had my back, I made my way down the hall.

"Go inside," I whispered when I reached the door. The act violated my father's privacy, but I needed to assure myself that he was at least working on a plan to retrieve my sisters. No longer would I remain in the dark.

Another shadow slipped from me, and slid through the crack at my feet. My lips parted. I half expected that the king would have up protections that would stop them. But now, apparently Gory had stronger wards around his headquarters. Not all wards were created equal.

Not a second later, the door eased open from the inside. I scurried into the room and shut the door, pressing my back to it. A nervous exhale left me.

"Thanks," I murmured, both astounded, and a little creeped out at all that my shadows could do.

The smokey figure didn't reply, only floated to the firlon. The fire glowed in the magical instrument, lower than usual but still ready for someone to view whatever they wished. I joined the shadow and peered into the flames. My heart hammered over what I was about to do—violate Father's privacy. Anyone would dislike that, but my father would hate it more than most. He was a king, used to having people fall in line.

I would not wait any longer.

"Show me the king."

The firlon zoomed into the city of Lyonesse, like I would on a tablet in the Old Land. I watched, my breath tight in my chest as it panned on a grand old villa. That had to be one of the nicest homes in the kingdom, if not the nicest. The next thing I knew I was inside that very home, streaking down a hallway and into a sitting room.

Father, Meegra, and the bald fae I'd seen taking blood from the dragon sat in different armchairs in front of the fireplace.

The fae's lips turned down as he smoothed his red robe. "If they're onto us, there's no reason to have them here. You'll have to do something about the brood you've brought to our realm."

I blinked at his tone. It was almost as if he was telling my father what to do. Who was that guy?

"I believe the others can still be useful," Father replied. "As long as we make the girls' deaths look like Queen Pari's fault."

"The soldiers I hired will get the job done. In fact, they might have already done so," Meegra assured them. "There will be no more letters. No hints of faltering loyalties."

My heart stopped, and I staggered back, shocked. Had I heard that right?

Was Father planning to kill Lana and Crystal?

For a moment, I lost track of the conversation happening in the firlon, but I needed answers, so I stepped back up toward the enchanted item. A yell in the hallway stopped me before I took in another word.

"Finn!" A man bellowed. "Call it off!"

My body stiffened. I recognized that voice. Bolting toward the door, I flung it open. "Stop!"

The shadow, which had been trying to suffocate Ryker, released him.

"Get away from him."

The shadow followed my command, but even as it did, a pit expanded in my stomach. I'd been able to keep my demon gift a secret, but that was no longer possible. My shadow had tried to strangle Ryker!

Instead of appearing upset, the guard marched toward me, fear lining his face. "What are you doing in there?"

"Uhhh." I cast a glance back at the firlon. The flames still danced, and although I was too far away to understand what was being said, voices continued to resonate from the enchanted object.

Ryker's eyes widened. "Sinkers . . . Finn, what are you watching?"

I gulped.

The guard cocked his head, listening. His sense of hearing was better than mine, because he drew in a sharp breath. "The king!" He reached out and grabbed my wrist. "Finn, look at me. What are you doing in your father's chambers? Does he know you are here?"

"I needed to know what was happening!" I blurted. "Something is off. He's taking forever to rescue my sisters, and he won't speak with me."

"I see." Relief flickered across Ryker's face. "I have answers."

"What? Tell me!"

"I will, but we can't stay here. Shut the door. We need to get you out of the castle."

"What?" I blinked. Was this *screw with Finn* day? That would sort of be a relief, to know what I'd heard was a joke.

Instead of replying, Ryker eased the door shut and stared at me, his dark eyes piercing.

"Do you suspect your father of foul play?"

"I-I-I'm not su—"

"Answer me. We don't have a lot of time."

"Yes," I blurted. After what I'd overheard, what else could I think?

"Then this will be much easier."

That got my attention. "What will be easier?"

Ryker exhaled a long breath. "Your father tried to have Lana and Crystal killed yesterday."

I stiffened. His claim tracked with what I'd just heard, but how did Ryker learn that?

My shadows swarmed around us, mirroring my

emotions. Ryker gulped, and I held out a hand, stilling them.

"Thanks." Ryker's shoulders loosened.

"I command them, so you don't have to fear them. But back to the point, how do you know?"

"That's why Meegra went to Zatus. To hire assassins. It wouldn't be the first time she did so."

Ice flew through my veins remembering her words. She'd suggested her assassins had already done the job.

"But the wards around Buyan," I said, trying to work it out. "They had to have strengthened them. Queen Pari would have been a fool not to tweak them to be sensitive to human blood."

"You're right. I'm sure the new wards will alert her if anyone rides into her kingdom. They can then send a troop to check them out. There will be stronger ones by the city, stronger still near the castle. But the Buyan bonegate, far north of the city, isn't the same. Wards can be specialized, and the protections are weaker there because magic flows into our world from the Old Land and it needs to reach all of the kingdom." Ryker shook his head. "Don't worry. The assassin failed, but Lana got stabbed."

I blinked. Stabbed?! "H-how did you learn all this?"

He leveled me with his gaze. "My family are spies. We act on behalf of the citizens of Lyonesse, keeping the most vulnerable safe. Specifically, those who see the truth. We even help citizens escape when we can, and we have connections in other kingdoms. Buyan included." His eyes narrowed, challenging me to rat him out to the others.

My mind whirled with about a million questions, but something told me I didn't have time for them. Not if our father tried to kill Lana and Crystal.

"Ryker, my siblings and I need to leave."

"I've got your back, bro," he assured, relief clear in his voice.

"How?" I had no bloody idea how to get eight people out of the castle unnoticed.

"Garret and Ebba are saddling gryphons for you to use. Let's move. We can't waste any more time."

We strode down the hallway with urgency. I brushed aside the fear of riding, flying, on a gryphon and focused on another matter.

"Are they spies too?" I asked when we turned down another corridor.

"Only me and Sai."

"What did you tell them?"

"Told them you got a secret mission to rescue Lana and Crystal and they needed to go with you. Once you're out of the kingdom, tell them the truth. The king knows about Lana and Garret, so I have to get him out. He's my bro, my family by choice. Sai feels the same about Ebba . . . not that you could leave her behind anyway."

He was right. She might not have the same feelings for me, but I couldn't leave her with my father—a man who tried to have his own daughters killed. The realization made my fists clench.

"Thank you. Now let's go find my siblings" We marched down the hallway, side by side, trying to look as if we weren't running for our lives. When we got to the section of the castle where most of my siblings and I lived—all except for Lana, who had stayed one corridor down, I listened closely.

A burst of laughter caught my ear, and I followed it to Maria's room. Inside, my rumbler sister was playing cards with Himari and Arlo. All three had nearly-empty glasses of elven wine in front of them.

Wonderful. They were probably half tanked, and we needed to sneak out of a kingdom.

"You need to be gone by the time the king returns," Ryker whispered.

His voice caught Maria's attention. She looked up and beamed. "Hey, boys. Wanna join? I'd be happy to take your coin too."

"Actually, no." I eased inside the room. Ryker followed, shutting the door behind him. "There's something I need to tell you guys. So, listen up. I don't have time to go over this twice."

I launched into my story. From seeing Meegra fly to Zatus to the firlon, and Ryker confirming it all. Their mouths fell open, but no one interrupted.

Ten minutes later, I led my siblings down the hall. Tension and shock riddled the group, but they'd believed my story more quickly than I'd dared hope. Had they, too, been wondering why we had not rescued Lana or Crystal yet? Or did something else tip them off that our father was rotten?

Now that I thought about it, he'd acted shady a million times. Each time I'd brushed it off as a cultural difference—which was probably exactly what he wanted.

"Does anyone know where the others are?" I asked.

"Gio said something about getting in some training," Maria mumbled. "I told him that would be stupid. He isn't healed all the way, even though he acts like he is. But I bet he did it, anyway."

She was probably right. Despite being severely injured in Buyan, Gio did not like being thought of as helpless. He'd been training, much to the dismay of the castle healers.

"Dak is with him," Himari added.

"The training room it is, then." I led the way, and soon enough, the sounds of people sparring rolled through the corridors. We were so close. Once we got them, we could leave and then we'd be safe.

I kept that line of thought intact until I stood in the doorway of the training room and it all came crashing down. Our siblings were in there, working out and sparring, but so were Prince Casimir and three Feathered Fae.

Casimir caught my entrance and his eyes lit up,

but thankfully he was in the middle of a session with Ash, an asshole Feathered Fae who barked for the prince to resume sparring. Casimir obliged, but still, I could tell he wanted me to be his next partner. He loved a challenge and as another full elemental, I certainly was a challenge. Shite! I backed up into the hallway and collided with Ryker.

"We can't waltz in and get them," I whispered. "Casimir will ask questions. He's devoted to the king."

"I know," Ryker's tone rumbled low, worried.

"What are we going to do?" Himari squeaked. "We can—"

Fast footsteps sounded down the hall, coming our way, and my alarmed gaze locked with Ryker's. Were we too late?

Sai swung around the corner, white hair streaking behind her. The moment she saw us, she gestured for us to join her. We did so quickly.

"The king is back," Sai whispered. "He knows someone was in his chambers. The firlon was still viewing Lord Tizu's sitting room. Anything to do with you?" She arched an eyebrow at her cousin.

"Fuck," I muttered. "No. That was me."

"Well, you need to move. He's questioning every-one." Sai leveled me with her gaze. "And asked for you. He might suspect your demon gift got you inside. No one has ever done that before."

I glanced back at the training room. "We need to warn the others."

Ryker placed a hand on my shoulder. "There's no time. You need to run. Now. If you tell them to leave, Casimir will be suspicious."

"We can fight him."

"No, you can't," Ryker argued. "He'll call more guards. You might be a demon born, but don't endanger yourself when you have a shot at surviving."

"He's right," Sai added. "Run to the stables. We'll take care of the others. Besides, they have an alibi. They've been training since the king left. He saw them and applauded their efforts."

"You'll get them out when you can?" Maria asked, her voice wobbly, troubled. "Keep them safe?"

"We promise," Sai vowed.

Tension hung thick in the air. More than anything, I wanted to turn and grab my other siblings and then go, but I suspected the guards were right. It would be idiotic.

Shouting and the sounds of boots hitting the ground came from somewhere deep in the castle. Our time was up.

"Go!" Ryker urged.

My heart ripping in half, I did as he said, and broke into a sprint toward the stables.

CHAPTER FOURTEEN

LANA

I groaned and squeezed my eyes tightly closed, wanting to continue sleeping. What hurt so bloody bad? Had someone punched me in the boob? Or . . .

Oh, right. I'd been stabbed.

"Darling? Are you alright?"

My eyes flew open to find Mam and Crystal at my bedside. Above me, Naela perched on the headboard.

A gut-wrenching sob tore up Mam's throat once her gaze met mine. "I'm so glad you're awake."

"Wish I wasn't," I croaked painfully. A pang of pain scrunched up my face as I pushed myself up; fire seared my chest.

"Don't you dare!" Mam held her hand over me. "Lay down, Lana! I need to look you over."

"I can have the castle healer come check on her if you want assistance." Another voice, Pari's, offered.

I gazed past my mother to find the queen at my window. Bright light filtered in from the outside, illuminating dark circles around her eyes.

"No need." Mam began unbuttoning my shirt. "I'll care for my daughter. The serious stuff has been tended to, darling, just tell me how you feel. I'll take care of the finer work."

Yesterday I would have been self-conscious over exposing my boob to everyone, but I suspected they'd all seen it already. Plus, Mam excelled at healing, and I wanted to get back on my feet quickly.

"I just feel sore and a bit inflamed." I could tell that people had been healing me while I rested, otherwise I probably wouldn't be able to sit up. "My boob is tender."

Mam got to work.

"What time is it?" I asked. "And what exactly happened?"

"It's the day after you were stabbed. Late afternoon, fourth bell," Pari answered and twisted to face the room. "We healed you just enough at the bonegate to bring you to the castle, where we have greater resources. Your mother has been doing most of the heavy lifting." As she spoke, she began walking to the door.

Only then did I notice Bellona standing guard in my room. She opened the door for Pari, who poked her head outside. Mumblings about fetching the healer and having him wait outside the door in case we needed him, filled my ears.

Judging by the way Mam's lips tightened, she'd heard them, but she didn't tell off the queen. She merely poured her magic into me. Slowly, the injured area went numb, and I exhaled with relief. My mother was a genius.

Feeling stronger and ready to get answers, my gaze veered back to the queen. "How did I get back?"

Riding on a gryphon had been precarious on the way to the bonegate, and on the return trip, I'd been unconscious. Apparently, for well over a day.

"You rode between Crystal and me. We supported you in flight." The queen gave me a soft smile.

"What happened to my attacker? You questioned him, right?"

It was all coming back to me slowly. The fae who'd fallen from the thick canopy. How Crystal and I had worked together to incapacitate him, while his accomplice died at the hands of one of Pari's ladies. Why were they there? And why attack me?

"We did question him," Queen Pari conceded. "Are you sure you don't want to rest right now? You've been through a lot."

Instantly, I stiffened. Something in her tone told me that whatever they'd learned from the fae wouldn't be pretty. What had he said?

"What did you learn?"

A huffed breath left Crystal's lips. "She *deserves* to know."

It was the first time she'd spoken, and instead of speaking softly—as one would over another person's sick bed—my sister sounded angry. Furious. My eyes met hers. "You tell me."

"Lana, I—" Mam started, but I held up a hand.

"I won't be kept in the dark." I slipped my hand toward Crystal's, feeling her take it and squeeze. "Why were those fae there?"

She gulped. Whatever she was about to say hurt her too.

"Our father sent them to get rid of us both. Queen Pari too, if they could manage." Tears flooded her eyes. "There were more of them before they tampered with the bonegate, which was a way to lure us there. Somehow assassins broke through the wards and entered the castle too, in case we weren't with the queen when she checked on the bonegate. And they probably knew Armina would be with Pari, so she wouldn't feel the tampering. They timed it just right, like real professionals. Father really covered all his bases."

"No," I whispered, barely audible above the sound of blood pounding in my ears.

Crystal drew in a sharp breath, swallowing. "Yes. I expect he was going to cover up the fact that we switched sides. He'd tell everyone that Queen Pari executed us or something."

"Undoubtedly," Pari muttered.

"Our father hired someone to assassinate us?" Acid bubbled in my gut, volatile. I'd come to terms with the terrible person he was, but this? It was beyond comprehension.

My heart shattered, and pain that had nothing to do with my stab wound shot through me. His letter had suggested that I go home. Did he learn I hadn't and decided to take care of me before I made trouble? Or had this been his plan all along?

A memory of speaking with Gory surfaced. I gasped. "Do you remember Gory?"

"How could I forget?" Crystal asked.

"He said then that Meegra had arrived to negotiate a deal a few weeks before us. She only asked for a few of his best soldiers on retainer. Do you think . . .?" The sentence stuck in my throat, too terrible to finish. I had been talking with, *trying to impress*, the fae who would later send hired swords to kill me.

"You might be onto something," Crystal replied, her voice breathy. "But even if he made the deal later, he's still a monster."

Mam's healing paused as a sob escaped her. "I'm so sorry, honey. I can't believe I ever loved him. What kind of man does that?"

"You are not the only one he has fooled," Pari assured her.

No. Father had personally hurt nearly every woman in the room. My fists clenched. The fecking bastard.

"What are we going to do about it?" Crystal asked after a long moment of silence. "Our other siblings are still there, at his mercy. They don't even know what he's really like. What if he kills them to be on the safe side? We need to get to them and tell them the truth."

My blood froze. She was right. An assassination attempt made it even more imperative that we extract our siblings from Lyonesse, before the king did something dire.

Above me, Naela flapped her wings for attention. My gaze snapped up to find her holding out her leg, as if asking me to send a letter.

"Oh no, you don't," I argued. "King Oberon said he'd kill you on sight if you returned, Boss. I can't risk it."

I'd already lost so much, losing Naela too might be my end. We had to figure out a different way. Mam threw my familiar a pointed look as if to second my opinion, before resuming healing my wound.

"You should not need to do that anyway," Pari interjected. "I spoke to my sources in Lyonesse early this morning about what happened—I find it best to keep them well informed. Although, I'm not sure they passed the information along already. I can try to get another message to them and tell them it's urgent. They will relay it to the castle as soon as they can."

That wasn't the first time she'd mentioned her sources. I wondered who they were. Had I met them? If they could get a word to my siblings, they must be well connected, but did it matter? As long as they saved my siblings, I didn't really care who they were.

"A message to Finn would be best," I agreed. "How do you deliver the messages, anyway?"

Pari smiled. "We use an item called an aqual to speak. It looks like a normal bowl, but it allows the owners of connected bowls to speak using water as a medium. No one will need to be injured or caught. The only question is when it will reach those in the castle."

My eyes widened. "I'm surprised the king never searched homes for one of those. It sounds so simple."

"My sources are excellent at pretending they're loyal. And as I have not attacked in years, he has no reason to think anyone is against him. Your father believes he has everyone tricked."

"He's not far from wrong," Crystal hissed.

"Yes. Of course, you're right, but there are those who know the truth." Pari gave her a weak smile. "After he told me his plans to infiltrate the Old Land, I placed an aqual in a location he never expected before I took control of his bonegate."

Wow. I knew fae lived for many centuries and as a

result often played the long game, but Queen Pari and my father took that to a whole other level. I was about to ask another question, when Mam removed her hands from where they'd hovered over me, and leaned back.

An exhausted breath gusted out of her. "All done for now. I'll check it again in a few hours, but you should be good to go by tomorrow, darling."

Stunned, I looked down at my chest. Where yesterday a gaping hole had gushed blood, now only pink skin stared back at me. The area was still numb, and it was far less red than before Mam started working. Most likely, I'd have a scar, but I'd rather have that than be dead. Tears filled my eyes when how close I'd come to dying really hit home.

"Thanks, Mam. You should rest." She looked knackered, which was not surprising. Intense healing took a lot of energy, and I was sure Mam had used everything she had to heal me. She'd probably been awake all night too.

"Are you tired, darling?"

Far from it. I was amped up and wanted to hear more about how we'd get my siblings out of there. Also, though I wasn't about to admit it to her, I wanted to talk to Queen Pari about getting Mam out of Faerie. If I wasn't safe here, she wasn't either. If my despicable father would kill Naela, he'd totally use Mam to get to me.

"I'm not, but we can move to Crystal's room so

you can sleep?" Mam had been sharing my room, as Celine shared her daughter's quarters.

"Actually, Mom is asleep in there," Crystal said apologetically. "We didn't get back till pretty late last night and she stayed up. Worrying."

"The room next door is free," Pari offered. "It's like this one but with no door connecting it to Lana's room."

Torn, my mom's gaze focused on me.

"You should take it." I pressed my finger to my stab wound. "You might need to perform more miraculous healing later."

Giving in, she patted my hand and stifled a yawn. "I will go rest, but don't you dare do anything other than relax, okay? You're still on the mend."

"I won't do anything."

Mam kissed me on the cheek and rose. "Love you, darling."

"Love you too." I smiled.

"Bellona, please ensure that Aileen has everything she needs in the next room," Pari commanded.

"As long as there's a bed, I'm fine," Mam said.

"Even so, Bellona, please show her to her quarters. Return once she's settled."

The guard gestured for Mam to follow, and she did, only throwing me one more worried glance.

"I'll be fine," I assured. "Promise. Go sleep."

With a kiss, Mam disappeared through the door, shutting it behind her.

"She hasn't slept at all since we got back," Crystal confessed when we were alone. "I'm glad she's resting."

I was glad too. Particularly because she wouldn't like what I was going to say next. "If your sources can tell our siblings to leave, how will they do so without attracting attention? If we need to help, I'd like a little more information."

Pari's lips twitched as if she'd known what I'd say. "We'll have to see. It depends on—"

A knock came at the door, halting the queen's words. Bellona would have entered and resumed her post, and no one else would dare interrupt the queen unless it was serious.

"I got it." Crystal rose from the bed.

"No. Allow me." Pari strode over before Crystal even took a step. Her shoulders tensed lightly, but the moment she saw whoever stood on the other side of the door, they relaxed. "Queen Maurette. This is a surprise. I asked Isis to inform you of the developments, but did not think you'd pay us a visit."

"She insisted, Your Majesty," Isis piped up from the hall.

"I sure did. And please, Queen Pari, it's Mauri. Only use the queen if you must, it's still weird for me."

Crystal gripped the bedspread, and my attention snapped to her. She looked like she'd seen, or more aptly, heard, a ghost. I sat up, not without a struggle, but easier than I had earlier.

"You okay?" I whispered as the other women kept chatting.

"I know that voice." My sister darted a frantic look to me before her gaze returned to the door. "No . . . is this real?!"

"What?" My eyebrows furrowed.

Crystal was already up, dashing across the room. When she got to where she could see the visitor, she shrieked. "Mauri! What the hell are you doing here?!"

"C-Crystal? This is where you've been?! I called you for months, you ho!"

Okay, now I was super confused, and as it seemed, Pari shared my bewilderment. Her eyebrows furrowed while her gaze volleyed between the women. Yet, before she could ask a single question, a woman barreled into my room and threw herself at Crystal.

My sister laughed so hard that tears leaked from her eyes. I had a million questions too, but I listened as the pair talked. Mauri, or Queen Maurette, was Crystal's bestie from the Old Land. She was half vampire and half fae, a nosferatu—whatever that meant—and now ruled over Ys. The pair hadn't been in touch since before Crystal got sucked into Faerie.

It was all too wild, too crazy to believe. I expected I still had a dumbfounded look on my face, when Mauri turned to me and smiled.

"Hey, I'm Mauri, the new Queen of Ys." She beamed. Mauri was a stunning black woman with the straightest, most perfect teeth I'd ever seen. I found it hard not to stare at her smile. "You must be one of the siblings. You've got that Old Land look all over you."

I snorted a laugh. She was one to talk. Mauri might be a queen, but she was wearing leggings. Real stretchy, *comfy* leggings. I missed those.

"Back at you. I'm Lana."

"We have a hell of a lot to catch you up on, girl." Crystal's tone dipped in a way that told me she was thinking of the Successional. Probably our tumultuous past, too.

"Well, as long as it's okay with Queen Pari, I'll stay a few days? I have a few things to do here, anyway."

Crystal cocked her head, but Mauri did not elaborate. For the first time, she looked uncomfortable. Oh, she had secrets. That pair had a lot to catch up on after all.

"I'd be honored," Pari said. "I'm happy to have brought two old friends back together."

She really looked it, too. I could understand. It was pretty damn heart-warming watching Crystal and Mauri talk. They were like sisters—even more so than Crystal and me, because they had so much history.

Feeling self-conscious, I squirmed. I hoped Mauri liked me.

As if calling for attention, my stomach rumbled loudly, pinning everyone's attention to me. "Sorry. Perhaps we can get an early tea brought in, so we can get to know each other better?" I suggested, not quite ready to be left alone yet, which was a novel experience for me. I loved my alone time.

"Of course, I can have something brought to you ladies," Pari agreed. "I should—" Halting mid-sentence, her head snapped toward the door.

Thunderous footsteps raced down the hall. My heart rate kicked up, mimicking their tempo just as Tau burst into the room, his eyes latching on the queen.

"What happened?" she asked. "Was the bonegate attacked again?"

"No, it's fine," Tau assured her. "Scouts sighted gryphon riders from the south. They'll breach our boundary line soon."

"How many?" Queen Pari asked.

"Three gryphons. They were being chased."

"Oh? By what?"

"Birds—but not normal ones. Feathered Fae."

I sucked in a breath. Who would the Feathered Fae be chasing? Only two options came to mind—rebel spies or my siblings.

"Were any of them doing magic?" I urged. "What kind?"

"Scouts reported fire magic," Tau replied.

"Fire! Possibly, Finn?" I looked at Crystal.

"It has to be them," she gasped. "Pari's sources must have told Finn already. We have to help!"

I pulled back the covers, barely noticing the pain through the rising fear that we'd be too late. "What are we waiting for? Let's go!"

CHAPTER FIFTEEN

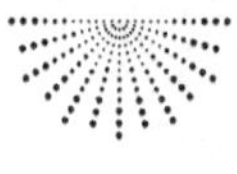

FINN

The gryphon's wings snapped against the wind, propelling us forward. I leaned over the beast's neck, to a more secure position, and chanced a glance behind me. My heart sank. We were still being chased.

"Himari! Got any more juice?"

"Not really!" She panted from where she sat, doubled up on the saddle behind me.

"Do what you can! They're gaining on us!"

"On it!" Himari yelled back and another wind gust caught our ride's wings, giving him a boost.

Nestled between our bodies, Kane shifted. He did not like being positioned there. I didn't blame him, but after Arlo spotted the Feathered Fae, I'd insisted my familiar take cover. Himari's winds could blow a bird off course. Even Arlo, who was larger than Kane in eagle aspect, sat behind Garret, instead of flying.

Hours ago, when we'd rushed into the stables to meet Ebba and Garret—unbeknownst to them we were trying to escape—the intention had been that we'd all pilot our own gryphons. However, Maria and Himari took one look at the beasts and refused to fly alone. In the end, doubling up had worked to our benefit.

Himari's air magic, while strong, had limits, and encompassing three gryphons in a gale was easier than six. Seeing as we were so close to the Buyan border, we needed to seize every advantage. If the Feathered Fae caught us, they'd snatch away our freedom, or perhaps even kill us . . .

I didn't want to find out.

"Why are they following us? They're going to blow our cover!" Garret bellowed again from where he flew with Arlo at my side. He shot me a bewildered expression, as if begging for me to explain why we were running from soldiers in our own army.

I gulped. While the two guards had bought Ryker's tale of a covert rescue mission, when the Feathered Fae showed up, they started to question what was happening. All I could do was insist that they not question my leadership and fall in line. Thank God, I outranked them and both Ebba and Garret were military fae to the core.

Still, they knew something was wrong with this picture. I would have a hell of a lot to answer for when we landed. That was, if we were still alive when that happened.

Glancing behind us again, I swore. The Feathered Fae were even closer! I kicked my heels into my gryphon's side. "More wind, Himari!"

"I'm trying!" She panted as another gale ripped by, chilling my face.

Her grip on me loosened, and I swallowed thickly. Himari would push herself to breaking to help us escape. If she passed out, I'd have to keep her on the gryphon.

Inside, my shadows surged, assuring me they'd keep her stable. "Yeah, let's not test the theory."

Wanting to be released, to fight the Feathered Fae, the shadows pressed harder. Although I was sure they'd be effective, that was the last thing I wanted. My shadows were not normal, and my siblings still didn't know I had them or how dark I had become. I still remembered the looks I'd received when it first came out that I was part demon born witch. If they learned about my shadows, I could expect even worse.

"They're gaining!" Maria screamed from where she sat behind Ebba, glued to the guard's back. Ebba's face scrunched up tightly. Like Garret, she was out of the loop, but something in her expression made me wonder if she suspected more than she'd revealed. Either way, she did not question my command.

Again, I scoured the horizon. The hills separating

Buyan and Lyonesse were within sight, and they called to me. We'd be safe once we crossed the boundary line. I had to believe that the Feathered Fae would not enter Buyan's land. Or at the very least, they'd question doing so. I dug my heels deeper into the gryphon's side, urging him forward. The beast shrieked but beat its wings harder.

"Himari!"

Another gust soared by me, giving our mounts a boost. Once it passed, I hurled streams of fire over my head. The Feathered Fae were too far away for it to hit them, but I hoped it would keep them back.

"Finn… I—" A weight hit my back as Himari passed out, and Kane squawked.

One of my hands released the reins, and I gripped her tightly, but we were moving too fast, and the gryphon's wings jostled us. Her slack body drooped to the side.

"Himari! Wake up!"

A groan came from behind me, announcing that was it. She'd spent all the energy she had trying to save us. I couldn't count on her waking up, and without her, we were royally screwed. I darted another glance backward. The Feathered Fae had gained even more ground.

"Fuck!"

"Is she okay?" Ebba screamed.

"No! Can you make wind?"

"Not like her! Together?"

That could work. I had all four elements, as did Ebba and Garret. Maybe working as one we'd be as strong as Himari. "Now!"

Winds surged around us. Immediately, I knew they were nowhere near as strong as the weaver witch, and yet, they were strong enough to make Himari slip a little more to the side. My heart lunged into my throat as between us, Kane screeched. The poor bloke was being crushed but there was nothing I could do about that now. I had to hold on to my sister and fend off the attackers.

"Kane! Don't move!"

He grew still, rigid—pissed off, no doubt—but if Kane slipped out at least he could fly. Himari could not.

Once more, my eyes traveled over my shoulder, the sight sending my pulse into overdrive. The Feathered Fae were so close I could make out Meegra's eyes, glinting with victory.

My shadows urged for me to set them free, and I had no choice. We were still at least a couple of kilometers from the mountain range. If we were going to make it, I had to use them.

I bit down on the side of my cheek, and spit out the blood. "Attack those chasing us. One of you, hold my sister in place."

From the flying droplets, shadows formed, taking the shape of men with horns.

"What the fuck is that thing!" Maria's accent

thickened with terror as the shadows shot backward to do my bidding "It's touching Himari!"

"It's my demon gift!" I yelled back, relieved because I could feel that Maria was right. Thanks to one of my shadows, Himari was sitting up straight once more. She wouldn't fall. "She was slipping!"

My rumbler sister's eyes were wide with fear, but she didn't say another word. Although I was sure I'd hear about it later. If we lived through this, I'd have to explain the darkness that lived inside me.

An eagle screamed, and I tossed a glance to our old army. A shadow was chasing Meegra. My heart leapt, and I gripped the reins tighter, urging the gryphon forward. It was working.

We're going to make it, I thought. We—what the bloody hell is that?!

Over the mountains a flock of gryphons surged, flying as fast as lightning. They were close enough for me to make out the riders. One had flaming red hair. Another pulsed light from her hands.

"Is that Crystal?" Arlo yelled.

"And Lan—argh!"

Talons ripped into my shoulder as a sparrowhawk, notoriously fast and agile birds of prey, dive-bombed my ride. I was about to retaliate when a blaze of light blasted by the bird.

The sparrowhawk swerved and fell back, though others in her group continued to lay chase. They were agile, outmaneuvering even my shadows. Nevertheless, they couldn't fight the shadows *and* the light—the latter of which Lana was now raining on them with wild abandon.

Shrieks flew from behind us, and then the sound ceased. Heart still pounding in my throat, I turned back and sighed. The Feathered Fae were retreating. One of my shadows was still chasing them off.

I hoped that the droplets of blood I'd given was enough to keep the shadow moving for a long time. They required a blood sacrifice to exist, and though I hadn't worked out the finer points, it seemed that some activities took more of a sacrifice than others.

"Finn!" Lana screamed, making me face forward once again.

The other group was close, already slowing their gryphons. I slowed mine too so we wouldn't crash. Following suit, Garret and Ebba fell in line. Relief rolled through me. Not only was help here, but Lana and Crystal were okay.

As I caught sight of a woman I recognized from paintings, I stiffened. Queen Pari. Oh . . . shite!

I didn't have time to utter a single syllable before Garret attacked, hurling a blaze of fire at the queen. The famed enemy of his kingdom.

A woman with gold-capped teeth deflected it, her attention pinned on the attacker. Two other warriors flanked the queen, murder burning in their eyes.

"Stop!" I commanded. "Stand down, Garret! Ebba, you, too!"

The fae soldiers turned toward me. A muscle fluttered in Garret's cheek. "She's the enemy!"

"No!" Lana positioned her gryphon right in front of us. "She's not. Garret, listen."

"What did she do to you?" Garret's eyes softened as he took in Lana. Pure love and worry shone through them. "Lana, we've come to take you home."

"No," I interjected. "We have not. I have something I need to tell you and Ebba."

"Well, spit it out," Ebba barked.

Finally, I told them what I'd seen in the firlon and what Ryker confirmed. When I brought up Garret's best friend, he looked shocked, then angry. Ebba's anger, however, seemed to fizzle swiftly, and a thoughtful expression slipped over her fine features.

"You know, it makes a bit of sense," she mused when I finished, though she didn't seem totally convinced. Something in her tone was hesitant, held back as if she was running up against a wall. It wasn't like her, but then again, Ebba had just had her world shattered. "The king has kept the whole of Lyonesse on such a tight leash. This could explain why. You are sure, Lana? Crystal?"

The queen and her warriors remained silent. They knew better than to interrupt.

"Positive," Crystal assured. "Father sent assassins yesterday to off us. They admitted to the crime."

"I wondered why Meegra went to Zatus when we

should have been marching north," Ebba replied. "That must be why Ryker mentioned it. He wanted to plant seeds."

The tension eased from my chest. Ebba was putting the pieces together fast. Not that I was surprised. She was a bloody genius. It was part of the reason I liked her so much.

"What?!" Garret roared. "You're insane!"

Lana urged her gryphon closer to him, her eyes pleading. "Garret, please!"

"What happened to you? What's really going on here?"

"Finn told the truth! Pari isn't holding us as prisoners or harming us. She's kind."

"How has she filled your head with lies?!" Garret, usually so stoic, looked like someone had slapped him across the face.

"If there's a liar in this tale, it's my father!" Lana replied.

Garret whirled his gryphon around, but Arlo, who was still sitting behind him, hit him upside the head. A shocked cry left Lana when Garret slumped forward, but Arlo moved quickly. Grabbing hold of our friend, he situated him securely over the thick neck of the gryphon.

"Garret," Lana murmured.

"He's out, cold," Arlo replied. "Sorry, but I don't think he'd come otherwise. He was vibrating with anger. We need to get to safety and get him off this beast. He's not going to be pleased when he wakes up."

"No. He's not," Ebba agreed. "We'll have to restrain him too."

"On it!" Maria yelled, and out of nowhere vines grew around Garret, binding his arms to his body, and his body to the gryphon.

"Can we trust no attack will come from you?" One of the women who flew next to the queen, addressed Ebba coldly—a blonde with ice-blue eyes.

Ebba loosed a breath, her gaze flickering to Garret for a moment. "I will not attack."

My racing heart slowed ever so slightly. This wasn't ideal, particularly the part about Arlo knocking Garret out, but it was the best we could do given the circumstances.

"Then I extend an invitation to all of you into my home," Queen Pari announced, sounding regal, strong. "I will assist you in any way possible and provide sanctuary."

Still hesitant, Ebba glanced at me.

"I accept," I declared. "And you, Captain Ebba?" I wanted her to come, but I'd be damned if she said I forced her into it. I already felt badly enough that Garret was being forced, even if it was for his own good.

"Besides the fact that I doubt we'd be welcome back home right now . . ." Ebba's eyebrows arched with intrigue. "There's something here. Something I want to learn more about, so yes, I accept your offer of sanctuary."

"Let's fly." Pari turned her gryphon to face the hills and took off, soaring.

Lana shot me a curious look, her gaze drifting back to the shadow still pressing Himari against me. Her lips parted, but then she seemed to think better of it. Closing her mouth she nodded.

Together, we followed the Queen of Buyan.

CHAPTER SIXTEEN

LANA

For the duration of the journey back to Buyan, I flew next to Arlo and Garret. A few times, my gaze strayed to the eerie shadow riding behind Finn and Himari like a servant, but mostly, my attention remained focused on Garret.

He'd been about to flee. Unlike Ebba, Garret did not connect the dots—or have any suspicions related to my father. As much as it sucked, I couldn't blame him. I'd been that way too.

When we touched down in front of the castle doors, Isis dismounted and hustled over to help her queen down, but Pari slid off gracefully without help.

"Get the male—Garret, you called him?—into a room of his own. Armina will ward it to his powers. What elements does he have?"

"Full elemental." Ebba's quick response sent a wave of shock through me. Then I realized it was her way of assuring the queen that she stood here willingly. That she would help, not fight.

"Put him near Crystal and me," I added. "All of them should be near us, but especially Garret."

Queen Pari studied me for a moment. "Very well. Once Armina wards his room, anyone who wishes to do so may visit. Lana, perhaps you should be the first to see him. He'll do better hearing the truth from you, rather than from me."

Ebba snorted. "You have no idea."

Pari turned to her ladies. "Carry Garret to his chambers."

"Are you sure, My Queen?" Isis asked. "You're okay being left alone with these people?"

"I am. Lana and Crystal trust them. I do, too."

The vote of confidence warmed my heart, although Pari's ladies did not seem so convinced. Still, they followed orders. Isis and Bellona took Garret's weight while Armina led the way into the castle.

I slid off of my gryphon, trying to muffle the groan that seeped from my lips. Riding the beast wasn't easy. Not only because I wasn't fully healed, a fact that was becoming more apparent now that my adrenaline rush had passed, but gryphons were large around the middle, even more so than horses. At least riding had been less scary than the first time. The idea of losing my family to the Feathered Fae had been much more terrifying.

"Where are the others?" Crystal asked, her tone tense as she faced our siblings.

Earlier, we'd been flying too fast to ask questions, but I'd been wondering where Gio, Dak, Victoria, and Wikolia were too.

"We didn't make it to them in time," Finn answered softly as he helped Himari down from their mount. She'd woken up about twenty minutes ago. Her return to consciousness had been quite eventful as she found a shadow-man pressed against her, making sure she didn't plummet to the ground. The shadow's presence was another question to be answered.

"Why?" I asked.

While Finn explained what had occurred, I stared at him, part of me still shocked at what my father was capable of, though I should know better. How wrong had I been to trust him.

Once finished, Finn dragged his hands over his pants, exhaling deeply. "So, yeah, I failed in saving them. It was either get half of us out, or none." Pain riddled his voice, and I couldn't help myself from rushing to him and throwing my arms around him.

"You did the right thing." I pressed my cheek into his shoulder.

"It doesn't feel like it," he whispered.

Pulling away to look at him, I noticed a dirty blond curl fell into his eyes. When had his hair gotten so long?

"Feels like when I left you behind," he added, anguished.

"Which changed everything in a way that I don't regret," I replied as we stepped back. I wouldn't say leaving behind four of our siblings had a silver lining, but I hoped it did.

"What I'd like to understand," Queen Pari broached softly, "is how your power works."

Finn stiffened. "I'm half demon born witch. What you saw is my demon gift."

"And you possess four elements? Do all demon born witches?" Pari inquired, fascinated. I suspected that if she did not know many illuminators, she knew even fewer demon born. They were the rarest type of witch.

"That's right. All four elements," Finn admitted. "Demon born get increased powers from their witch blood, and a little something extra from the demon blood. Too bad it's dark magic."

"But it can't be all that dark, if it saved me," Himari interceded. "It does what you say, which means you have the choice to use it for evil or good."

"I suppose so." He didn't sound sure.

"I know so," Himari assured. "Thank you for saving me, Finn."

The tension in his shoulders loosened. "You wouldn't have needed them to save you, if I had not pushed you so hard."

"If you hadn't pushed me to use wind, we

wouldn't have made it as far," Himari countered. "We might not be here. Safe."

As she spoke, my heart cracked open a little more. It was obvious that Finn had been worried about exposing his demon gift, but as far as I could tell, no one was against it. Initially, the shadows might have startled them, which was understandable, but Himari was right. His power could also be used for good. Finn was the deciding factor.

"They were remarkable," Pari added. "I'd love a demonstration, if you're not too tired?"

"Y-you would?" Finn, usually sure and charming, could not hide his shock.

The queen smiled. "Yes, but first, let's go inside. You've told your story. Now, I believe it's time I told you mine."

AN HOUR LATER, MY NERVES MOUNTED AS I SHUFFLED down the hallway. The others, Mam and Celine included, were still speaking with Queen Pari. There was a lot to fill them in on, and so far, everyone was seeing the light faster than I had. Even Ebba, a soldier who had served my father for years.

There was only one person who hadn't heard the truth. According to a guard watching over him, Garret had woken up, and he was pissed. I couldn't blame him. Finn had not offered them all the information that he'd discovered, opting instead to allow Garret and Ebba to believe they were flying north to save me and Crystal. Ebba forgave him easily, but Garret didn't know Finn's reasons. I could only hope that once he did, he'd forgive too.

My steps stopped at the end of the hallway where my room was located. Halfway down the corridor three guards were positioned outside a door—their weapons at the ready.

"Be careful, princess," one cautioned, his eyes wary at my approach. "The soldier is spitting mad."

That they cared enough to even say that spoke volumes about how my reputation had morphed. Days ago, no one would have given two hoots about my safety. No one, that was, except for the queen. The rest of the castle was coming around to the idea that I believed their queen.

"I will. Thank you." I opened the door.

The bedroom I entered was smaller than my own, the bed about the size of a full, but the room was still comfortable and nice. Not regal, but had I stayed in a hotel room like this in the Old Land, I would have been happy.

A red-faced Garret was across the room, trying to shove himself out the window. Thanks to Armina's Garret-specific warding, all he was doing was hitting an invisible wall. I would have laughed except I'd tried to do the same too many times to count. At the time I hadn't found my failures funny in the slightest.

"It won't work." I shut the door behind us, sealing the ward. I needed him to stay and listen. "Armina is a powerful wardmaker. You won't break out."

His head turned, and his gaze latched on me. "Lana."

Garret rushed across the room, his arms spread. Apparently, he'd forgotten what I told him before Arlo knocked him unconscious. I wasn't sure if that was a good or bad thing, only that we were starting at zero.

His arms pulled me close, enveloping me until my nose filled with his scent—masculine, with hints of leather and hay from the gryphon ride. I pressed my cheek to his chest, and for a moment, allowed us to soak in the togetherness.

"Are you hurt?" he whispered.

"I'm fine. Pari has been treating us well."

An unburdened breath left him, and he pulled away. The relief on his face lasted for another few seconds before his eyebrows knitted together. "They let you into this room—a room that's far too nice for the likes of someone who tried to infiltrate an enemy kingdom. Too nice for a soldier in general. Why am I here and not in a dungeon? And why are *you* not chained? None of this makes any sense. Is she trying to trick us?"

"You should sit down. There's a lot to tell."

For a second, Garret studied me, his mercurial gray eyes questioning, but then he perched on the bed. "Tell me."

Heart tightening, I explained everything I'd been through here, starting with how I too had believed that the overly grand rooms were a trick. I admitted to how I'd tried to gather evidence against the queen, and about my flock of chaos. I wanted to make sure he didn't feel stupid for being tricked by the king like we had been.

"It took a while," I ventured. "But once I got that letter from my father and put it next to the other one —the one the queen thought she'd lost—I knew she was right. King Oberon is a liar, Garret. The horrific state of Lyonesse is all his own doing. He has put his people, *you*, in danger for his greedy desire to conquer my world. Not only that, but he tried to have me and Crystal killed yesterday."

"What?!"

"He hired assassins from Zatus and sent them here and to tamper with the Buyan bonegate. Crystal and I flew to the bonegate with Queen Pari to check on it and two winged fae tried to kill us. Ryker learned about it, as did Finn, straight from Meegra's mouth."

"Why didn't Ryker tell me this?" Garret seethed.

I was not totally sure, though I had a good guess. "You're his best friend. He wanted to protect you."

"What about him? And Sai?"

"I'm not sure," I admitted. "They must have some reason for staying."

Garret fell silent, head dropping to stare at his hands that rested over his muscular legs. As much as I wanted to fill the air with more explanations and assurances, I didn't. People had to draw certain conclusions on their own. Matters such as these required delicacy. I knew that firsthand.

The seconds ticked by, transforming into minutes. The sounds of the city seeped through the window and into my ears, a welcome distraction, and yet, I could not take my eyes off of Garret's face. A million emotions flashed across it.

When he finally looked up at me, tears shone in his eyes. "I have to go home."

"What?! After what I told you?" I darted over to perch on the bed next to him. "Do you believe me?"

Garret swallowed, the sound thick. "My predicament is the same no matter what."

"What's that?" I whispered. "You're safe here. I promise."

"You have to understand, Lana, my father and brother died fighting for your father. *Died.* And my mother is still in Lyonesse. If you're right, I can't leave her there. And if you're wrong—"

"I'm not wrong," I said. "I swear to you."

He nodded, a gesture I couldn't entirely read. "Because of my actions, my mother is in danger. She's too old to fight. I have to leave."

My heart squeezed. I did not want him to leave, but he was right. His mother, Alvina, was in grave danger. By now, the castle would know that Garret and Ebba left with my siblings. Had Ryker considered their families too? I wanted to believe he would. After all, Garret and Ebba were two of his best friends.

"Wouldn't Ryker have sent word to your mother to hide? Or even have hidden her?" There must be other spies in Lyonesse. And they would help protect those who needed protecting. The job loomed too large for two people.

"Perhaps," Garret replied. "But I can't take that chance. She's the only family I have left, Lana. You must understand."

"I do. My mam is everything to me, too. But what if you go and you're injured? Or worse, killed?"

The idea made me want to weep. A world without Garret sounded like utter shite.

Garret stared into my eyes, and for the first time since I entered his room, we connected on a different level. A deeper one. My emotions flipped. I went from frantically needing him to believe me, to wanting to be as close to him as possible. How in the world had that even happened?

He inched closer. His lips parted. I drew in a breath as fire seemed to encompass the room.

"Garret," I breathed. "Do you believe me?" I had to know. Had to be sure. Even if I desperately wanted to let go and throw myself in the man's arms, that was important.

"I do." He came even closer. "There are holes, things I can't figure out." Confusion flashed across his face for a moment, but he shook his head as if to push them away. "But if there's one thing in this world I'm sure about, it's you."

Relief crashed into me, heat washing over me simultaneously, and stealing my breath. A lifetime ago, Garret and I said we wouldn't get together. We claimed to be just friends. That had never been true, and if it had, screw that lifetime.

So much had changed. I'd lost a dream I once held dear, and in another kingdom, maybe people I loved might be suffering at this very second. I was done pretending that Garret and I were only friends. I wanted him, and he wanted me, and that had always been the truth of it.

That truth had never been more apparent than when our lips finally met, and a blaze of fire seared through my blood. Our tongues danced, exploring, hot and needy. Garret's hand landed on my cheek, cupping it. Wanting to explore every bit of him, I leaned into him and felt him respond, pulling me closer. My hands threaded through his black hair and a moan escaped his lips. Desire surged through me. I wanted him more than I'd ever wanted anyone.

Unexpectedly, Garret pulled back. Unbridled passion lingered in his mercurial gray eyes, but it dimmed quickly, as if he were pulling himself out of a trance.

"I apologize. We said we were friends."

"Fuck what we said." I leaned closer, but he stopped me. "Is this not what you wan—"

He pressed a finger to my lips, halting me. "Lana," he rasped. "I love you."

Holy shite. I sucked in air. I'd thought those same words before, but never, *never*, allowed myself to say them. Yet, here was Garret, proclaiming that he loved me. My heart squeezed so hard it might burst.

"I love you too, Garret."

My lips tingled as the words slipped out of me. A sense of lightness, of wholeness, wrapped around me.

He smiled. It was so beautiful I wanted to cry. His hand found my face again, and he tucked a stray hair behind my ear. "I've never wanted to hear that from anyone but you. I never thought it would happen. Or that us being together was truly possible."

"Same," I confessed, the heat inside me building again.

Now that we knew where we stood, I wanted to be as close to him as a man and woman could be. My hand landed on his chest, and I pushed him back onto the bed. "Take off your shirt."

Garret's eyes widened. "Are you sure?"

"I've never been more sure of anything in my life." I straddled him. "Do as your princess commands."

A slow smile spread across his lips as Garret lifted his shirt and tossed it on the floor. "I'm yours to command, my lady."

CHAPTER SEVENTEEN

LANA

Garret and I strode side by side to find Queen Pari. His scent clung to me, which both gave me happy chills and made me hope others couldn't smell it. I didn't regret what had happened between us, I could never regret us being so open and honest with how we felt, but that didn't mean I wanted to advertise it to others. Not yet, anyway.

"Do you truly think she'll help?" Garret asked, trepidation dripping from his tone.

I understood. That he was willing to face Queen Pari and ask for help, spoke volumes. Garret had grown up thinking of the Queen of Buyan as the ultimate evil. It was even more indoctrinated in him than it had been in me.

"She will help," I assured him. "Pari is kind and level-headed. Everyone here loves her. It wouldn't surprise me if the others have already started planning to extract our siblings from Lyonesse. We can get your mother out at the same time."

Garret said nothing more as we approached the queen's study.

"Is the queen in her den?" I asked when we reached the soldiers guarding the gilded hallway.

"She is," a man answered. "As are a few others of your party. Shall I announce you?"

"Sure." We followed the guard to the door where he announced Garret and me.

"They may enter," Pari replied.

Once we moved inside the room, we found Finn and Ebba present. Isis was there too, leaning against the wall behind Pari, ever so watchful. Bellona and Armina were absent, though.

My gaze found Finn's. "Where is everyone else?"

"They needed a rest," Finn informed me. "Our journey was stressful. Himari and Maria were terrified the entire flight. They're coming down from an adrenaline rush. Arlo didn't want to leave them."

"And why are you still here?" I wanted him there, but from what I'd heard, Finn had the most stressful day of them all. I couldn't imagine how scared he must have been breaking into our father's private chamber. Honestly, I wasn't sure I would have had the balls.

"We're making a plan to save the others," Finn explained. "I can't rest until I know what we're going to do."

"We are here to help." My attention shifted to Ebba. "Garret is worried about his mother. Are you worried about your family?"

Perhaps Ebba's family was part of the spy ring? Seemed unlikely, but not off the table.

"I am." Ebba glanced at Pari. "Although I know there are more important matters. Saving your siblings, for instance."

Her statement made me bristle. Her guard training, to value the lives of royals more than her own—and even her family—shone through the words. The crown had brainwashed her into that line of thinking since she was very small. I hated that she'd been trained to think that way.

"Nothing is more important than family." Pari stood. "Let's check in on your loved ones."

"How?" Ebba blinked.

"She has an aqual," I explained. "It's how she speaks to people in Lyonesse."

Ebba and Garret exchanged glances. It must feel weird for them to be tossed into a world of spies who worked against the king they had served for years.

Queen Pari sashayed to the far side of her study and pulled a bowl from a shelf, and as her hand hovered over it, the depression filled with water. She set the bowl on top of a circular dais. "Join me."

We gathered round the platform, and Pari turned her face to the bowl. "Contact, Posy."

The water shimmered and moved like waves

churning atop a tiny ocean. Sounds came from the other side, like someone was speaking through a pad of foam.

I tilted my head. "That sounds . . . off."

"She needs to fill hers with water," Pari explained. "Otherwise, her words, and any sounds we might hear, will be garbled."

"Wicked," Finn whispered. "The water is a conduit for sight and sound. Like a video chat, but with magic."

Pari shrugged. "If you say so. I have no idea what a video chat is."

"Why doesn't she keep it filled with water at all times?" Finn asked.

"What if a raid occurred?" Pari countered. "The aqual might give her away, particularly if it was full of water and waiting on a table. Posy is attuned to the magic of the bowl, and knows when I'm calling her. Just as I am in tune with her aqual, but keeping it void of water means no one will suspect it's anything other than a bowl. And I won't accidentally blow her cover by calling for her at inopportune times."

"A minute, Your Majesty!"

"You're fine, Posy. Don't rush," Pari replied. There was a sound of water being poured, and the face of an old woman wearing a bright red headscarf came into view.

At the sight, I sucked in a breath. I recognized that woman! "You're Ryker's grandmother!"

Posy smiled. "That I am, Princess. Good to see you are now enlightened." Her gaze traveled around the group, stopping the longest on Garret and Ebba. "My grandchildren wanted to tell you two so many times. Please believe it was difficult for them to keep our family secret. I'm glad you're safe."

The guards looked gob smacked, but Ebba recovered quickly. "I understand. They're loyal friends, and it would have been unwise to tell us in the past."

Garret merely nodded, perhaps stunned into silence.

"Posy," the queen spoke, "we're getting in touch because these soldiers, Ebba and Garret, are concerned about their families. Did you put a plan in place to help them once your grandson engineered the escape of Oberon's children?"

Posy's face fell. "Yes, but unfortunately, we only got to one in time. Ebba, your family is being kept in a safe house. We extracted them moments before the Feathered Fae arrived at your home."

Ebba's shoulders relaxed. "Thank you."

Posy's attention turned to Garret. "I'm so sorry, my boy, but we couldn't rescue Alvina in time. Meegra, herself, came for her."

Horror washed over me. Had Meegra killed Garret's mother?

"Is she alive?" Garret whispered, echoing my thoughts.

My hand found his, and I squeezed, trying to give

him my strength. Truth be told, it wasn't much. I felt sick at the idea that Meegra would kill someone who had done nothing wrong.

"I heard from Sai not long ago. Your mother is alive," Posy assured Garret. "She's being kept in the dungeons."

"Oberon will use her as a lure." Queen Pari's lips twisted in concern. "As I suspect he will use your siblings too."

Posy's old eyes looked more tired by the second. "Yes. Sai tells me that the other royal heirs had an alibi. They were with Prince Casimir at the time of the escape. And yet, their father has locked them away too."

"In the dungeons?" I asked, my tone high. What would he tell others to justify it?

"Their rooms, for now. They will be guarded around the clock," Posy replied. "There will be a royal trial, and soon. You lot are on trial too."

My gaze found the queen's. "What does that mean? We're not even there."

"Your father will try you without your presence."

"With a jury?" Finn asked. "Even though Lyonesse is a monarchy?"

"In instances of royal blood, the king, his head advisor, and a few other influential fae come to a consensus. It's a way of making sure personal issues don't taint a king, or queen's, judgment. Although, there can be no question what they'll decide, and your father will use the verdict to wage war on Buyan. True war. Which means we must act quickly; stop him before you are deemed traitors."

I didn't want to ask what the sentence for a traitor was, couldn't ask. From the look on Garret's face, it was obvious. Death.

Pari's fingers gripped the side of the dais. "Any other news, Posy?"

"Two Feathered Fae are walking the city, searching for other traitors. But that is to be expected. No one has found our headquarters, though. I don't believe that they will."

"Good," Pari sighed. "If that's all, we must go. We have much planning to do if we are to help in Lyonesse."

"Best of luck. I hope to see you in the flesh soon." With that, the women severed their connection.

"I have to leave." Garret spoke before I could ask the queen what our next steps should be. His eyes burned into Pari's. "My mother is the only family I have left. I cannot allow her to rot in a cell. If you cannot spare a gryphon, I'll walk, but please, let me leave now."

"Garret, you can't walk to Lyonesse," I interjected. "That will take days."

"And it is unnecessary," Pari commented. "I plan on providing a force to fight Oberon. I will call my allies too. We'll show up with a sizable army. You should wait until they are ready to mobilize. It will not take long. A few days at the most."

My lips parted in shock. While I'd known that Queen Pari was an ally, I hadn't expected her to risk the lives of her countrymen and women for us.

"Why would you sacrifice your soldiers for Fullfeather heirs or Garret's mother?" Ebba asked, her eyes narrowed.

A knowing smile curved Pari's lips. "This day has been marching toward me for years. I signed my fate the moment I seized Lyonesse's bonegate. When I captured Lana and Crystal, I figured it could only be a matter of weeks. The kingdom of Lyonesse knows them, trusts them, do they not?"

"They do," Ebba admitted slowly.

"Then when word spreads about what Oberon has done, from the lips of his own children, no less, who will stand with him?"

"The people *love* the king. Adore him," Garret argued.

"As did you," Pari countered, her eyebrows arched. "But it did not take you long to see that he has manipulated you. Others might take longer, but not all. And if we're already in control of the kingdom . . . Well, then they'll see how he has used them with their own eyes."

"Do you mean that you'll allow the magic of our bonegate to reach the city?" Ebba gasped.

"I will," Pari confirmed. "As long as someone I

trust is in charge, someone who will not use the portal to infiltrate another world, and control those who live there, I see no reason not to hand it over. I'll supply evidence of his treachery too." As she spoke, her eyes grazed me, and I shivered.

Her implication was obvious. Prince Casimir could not rule Lyonesse, someone else had to do it. As I was the highest ranked heir, I was the natural choice.

Except, I didn't want to rule. I wondered how much Casimir knew of our father's lies. Was he complicit? Or a pawn like me? Something told me he didn't know the whole story, but was I just being hopeful and naïve? It wouldn't be the first time. Were both my father and brother rotten to the core?

"Having control of our bonegate would be astonishing. Revelatory," Ebba murmured. "The Feathered Fae would no longer have to retrieve magic."

"How do they do that, anyway?" I asked. I understood that somehow the Feathered Fae gathered magic and brought it back. Of course, a small amount seeped through to Lyonesse—Armina's wards were not powerful enough to stop *all* the magic flowing over from the Old Land, but I'd never seen the exact retrieval process.

"They use enchanted thuribles," Ebba replied. "The first time I saw Ash return with one in his beak, I felt noticeably stronger that day. Occasionally, I would see another Feathered Fae return with another thurible in their beak, and the same thing happened. That's all I know about them though."

"Oh my god . . ." I trailed off, mind whirling.

In the heart of Castle Phoenix there was a room unlike any other. A place forbidden to all but my father, Prince Casimir, and the guards who accompanied them. The room radiated power, and had a fountain of flames from which thuribles hung. In the same room, maps hung—one of which showed the Old Land—and a painted portrait of Queen Pari rested on the fountain.

I drew in a breath. That space wasn't a place of reverence, as Garret had guessed. Or a burial ground for Casimir's mother, as some believed. It was a courtyard where my father housed magic, the strongest place in the kingdom. In the same room that he absorbed power, he planned and concocted ways to infiltrate my world and defeat Pari.

Since the courtyard was open, it would be easy enough for a bird to fly straight to it. The king not only lied, he hoarded magic in his castle, likely allowing only the smallest trickle to leave so his subjects could use it too. No doubt he did it so they'd remember what it felt like and wish they had more. He gave the downtrodden and weak hope, but all along, he could have shared so much more than that.

What a bastard.

"Lana, are you alright?" Garret asked.

"Do you remember the room I explored?" I asked.

"Before the Successional? The one only my father and Casimir can enter."

"Yes, of course. Oh . . ." Garret's eyes widened as understanding cut him to the core.

"What's that about? Spill, Lan," Finn ordered.

Without hesitation, I told them about the room and my suspicions. By the end, everyone's jaws were set tight.

"He has magic whenever he needs it," Ebba concluded, "but he allows his people to remain weak."

"He's horrible," Pari agreed. "If he had not devised that workaround, he would have had to give in to my demands years ago. Instead, he came up with a way to remain powerful while his people suffered." The queen swallowed thickly, the repulsion on her face, plain. "Which is why we must stop him."

"We must." Though I didn't have the slightest idea of where to start.

Pari's gaze sought Garret. "Please remain here until my forces can move out. Oberon does not deserve another prize, and my soldiers will need your expertise to attack Lyonesse."

"And I couldn't bear it if they caught you before we got there." My hand held his tightly.

Finn's and Ebba's gaze flickered down to our joined hands, and their lips twitched, but neither commented.

Garret drew in a shallow breath. "You promise that we'll leave soon?"

"As soon as I can mobilize," Pari assured him. "If we're to breach the walls and fight, we'll want the right people at our side. As you know, Lyonesse's defenses are quite good. I only ask for a few days to prepare."

"Yes," I blurted. "We need to be smart about this. We can't rush forward into battle. Not when the enemy will probably assume we are coming."

"Fine," Garret exhaled, his shoulders loosening with the motion. "Four days. After that, I leave."

"I will send envoys to my allies immediately," Pari assured him. "They will request that their armies join us on the way. Soon, it will be time to settle the strife between our kingdoms once and for all."

CHAPTER EIGHTEEN

FINN

After hours of tossing and turning, I finally gave up on sleeping. I rose, dressed, and left my room, intent on taking a stroll to settle my mind.

"Can I help you?" A guard posted at the end of the hallway asked when I neared.

"I don't suppose you have a forest to walk in?"

"We have gardens."

"That'll do. Can you show me the way?"

He escorted me there in silence, and when we arrived, I breathed in the humid air. The scent of tropical flowers and—possibly fruit?—filled my nostrils.

"Smells like a sweet shop out here," I commented.

The guard shrugged as if the lovely scent was the most mundane thing in the world. "If you're fine by yourself, I'll take my leave. The queen no longer insists chaperones follow the Fullfeather heirs."

Clearly, I was not about to become best mates with the guy. Though, I couldn't blame him. Tales of my demon gift had to have spread through the castle by now. I was the darkest soul on the block.

"I'll be alright," I said. "Will someone find me if anyone else plans a meeting?"

We were going to infiltrate Lyonesse in a few days. There better be a few damn meetings.

"We will." The guard inclined his head. "Good day."

The moment he left a shroud of loneliness draped over me. I had never been comfortable being alone for too long. Unlike Lana, I much preferred a boisterous gathering to solitude, which made my new power more ironic.

Who in the world would want to be around someone who controlled shadows of death?

Even though my siblings seemed okay with it, I still couldn't wrap my head around their acceptance. I was still so far from accepting myself.

With a huffed breath, I walked the garden paths. It didn't take long to discover the fruits I had smelled earlier. They resembled pomegranates, but with purple skin and the seeds along the outside. Equally odd and tantalizing. My fingers itched to pluck one from a tree and taste it, but I suspected it would be smart to make sure they weren't poisonous first. I didn't want to be the idiot prince who poisoned himself because he was curious.

It wasn't long until tropical trees, ferns, and vines enveloped the trail, nearly enclosing me in a sort of lush tunnel. It gave the impression of walking through the forest, which was nearly as good as being in one. I peered up at the sliver of blue sky that the greenery had not overtaken. Speaking of back home . . . where was that bird?

Placing two fingers in my mouth, I blew a whistle. A screech rang out from somewhere in the distance, and I scanned the sky above. Not a minute later, Kane appeared, soaring through the air.

"Hey, mate!" I waved and smiled. The bit of me that was still wary of Buyan loosened. Although Lana and Crystal assured me we were safe here, it was difficult to come to terms with it so fast. I couldn't imagine how Ebba and Garret felt.

He began to descend, so I shook my head. "No glove. I was checking on you. Go on now, have fun."

"Is that Finnegan Fairchild, I hear?" A feminine voice pierced the air.

My eyes widened. "Aileen?"

Lana's mother laughed, the sound musical, like wind chimes in a soft Irish breeze. "Where are you in this maze of jungle?"

"Stay there. I'll find you."

"Okay." She sounded close. Still, I used my shadows to find her, pulling them back into my body right before she saw them.

Lana's mother beamed at me. "Finn, we haven't gotten to speak properly yet."

That was true. We had spoken and embraced the night before when everyone else met up for the first time in weeks, actually months in the case of Aileen and me. Yet, there'd been too much excitement, for a proper chat.

"It's been an age." I walked to stand with her. "Want to stroll?"

"Certainly. I take it you couldn't sleep either?"

"I should be dead on my feet, but recent events make catching a kip more difficult."

"I know what you mean. At least this garden is lovely. A nice place to pass the time."

We fell into an odd silence, which was weird because Aileen and I rarely found ourselves speechless. I'd known her for most of my life. I'd stayed in her home when neither parent wanted a holiday in the West country so that I could fly Kane in the wilds of Ireland. In the Shea household I had always had a place, a bed, a table to take tea.

"Did you know Lana wants me to leave? Tomorrow, at the latest." Aileen's lips twisted. "She thinks it's not safe for me here, now that you are marching back on Lyonesse." Her tone tightened, not at all pleased that her daughter would give her such stipulations.

Lana and her mam had always gotten along famously, but I sensed this was a sticking point on which neither would budge.

"It's not that she doesn't want you here." I knew that to be true without having to ask. "She fears for your safety. Our father . . . "

My eyes flashed to Aileen. It felt so strange to say certain things to her. To acknowledge that Lana and I were siblings. I'd had months to get used to the idea, but knowing that Aileen and my mother had loved the same man at one point was so strange. Ms. Shea and my mother were very different. How had Oberon seduced them both?

"He's a monster," Aileen finished. "I never suspected it when we were together, but it's clear as day now. I'm so glad everyone has seen him for what he is. Still, I don't want to go. I worry about you guys."

I stopped and placed a hand on her shoulder. "I worry about us too. But I would worry more if you were here. It's not safe in this realm for those we love. Given half a chance, my father will use you against us. It gives me relief that my mum isn't here."

"You always took her side," Aileen commented softly.

"You're her only family."

"That's not true." Her lips twitched up as her eyes, the same color of gray that Lana's used to be before we came to Faerie, focused on me. "You were always family. Always one of her favorite people."

"Yeah," I muttered, and fell silent. We were nearing uncomfortable territory.

"Lana told me you fancied her," Aileen whispered, as if knowing what I was thinking. "Of course, I already knew that."

"She did? *You* did?" That surprised me. Lana kept quiet about things like that, and everything had come to a head months ago. Was she still worried about it?

"Last night, after you arrived," she continued. "She thought it was one big secret that you had feelings for her, but asked if I'd known." She chuckled. "Of course, I did. You loved her for years, and only my darling girl didn't realize it."

Heat filled my cheeks. "Was I that obvious?"

Lana's Mam shook her head and continued walking. The sound of running water filled my ears. Soon we would come across a fountain or stream, or maybe a majestic waterfall—I didn't know, anything seemed plausible here.

"You weren't obvious at all, but I know you. I always thought one day Lana would figure it out. Now I'm glad she didn't, but are you okay?"

"I am," I admitted. "It hurt for a while. But I've moved on."

"Good," Aileen conceded. "I hope the new girl knows how lucky she is."

I didn't reply to that. Ebba remained a mystery I wanted to unravel. She was even more difficult to crack than Lana, and that was saying something.

Out of the blue, a pegasus soared above us. It gleamed white with gold feathers.

A delighted gasp left Aileen's mouth. "Isn't it amazing, Finn?" Together, we stopped walking to admire the creature. "Does it belong to the queen?"

"I suspect so."

"It's so beautiful! I'm not leaving until I meet it." Aileen's eyes shimmered like a teenage girl seeing a dream come to life.

"It might have landed. Let's go see."

We rushed down the trail until it opened into a clearing. The water we'd heard trickle was exposed as a gold, glorious, three-tiered fountain. It gleamed in the sunlight, striking against the deep green of the garden. The pegasus drank from the blue water, taking no notice of us.

When my gaze fell over Ebba sitting on the edge of the fountain, I stopped and sucked in a breath. To my surprise, Kane perched beside her, content to sit with the fae. I'd never seen him do that with anyone, except Lana and me. The petite soldier brushed herself off as the pegasus took to the skies again.

"Hello," Aileen greeted, her smile wide as her gaze flicked up to me and then back to Ebba. "Seems everyone's out this morning. You arrived yesterday too, is that right?"

"I did." Ebba bowed but Aileen looked away, feeling uncomfortable over being a person linked to royalty. Ebba rose and turned her gaze upon me. "The guard told me you were out here. I came to have a word."

"Oh, right. Well, I-I guess that can be arranged." Bloody hell. Back home I was known as a bit of a ladies' man. How did this woman reduce me to a stammering boy?

A smirk crossed Aileen's face. "Right. I need to check on Lana anyway. She might need one more healing session before she's set to rights." She squeezed my wrist and winked.

"The guard who showed me to the garden mentioned that all trails lead to the middle." Ebba offered. "I suspect this is the middle."

"Right. Thanks." Aileen threw a wave and trailed back the way we'd come.

I was alone with Ebba. That almost never happened. Usually, my siblings or other guards surrounded us. Almost always Gio was there, vying for her attention too. In those cases, earning her attention felt more like a game. Who could get her to laugh first? To smile? Would she show either of us favor?

Now, with her sharp gaze on me, I felt awkward. Like a teen working up the courage to ask his first crush on a date.

Clearing my throat, I looked to Kane, who remained perched on the fountain. "Was he being a bother?"

"What?" Her brows pinched together adorably.

"My hawk," I clarified. "Was Kane being a pest?"

Behind her, Kane ruffled his feathers indignantly,

and guilt trickled through me. He was submissive, particularly to Naela, and never pushy.

Sorry, mate. Take one for the team, I thought. I needed some way to smooth over my awkwardness.

"Oh, no. He's quite calm." Ebba glanced at my familiar.

"Would you care for a stroll?"

Walking would be better than standing there, staring at her face, wanting to cup her cheek with my hand. Movement meant I had something else to look at, something to do.

"Sure." She turned, choosing a path for us.

A soft breath escaped out of me as I followed. A tree-lined trail ensconced us while I built up the courage to speak. "You said you wanted to talk?"

Ebba exhaled a relieved breath. "To thank you, really."

"Bout what?"

"For getting us out of there."

"Honestly, I probably put you in more danger. Once my father learns that you're with us, you'll be criminals." I hated the idea, but it was true. Still, Ryker had had a point. Garret would have had a target on his back either way, and I would have hated leaving Ebba. Knowing she was here, safe, let me rest easier.

Unlike half of my siblings.

The guilt snuck in again, my unwelcome companion. I hated the fact that I'd deserted them, even if temporarily.

"We will be. But neither Garret, nor I, care about being seen as traitors. Not when so much is on the line, and we finally know the truth. Only our families . . ." she trailed off, conflict rippling across her fine-boned features. Her family was safe, but Garret's mother was not.

"We'll get to her in time."

"I trust we will," Ebba agreed. "I wish they'd have gotten to her first. She's older than my parents, but I understand it wasn't possible. We're all doing the best we can, given the circumstances of our escape." A resigned sigh escaped through her rosebud lips. "What I'm trying to say is thank you for getting us out of there so we could learn the truth. It hurts, knowing the king deceived me for so long, but it's better this way. Now I need the rest of my homeland to see the truth too."

That would be a feat. Even if we saved my siblings and took back Lyonesse, the fae of the kingdom were devoted to King Oberon. His family, my bloodline, had risen from poor fae to royalty and many found hope in that rise. I knew that if we took the castle, we'd surely have disgruntled citizens on our hands.

"I hope they'll see it as quickly as you did." My gaze darted around the tunnel of green we strolled through together. Vines and flowers filled the spaces between trees, creating an impenetrable wall of vegetation. "Did you ever suspect?"

"No," Ebba admitted flatly. "If I'm being honest, there's a part of me that doesn't want to believe it. Like an unnerving mental resistance." She shook her head, annoyed with herself. "History plays a large part, I suppose. Your family is well-loved and always has been. Still, I'm furious that I allowed myself to be taken in."

Understanding exactly how she felt, I nodded. I'd only known my biological father for months and I was fecking furious too. "He—shite!"

My arms caught Ebba when she leapt straight into me, my gaze latching on a projectile aimed straight at her. Instantly, my shadows stirred, and I nearly released them, when the bloody thing croaked.

"It's a frog," I said, my tone dipping with relief. A smile tilted my lips as I shooed it away with a flick of my wrist.

In my arms, Ebba shifted. Shite. I loosened my grip on her. She probably didn't want to be touched.

"Oh, sorry. I—"

"I'm the one who leapt on top of you. Over a damned frog!" Her cheeks grew rosy as she pulled away. "We don't have those back home. Although that's not a very good excuse. I'm a soldier."

Of course, in Lyonesse, no frogs would leap at people. The only animals that could live in the barren wasteland of Lyonesse were scavengers. They stayed hidden, preferring dark corners and blackened woods to leaping joyously through a lush garden.

"That's alright. I don't mind a pretty lady throwing herself at me."

A laugh burst out of Ebba. Her voice, her laugh, were music to my ears. An urge to woo her came over me. Flowers lined the tunnel and I reached to pluck one that looked like a peony.

"Usually, I like to get her flowers first though." I winked, acting more like myself.

Ebba stared at me, and for a moment, I was sure she wouldn't take the flower. I prepared to tuck it behind my ear to hear her laugh again, but then she accepted the bloom and sniffed it.

"Lovely." She glanced up at me from beneath thick lashes. "We don't have these back home either. I wonder what they're called?"

"Arathacanum," a voice barked.

My head snapped up, breaking the hold Ebba had on me. Bellona, one of Pari's ladies, stood down the trail from us, her arms crossed over her chest.

"That's quite the name for such a pretty flower. It would be better if it were something short and sweet." I tried to salvage the moment by catching Ebba's eye, but the heat that had simmered between us fizzled.

She still held the flower, but lower, her cheeks pink and eyes downcast. I could imagine what she was thinking—another soldier had caught her flirting with a prince. Captain Ebba would not like that.

"Well, it's not short, nor sweet," Bellona retorted, her eyebrows arched high. "And if you wouldn't mind coming with me, the queen wishes for you to join her for breakfast. There's much planning to be done before we march south."

"Of course." Ebba's tone became harsher. The Captain was back, doing away with the other side of the woman I'd glimpsed.

Together, we followed Bellona. Though the lady in waiting had ruined the moment, I couldn't help but feel excited.

For the first time, Ebba had flirted with me. Not only that, but she had not seemed freaked out by my shadows. Despite the knowledge that we would soon embark on a dangerous mission, the hope that the woman I fancied might return my affections bloomed inside me.

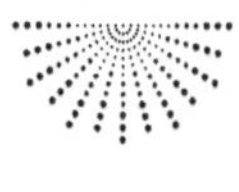

CHAPTER NINETEEN

LANA

The wind whipped through my hair as my gold-dappled gryphon, Taima, descended with the speed of a bullet. Soaring beside us, Naela released a joyous screech, and I whooped back, waving to her.

Mere days ago, the idea of piloting a gryphon terrified me. One brush with death, a race to save my family, a proper flying lesson later, and I was a convert.

Flying was amazing.

"Oh my God, Lan. Are your hands still on the saddle-knob-thing?" Mam's arms wrapped around me tighter.

I settled my hand back on the horn. The other hand clenched the leather reins wrapped around Taima's beak. A shriek of laughter came from somewhere behind me.

"Safety first," I lied.

Mam relaxed, her grip loosening ever so slightly. The poor woman had been so happy to pet the gryphons and the pegasi on the ground, but once we got her in the air she was a right mess. Since my first journey on a gryphon had been terrifying, I could relate. Perhaps if Mam returned to Faerie, we'd give flying another go, and she'd like it more too.

But first, I had to get through a battle and win.

"Okay, Mam, get ready. Taima's about to hit the ground," I warned.

Her grip around me tightened so much that I struggled to breathe, but said nothing. If Mam needed to squeeze me to death to feel safe, then so be it.

Taima's talons hit ground, followed a second later by her lion's paws, and Mam whispered a thanks to the universe. I guided Taima to the group gathering around Pari, the leader of our flock. All around, others landed too—some gracefully, some not. Poor Celine rode with her daughter and yelped loudly the moment her beast touched down.

"Good girl." I ran my hand over Taima's neck.

The gryphon didn't acknowledge me, but pushed her way through the crowd to stand next to Ra, the queen's mount. I eyed Pari sidelong, lips twitching upward, while she chuckled and stroked Ra's feathers.

Early in the flight we had decided Taima and Ra were a couple, because they always wanted to fly next to each other. The gryphons solidified that assumption now, as Taima rubbed up against Ra and clicked her beak flirtatiously.

"Let's stretch our legs before we say goodbye." The queen studied Mam and Celine, both of whom looked like they might be sick. "Feel free to explore."

"Excellent." Finn hopped off his beast and went to speak with a few soldiers.

I watched him, amused. Knowing Finn, he wanted to get the history of the area. That was probably why he'd come with us. What a nerd.

When we dismounted, Mam collapsed to the ground and lay looking up at the sky. She needed time to collect herself.

"Mam, I want to explore, but are you okay alone?"

"Fine, darling. Just need a mo' to catch my breath. Go on then."

My lips landed on top of her head. "I'll be right back."

King Oberon's bonegate was completely different from what I'd imagined. As a mere hole in the ground, it was much more mundane than Buyan's bonegate. Although, if I peered into it deeply, I could see the tips of white bone protruding from the dirt. I shook my head. The literal bones of one of my long dead ancestors, the Fullfeather Sinker sat there, imbued with powerful magic that kept the veil between Faerie and my own world open.

Still, it wasn't just the portal that shocked me.

Where the kingdoms met, the contrast between Pari and my father's territory was stark. On one side—the side where magic was traditionally supposed to flow into Lyonesse—the black sand I used to gaze upon from the windows of Castle Phoenix ruled the landscape. Only sparse tufts of grass and shabby shrubs dotted the area.

Where I stood, however, lush vegetation rose out of nowhere. Buyan's bonegate, though far away, kept its kingdom alive with magic. So, what was stopping the magic from flowing deeper into Lyonesse? Just wards? That seemed like a huge job. Could one ward-maker really do it all?

"Crow! Stop it!' A chorus of shouts followed, hitching my shoulders up with tension.

Crow? What did that mean? I turned just in time for a bird to soar by me, it's wing clipping me in the face.

"Ow!"

I twisted, and would have fallen through the bonegate, had I not caught myself with my hands. A squawk interrupted my relief, and my gaze shot up to catch a flash of black feathers and a glimmer of dark eyes as the crow disappeared through the portal with a white rock clutched in its beak.

My stomach dipped. That was no regular crow. It had to be a Feathered Fae, and in its beak was not a rock, but a bonekey.

Footsteps rushed over to me.

"Are you alright, Princess?" a soldier asked, holding out his hand to help me stand.

"Was that a Feathered Fae?" I rubbed at my face, which stung a little, but not as much as my pride.

"Undoubtedly." The soldier's lips turned down.

"How do they get by you so easily?" The words came out accusatory, though I didn't mean them that way.

"They hide in the trees, sometimes for hours waiting for the right moment." The guard glanced behind him, to where Pari was rushing over, her dark brown eyes wide.

Not far away, still on the ground, Mam's face was pale.

"We were distracted by our queen's arrival," the soldier continued, "and the Feathered Fae, who snuck through the bonegate, took advantage of that."

"I understand." Though I wasn't sure that was completely true. They were guards and should always be 'on'. Yes, their queen was here, but a priceless opportunity had slipped through their fingers. The crow was probably already soaring in the wind in the human world.

Where had it been taking the bonekey to? And why?

"Lana." Pari reached my side. "Are you okay?"

"Fine." I admitted. "Embarrassed, but more than that, concerned. How do they get through so easily?"

Pari looked at the soldier who took his leave. Her dark gaze returned to me. "We don't know how they get through Armina's wards. We suspect with an elixir that Oberon, or someone else created, but we can't be sure."

"Like a potion?"

When I was in the healing ward, I received what I would call a potion, or an elixir, but I didn't know the fae used them for other things.

"Exactly. Your father's Sinker Divine was an excellent potion maker. I wouldn't be surprised if Oberon uses his skills to keep people enchanted."

I blinked. "What is a Sinker Divine?"

Pari cocked her head. "They're the religious figures in Faerie. When I frequented the kingdom, his name was Thamula, but your father was going to appoint Tizu as his when he came of age. Tizu is actually your uncle, Oberon's youngest brother. He was quite gifted in potions."

"Never heard of him. Actually, Meegra told us that all of my father's siblings died."

"He might not be there any longer. It's been so long . . . perhaps he did die." Pari hedged. "The king could be using another potion master to confuse Armina's wards."

"Right." I felt stupid and too analyzed beneath her gaze. Turning, I took in the scenery. The questions I'd had before came rushing back, and keen to change the subject, I went for it. "Are the wards what stops the magic? I can feel it in the air and your land is so lush. But Lyonesse is a hell hole."

"There are wards up to protect the soldiers here," Pari replied. She seemed slightly relieved for the change of subject. Knowing that enemies could slip by her forces was probably not something on which she liked to dwell.

"Not to affect the magic?"

"Some of it is affected," Pari answered. "But mostly, the magic from the Old Land that would flow into Lyonesse knows the bonegate no longer belongs to Oberon. Hence, most of it is blocked. He would need to claim the portal for it to work properly for him again."

"And what little magic comes through, his Feathered Fae collect and return to the castle."

I'd seen evidence of the magic they retrieved in the palace. Now I'd seen how easily they could hide and slip through the portals too. Their feathered forms really were an asset. More so than I'd ever realized.

"Everything is a give and take." Pari inhaled deeply. "We absorb the magic of our surroundings and vice versa. Faerie has its own type of magic, but as we are nothing more than a derivative of the Old Land, the bulk of it comes from there. It's an exchange. Our power flows the other way, too. It's what keeps the portals alive."

Before that moment, I hadn't thought of the gates

as alive or sentient, but the queen certainly made them seem that way.

"Remain here. I wish to speak with Lana privately," Pari addressed her ladies.

"Are you sure, My Queen?" Isis asked, looking peeved.

"Positive."

"The gates differ from the bonekeys your father used to get you here," she explained, once we strolled out of earshot. "Those must be charmed in advance to certain locations. Theoretically, they can go anywhere, but they only work with one or two people. Bonegates, however, can accommodate mass movements of fae."

Ice brushed across my nape. Her implications were clear. If Oberon took his back, he could have an army on earth within minutes.

"I see you understand the severity of the situation. That your father has attempted three large-scale attacks in two months, is quite telling to me. It's harder than he's tried in years. He's no longer willing to wait to dominate the Old Land."

I didn't know how it was possible for my blood to get colder, but it did. I hated hearing how long he'd planned that, but then again, what did I expect? Fae lived for centuries. To him, a few years, even twenty years, was nothing.

"If he knows your people guard this one so well, why not use another?"

"Unless permission is granted, we can only use the bonegates that belong to our homeland. As it stands now, the Lyonesse gate recognizes me as its holder by right, but your father and those of Lyonesse as a holder by blood. Or history, perhaps. If your father, or his minions, asked to use one of the bonegates in the Free Realm or Beast Realm, guides would be needed. Not to mention, not every free city or kingdom has a bonegate in those realms. Either way, that would mean telling others his plan to take over the Old Land."

"Would they care?"

"Perhaps." Pari looked uncertain. "Even if they are allies, it is a risky move. They would demand a share of the power. I have reason to believe he offered shares to the demi-fae in the Old Land."

"So they would help him take over?"

"Precisely."

"And the only other time he confided in someone it didn't go so well."

"True. Nowadays, I doubt anyone other than his Master Feathered Fae knows of Oberon's true plan."

Prince Casimir, keen on getting on my good side, had confided that Meegra was sleeping with our father. Pari might not know that, but either way, I wouldn't doubt her assessment. Meegra was powerful and devoted to her king. Whether it was because she saw a crown in her future, or her own continent to rule over in the Old Land, I wasn't sure. Though, I was certain the king had promised her something in return for her loyalty.

"You don't think Casimir knows?" I asked.

Though I had less love for the crown prince than the rest of my siblings, I still didn't want to think of him as *that* manipulative. That keen to hurt and dominate an entire world. Could a boy who had grown up weak, do that to others?

"I'm not sure," Pari admitted. "What are your opinions on the matter?"

"I don't think so," I ventured. "Oberon has never seen him as a leader. He belittles him sometimes. In public even."

"I've heard that too. Casimir is now more powerful than his father, but Oberon still treats him poorly," the queen agreed. "He believes, as he always has, that he's the only person who can get the job done properly."

We continued walking along a wall surrounded by dwellings. Those buildings were where the fae who guarded the bonegate lived. They were small shacks, and judging by the divots in the walls, victims of the recent attack.

Were there no strong earth fae here to fix the holes? I eyed the gaps in the buildings. With the help of flowered curtains and colored doors they still maintained a cheery appearance.

"Did Ryker and Sai tell you all this? Or Posy?"

A smirk curved Pari's lips. "Most of it. Their families are among the ones I have counted on for centuries. Families broke apart when Oberon and I ended our betrothal, but some in my kingdom were able to get the truth to their blood in Lyonesse. They've been spies since then."

"I hadn't considered how many families must be split," I admitted.

"Have you met Tau's sweetheart?" Pari's dark eyes twinkled with mischief.

My face turned red. I hated recalling how stupid I'd been, going around interrogating citizens of Buyan.

"Petal. Yes, she is charming." I recalled the fae with pastel pink hair and curious, crystalline pink eyes. "Even when I was interrogating her to get the dirt on you. Sorry for that, by the way."

A tinkle of laughter left Pari's lips, and she rubbed my shoulder. "Do not be embarrassed. While I wanted you to believe me, I was a little relieved you didn't right away. Those who are swayed too quickly often change sides just as fast. You were doing your due diligence, gathering information."

"That's one way to look at it. So, Petal's family are spies too?" I wanted to get off the topic of how thick I'd been.

"She is a cousin to Ryker and Sai."

"What? No way!" Now that she mentioned it, I supposed I could sort of see the resemblance between Petal and Sai.

"Indeed. That pair has been a wealth of knowledge over the years. Although, they didn't see you coming."

"What does that mean?"

"Once you and your siblings arrived, it became more difficult to give information. They were on guard all the time, and others, those who believe in Oberon, were on high alert."

Like Garret. He'd been so attentive, so set on doing right by me. His vigilance would have made it harder for his friends to relay information.

We strolled the rest of the way in silence, allowing me to mull over everything Pari had told me. When we returned to the group, Mam was standing and talking with Finn. Tears welled in her eyes. Her time here was drawing to a close.

"I've kept you from your mother long enough." Pari nudged me. "Have your time before she leaves."

"Hey," I said as I approached my best friend and mother.

"Hey," Finn replied, his tone tight. "I was telling your mam to make sure she caught up with my mother . . . I want her to know what's happening. But not to worry."

"I will," Mam promised.

"Thanks, Aileen. If I can't see her, this is the next best thing." Finn looked away, sadness rippling across his face. I could tell that he missed his mother. I'd been so lucky to see Mam, if only for a short while.

"Want to walk for a moment before you have to go?" I held my arm out for her, and she took it, but not before squeezing Finn one last time and kissing his cheek.

We walked a different direction than Pari and I had gone. I didn't need her seeing the magic-shocked homes, and equate them with the battle I was preparing to throw myself into soon. When we neared the boundary of the jungle, Pari's land, Mam glanced at me.

"I never wanted you to despise your father. It's one thing that I do, but . . . you're his daughter," she confessed, breaking the silence. Tears glinted in her eyes. "This is all my fault. Had I listened to your Gran and not run off with him—"

"Then I wouldn't even be here. There's no need to feel sorry for falling in love. You are not the one at fault, and I know you didn't want me to hate him. You gave me twenty-one years of believing my father may be alright. But some dreams have to end eventually, right?"

Mam choked on a watery laugh. "Uncanny."

My head tilted in question.

"Your gran said the same thing to me when he left me. Since the start, she sensed he wasn't what he seemed. Though I doubted she'd ever imagined this degree of deception."

"What did she say about him?"

"Not much. I'd told him she was a psychic, and he

made a point never to meet her. Probably didn't want her rummaging around in his head. Still, your Gran heard stories and that was enough. She took it as a bad omen when he left. Did her tarot cards and everything. They always pointed to death."

"What?" I'd never heard any of that.

"It is the reason she was always so diligent with your lessons. She sensed he'd return, and when he did, she wanted you to be prepared. It's why she taught you how to keep out psychics, too. I claimed it was a bunch of nonsense." She shook her head. "I was a fool."

"I am what I am, and this is going to happen. I suppose all we can do is be pleased that Gran pushed me so hard, even though I was still an awful student." I grinned, and Mam laughed.

Until I came to Faerie, I'd been a lackluster witch. I'd always tried, but nothing ever clicked. Not until I arrived here.

A chill set in as the afternoon slipped away, and I knew we should get back to Buyan soon. I didn't want to fly in the dark.

Mam's hand extended, running over a strange tree with both leaves and needles. "This place is so amazing, Lan. I can see why you love it. You feel right here, don't you?"

My throat tightened because I knew what she was really asking. Mam wondered if I'd ever return to Ireland. "I've found where I belong."

Nodding, Mam gave me a sad smile. "I'll miss you so much."

I moved in for a hug, squeezing her tightly. "I'll miss you too. And even though I worry, I'm happy too."

She pulled away and looked me in the eye. "It's so clear that you've found your place."

"Thanks, Mam," I choked.

My mother kissed me on the cheek and squeezed me again. "You'll be a fabulous leader, darling," her whisper brushed my ear. "You were born to bring the light."

CHAPTER TWENTY

LANA

After Mam left, I couldn't stop worrying about her.

The appearance of the Feathered Fae at the bonegate made me doubt myself. Had my father sent the crow after Mam, not knowing she was already here? If it went after her, I wouldn't be able to forgive myself for sending her back home.

I strode down the corridor and inhaled a shaky breath, trying to break the cycle of dread gripping me before I reported for training. Trusting that my mother would be safer in Ireland was difficult but necessary. I needed to do my best to move forward and create a better future.

Despite all the platitudes I fed myself, my heart rate was still accelerated as I entered the training space. Isis, Armina, and Bellona stood in the center of the vast room, among the small army surrounding Queen Pari.

Queen Mauri was there too, talking animatedly with Crystal. A very attractive man, who resembled a Viking stood next to her, admiration, and maybe something resembling adoration, lining his face. I'd seen him around the castle, always by Mauri's side.

Surprisingly, Pari did not wear the loose-fitting clothing she favored. Today her attire resembled the closest thing I'd seen to activewear in Faerie. Tighter pants and a curve-hugging tank top, white of course, would allow the queen greater freedom of movement.

Obstacles and training props lay scattered across the floor. I jogged toward the center of the room, ready to throw myself into activity to dull the pain of Mam's absence. I was almost to the group when a bark of laughter came from on high. Glancing up, I blinked.

Guards, servants, and perhaps even fae lords and ladies, judging by their clothes, lined the hallways above the training space, which was open like a court-yard. Curiosity lined each of their expressions. Of course, we would draw a crowd. We were King Oberon's children from the Old Land. One of us was an illuminator. Another was a demon born. Both were rare, no matter what realm you called home.

A bout of nerves rushed through me. The

atmosphere felt a lot like it had before the Successional.

"Pay them no attention." Pari placed a light hand on my arm, redirecting my attention. "A dozen are officers in my army, a few others are soldiers who want to know your powers for when they fight along-side you. The rest are curious courtiers and servants." Her head shook in amusement. "No one is judging you, and I won't hear a word against you, but not everyone can train at the same time. There isn't enough space. And it *is* best they know all your capabilities. The more familiar we are with each other, the better."

I nodded, and Pari branched off to split people into smaller training groups. She saved me for last, putting me on her team, along with Armina, Isis, and Bellona. I tried to consider the grouping a compliment, but wished I was with any other group.

We claimed a spot near the edge of the room, far away from anyone else, and warmed up together. Though I was meant to be concentrating on myself, after a few minutes, my attention drifted. Aside from hearing that Pari's ladies in waiting were excellent fighters, I knew little about their skills. What I was witnessing, however, made me believe all the rumors.

With her blond hair pulled high in a tight pony-tail, Isis moved one of the car-sized boulders in the air with an ease I'd never seen from an Old Land rumbler. She was having fun with it too, flinging metal blades at the rock and chipping it away bit by bit.

Bellona put on a production too, with her four tornados circling her as she darted out of their way with feline grace.

"Wow," I breathed.

Her violet eyes shot straight toward me. "Can I help you?"

"Uh, no," I mumbled, embarrassed. As well as fighting with air, she could hear whispers on the wind. That was a valuable talent for a queen to utilize.

Focusing on myself, I called balls of infrared light and juggled them. They were my props, so I could pretend like I was working on dexterity rather than snooping. My attention turned to Armina, her blades whizzing through the air and spinning from one hand to the other with unnatural speed. It was mesmerizing, although she seemed content to keep her training physical, not magical.

I wondered why. Did Armina have such a destructive talent that performing it around others would be dangerous?

If you're curious, I can show you.

Staggering back, I shrieked, and the infrared light I'd been playing with disappeared.

Armina laughed coldly, making me suck in a breath. Had that been her?

"What is going on?" Pari ran up to me.

"Nothing, My Queen. The illuminator wondered

why I was not using my magic. I merely answered her." Armina's terrifying golden smile flashed.

My mouth gaped. Armina was a psychic, and she was the most dangerous kind. She didn't just possess the ability to read minds, she could also speak into other's minds, and likely alter them too.

"Armina!" Pari scolded.

"I promise I did not hurt her. Only spoke to her."

As Pari met my eyes, I nodded. Though it had terrified me, as Armina intended, that was all she'd done.

"Fine. Keep inside your own head and continue practicing. Lana, please join me." Holding my arm, Pari pulled me away from her ladies. Once we stood a good distance away, she stopped.

"She's psychic," I whispered. "That's massive."

"We call them mind fae, but from what I hear, the powers are the same as psychic witches in your world. I apologize for her actions." Pari's lips flattened in annoyance. "You are Oberon's daughter, and my ladies are trained to be distrustful. They were with me after we ended our engagement, so they remember firsthand how it affected me. Hence, why they dislike that I have been talking to you so much. It threatens them, especially Armina. They're so used to being the only ones allowed to be in my presence alone, a practice I have broken with you many times."

"It's okay," I assured. "I understand. Should we practice?"

Pari nodded, and we split to resume our activities.

Once everyone had time to warm up, we moved to practice in a larger, warded ring so everyone could get a sense of everyone else's magic. When my turn came, Pari eyed me carefully.

"Lana and Armina, in the circle."

The mind fae snorted. "Are you sure, My Queen?"

"Lana?"

If I backed down, I'd look like a weakling, and I knew that wasn't Pari's intent. She wanted to show her ladies that I was a force to be reckoned with too. It was a strange way to go about it, but from the confident way she held my gaze, I was sure that was her intent.

"I'm ready," I replied, making my way into the ring.

My hands trembled as Armina's dark eyes took me in like she was going to eat me. The days when I dreaded sparring against Crystal seemed laughable. Armina smirked as if she knew what I was thinking, and the pressure against my skull alerted me to the fact that she was there, waiting to break into my mind.

Fecking hell.

The starting flag waved, and I didn't have time to be scared anymore. I launched into action, hurling myself at Armina as I flashed visible light straight into her eyes. My best hope was to attack quickly, to prevent her from latching onto my mind.

Armina didn't even blink as the light flooded her retinas. Her black eyes grew wider, and she surged to meet me, sharp teeth glinting. Her blades flashed so fast, forcing me to leap back seconds before she swiped at my gut.

Armina was not playing around.

That's right, I'm not, little light witch. And you shouldn't be either.

I darted to the edge of the sparring ring, my heart racing. Armina followed me, her gait slow and measured, like a serial killer in a movie.

"You're going to cower like a little lamb?" she teased.

Her words hit me hard, knocking sense back into me. Yes, Armina intimidated me, but I was no lamb. I had to show her that, had to earn her respect.

Calling on my power, my infrared sword flared in my hand.

Gasps arose from the crowd. I hadn't shown them that trick yet, but Armina didn't seem impressed. She kept coming—blades locked in her hand, their edges jagged and cruel. When her dark eyes pinned me, a faint push grazed my skull. She was at it again, trying to infiltrate my mind. I needed to give Armina something to think about so her concentration fractured. It was time to pull out all the stops.

Pulling an illusion around me, I vanished.

The press on my head lessened as Armina's eyes widened in shock.

Go figure. My most basic trick was the one to stun her.

On light feet, I distanced myself from the ward-maker. When I struck, the timing had to be right. Armina's black hair whipped around her shoulders as she searched for me.

"Did you see that, my queen?" Armina roared. "For all we know since you've lifted her powers, she's been sneaking around the castle, gathering information for her father. How can you be so sure we can trust her?"

A roar of indignation rose beyond the sparring wall from Finn and Garret, sticking up for me.

If I hadn't been hiding from her, I would have done the same, but I couldn't risk giving myself away. Easing into position, I lifted my infrared sword high behind my illusion to take it down on her shoulder—incapacitating Armina without injuring her—when the mind fae whirled around, her blades slicing through the air.

"Shouldn't think so loudly, witch." Her words sizzled with ferocity.

The illusion dropped, and we danced in the circle. Metal against light, no one so much as nicking the other, but both coming dangerously close. My chest heaved and sweat poured down my face as Armina's daggers swirled and spun in the surrounding air. Her mind pressed in on mine.

I fought back, but another threat caught my attention. One knife soaring high, prepared to strike. I tried to shield myself, but then she dropped one blade, and lightning fast caught it, slamming it into my exposed triceps.

A howl of pain parted my lips. The infrared sword flickered and died, and I stood before her, defenseless. I whimpered, and Armina's sharp teeth glinted. Panicking, I flashed a beam of visible light at her, hoping it would blind her. Instead, she lifted her dagger in front of her face, reflecting my light back into my eyes.

My hands flew up to shield my vision.

"Is this how easy you'll fall if we fight with you? If so, tell me now. I must make sure my queen is nowhere near you. Pathetic."

Pressure gripped my skull as my mind latched onto one word.

Pathetic.

After everything I'd done, all I'd learned, that pissed me off to no end. No. It *infuriated* me. Did the others agree? I'd show them.

Light hung all around me. I ripped it from the air and the blaze tunneled toward me and then from my body, the conduit of magic. The conductor of the show. It filled the room, expanding all the way to where those above stood. Cries rose, but I pressed on, calling infrared to my aid. When the red light came, I grabbed it and flung it forward. The blaze seared Armina's skin, precise and cruel.

A scream tore up her throat as she launched herself at me. Her eyes wide, blades glinting.

I reached again and grabbed more light. Enraged this time; riled up from her mocking. A sword flashed in my hand, and I pivoted away from Armina, striking her back as she flew past.

She collapsed to the ground with a whimper, and then, Armina did the unthinkable. Her hand lifted in defeat.

My hands flew to my mouth. There, across her back in a diagonal line from shoulder blade to hipbone, gaped a foot long slice surrounded by bubbling, mutated flesh.

I had accessed the ultraviolet spectrum for the first time.

CHAPTER TWENTY-ONE

FINN

My best friend fell to her knees, her chest heaving with each breath.

"Lana!" I dashed forward, thankful the wardmaker's fancy sparring protections kept the danger inside, but allowed me to slip in and help. "Are you okay?"

Gold eyes flickered up to me, and then back at the person on the ground. Armina moaned as a crowd gathered around her to help.

"What happened?" I knelt in front of Lana.

"I-I—ultraviolet." Her lip trembled. "I didn't mean to."

My eyes widened. Back home I'd heard Lana talk about the spectrums plenty of times. Usually, she was complaining she couldn't access them, but now she had, and she might have done serious damage.

"We'll figure it out." I pressed a hand on her

shoulder, pushing into it so she felt weighted, grounded.

"Lana, come with us," Queen Pari called. She and her two other ladies were among those circling the wardmaker. Armina sobbed, and from what I could tell, the show of emotion was more than warranted.

Her skin was bubbling and smoking. A violent gash cut through her, exposing her insides to daylight.

Ultraviolet radiation was like infrared in the sense that it burned, but it went deeper too, hurt more, even with little effort from the lightworker. In short, it was more powerful—more detrimental.

"You want me to come?" Lana whispered. "Are you sure?"

Queen Pari turned. "Of course, I'm sure. I'm not mad, you were sparring, and something happened you did not expect. Later, that might turn out to be good for our side, but for now, my lady needs help. Tell me about your magic. Any small detail could help heal her."

"I'm not a healer. That's my mam."

"Go," I urged. "Tell them what it does. They might know nothing about your powers. They need help."

Garret, who had been hovering somewhere behind me, stepped closer to offer Lana his hand. "I'm coming with you."

With his help, Lana stood slowly. Other soldiers had already pulled Armina onto a stretcher. I would have expected the wardmaker to snarl a growl at my sister, but she continued to sob. Her eyes found Lana's and latched on to her.

"I'm so sorry," Lana blurted. "I—"

"*Stop.*" Armina spat. "Never apologize for your magic. Learn to control it. If you can do that, it might do us some good," she gasped, closing her eyes.

A stunned expression crossed Lana's face, but the moment Queen Pari commanded her soldiers to sweep Armina from the room, my best friend followed. Garret marched next to her, holding her hand. I was glad he was with her.

When the queen and those who assisted disappeared, I glanced around the room, and wondered if we should keep training.

A woman marched up to me and extended her hand. "We haven't officially met. I'm Mauri."

"Finn." We shook. "You're Crystal's mate from back home, right?"

"That's me. A lot has changed since I saw my friend last, but not our bond." Mauri's lips lifted into a smile. She is a beautiful woman, if my heart wasn't already taken, I could see myself falling for her in a heartbeat.

"Are you coming with us to Lyonesse?"

"I believe so. I sent a message to my grandmother, asking for soldiers to accompany your forces."

"Queen Merenith will surely say yes." A man who looked like a Viking, blond with ice-blue eyes, came up behind Mauri and placed his hand on her shoulder. He pulled her in close. "King Oberon's actions will affect us also."

"They already have," Mauri agreed, her brown eyes darkening dangerously.

"You're from Ys?" I asked. "I haven't been there, but have read about it."

"You are speaking with the newest Queen of Ys," the guy informed. "I'm her guardian, Anders. The other queen I speak of is her grandmother. She's no longer actively ruling."

"It's a long story." Mauri leaned into the man, her gaze flicking away. I recognized that look. Whatever had occurred, no matter how comfortable she seemed in her skin, Mauri wasn't ready to talk about it. At least not to me, a stranger.

"Okay. Should we keep training?"

In my experience, moving my body helped the most in working things out. I preferred hiking and hawking, but sparring worked too. Actually, it was more effective than I liked to admit. I'd always fancied myself a scholar, but was wondering if I wasn't a bit of a warrior too.

"That's what I was hoping," Mauri replied. "Be my partner?"

"I don't know if you want that." I gulped.

So far, I had been careful to only practice with my siblings, because they knew what I was. Still, I didn't use my shadows. I'd watched others a bit too, but not

Mauri. She'd been on the far side of the room. What if she wasn't a good fighter?

Mauri arched an eyebrow. "I do want that. Your kind is as rare as mine, and I love a challenge."

I blinked. "You're not fae?"

"Half fae, half vampire. They call my supernatural race nosferatu. We're the deadliest creature around."

For some reason that made me feel a lot better. Like we were both damned. "Demon born witch and elf. And if you're positive, I say let's try it."

Mauri grinned. "Let's get in the ring."

Once we faced off, Crystal took up position as the caller. "On three," she began. "One. Two. Three!"

There was a flash of motion, and before I could so much as blink, Mauri stood behind me. She gripped my chin upward, her fangs poised to rip out my throat.

My heart raced, and I gasped. "Shite! You're fast!"

"Which means you have to be faster. Again?"

We started over, and this time I didn't hesitate to blast fire at her. I knew the vampires were susceptible to flames, but Mauri was part fae too. Still, she darted out of their way. The detour slowed her down, giving me time to strike with air. I lifted Mauri off the ground, hovering her high above us. Her joyous laughter rang through the room.

Then, in a turn of events, her magic blew her

over, making me tumble, and the wind I controlled receded. A second later, the Queen of Ys was there once more, grabbing me, fangs exposed. "If this were an actual fight, I would have already snapped your neck and had a taste."

I gulped. "Do you drink that often?" Curiosity gripped me, because I had never met a vampire, at least not to my knowledge.

"Once every couple of weeks. And always from donor bags we get from the Old Land."

"She has excellent control," the Viking guy, Anders, said from the sideline. Whenever he spoke of Mauri, his eyes went all soft and googly. They were totally an item, and a striking one at that.

"Why haven't you used your demon gift?" the queen pried.

"I don't like using it," I confessed, squirming. "Too dark."

"Oh yeah, and I'm all unicorns and rainbows."

At that, I snorted. "Point taken. But I have to spill my blood to do it. If I pricked myself, would you be able to control your urges?"

Anders mentioned she was good at doing that, but it would be smarter to ask the source. It was my life on the line, after all.

"You smell good, but not good enough for me to go all blood lusty on you, Finn." A twinkle played in Mauri's eyes. I suspected that Crystal might have told her I was a bit of a flirt. "I want to see what you can do. We all do."

Agreeing, I pulled my dagger from its scabbard, and pierced one of the scars on my palm. Though opening older injuries was gross, I'd rather do that instead of making new ones. I didn't want to be the guy walking around with the million scars on my hands and arms when I was old.

Mauri watched me with interest, but there wasn't a hint of blood lust in her eyes.

"Come out," I whispered, hoping I wouldn't regret it.

Only one shadow appeared, but everyone gasped as if I had unleashed an army. Most of them had never seen that before today.

"Can you make more?" Mauri asked.

"Yeah. I don't know what my limit is, but I usually handle two at a time."

Giving me an understanding nod, she resumed her position at the far side of the sparring circle. "Alright, let's do this, for real this time. Come at me with all you got."

Two hours later, we trailed out of the training facility, all of us bone weary. Well, maybe not all of us. As Mauri walked in front of me, with Anders by her side, she didn't seem at all tired.

If we had an army of nosferatu, we would hands down win this fight. Just having Mauri by our side could turn the tides considerably. I hoped her grandmother was in the process of sending the army. Mauri might be the queen, and she seemed quite confident, but if her grandmother said no, perhaps she'd return home. I hoped that didn't happen.

Ebba came up alongside me. "Good practice today."

"Yeah." It really had been. I'd learned a lot about fae magic today. "Although I wanted us to leave faster, I have to admit that getting to see other people's powers was smart. In a battle, you want to know you can trust others."

Her lips curled up in a smile. "You guys haven't been part of our military for long, but no one would guess it from the way you talk. You really do understand how to lead. And what's at stake."

"I'm getting the hang of it."

We chatted lightly, and others peeled off around us, heading to their rooms, the kitchens, or elsewhere. After a few twists and turns, Ebba and I entered a lush courtyard—she enjoyed the outdoors too.

"You should know," Ebba began after a moment of silence, in which we'd been watching an array of colorful birds above, "I'm not scared of your demon gift. I think the rest were startled by it at first, but they're not frightened either. We need all the power we can get if we're going to beat King Oberon."

"Thank you . . . do you think it will be an even fight?"

Ebba worried at her lip. "I don't know. I doubt we're going to go with a full army, as that leaves Buyan at risk. King Oberon has allies too, though mostly they are in Beast Realm."

"What kind of allies? I haven't learned mu—"

"Finn! Can I have a word?"

Queen Mauri's voice cut through mine. Ebba and I turned to find her entering the garden. I glanced at Ebba, who shrugged. "I'll catch you later."

"Sorry." The queen approached. "I could tell that you wanted to keep talking to her, but time is short. And I have an idea that might help you."

Intrigue arched my eyebrows. "What's that?"

As far as I could tell, my problems and the shame that I harbored around my shadows, were unsolvable by anyone but myself.

"I have a tactical suggestion," Mauri admitted. "In battle it might not be such a big issue, you might be bleeding anyways, but what if you're not cut? What if you're weaponless?"

"I can bite my cheek."

Mauri looked amused. "Of course, you can. But what if you're gagged? Or, what if the amount of blood your shadows need increases during battle? I noticed you needed to keep reopening your wounds."

"Yeah," I inhaled. Since we'd been training, I'd learned a few important things about my shadows. "It seems when I have them fight for long periods, they can't always sustain themselves from the first draw of blood, not like they can when they're flying around the woods."

"And how much blood can you afford to lose before it weakens you?"

Okay, I could see what she was trying to say. If I was weaponless and someone stuck a rag in my mouth, preventing me from biting my cheek, I'd be fucked. She absolutely had a point about my shadows needing too much blood.

"You seem to have considered many angles."

The queen smiled. "You might say I think about blood a lot."

"Right, so . . . I need to learn some way I can inflict a cut on myself at any time. Maybe a burn? Fire is my strongest element."

"I have a better idea," Mauri replied. "One that doesn't involve mutilating yourself, and your shadows will always be at your disposal. Interested?"

"Absolutely."

"Follow me."

Mauri led me back inside the castle, through a series of wondrous jeweled halls.

"How do you know your way around so well?" I asked while we turned into a corridor that looked less traveled.

"Queen Pari and I are allies. She's . . . holding an important prisoner for me, so I come to check on the prisoner often." Her steps halted in front of a door. "The Queen of Buyan does a lot of experimenting, some of it on my behalf. I don't necessarily like the reputation that nosferatu have, and would like to revert back to fae, if I can. So far she has not come up with anything to reverse the bite that made me what I am."

"You don't want to be a vampire?" I could relate. I didn't particularly like the demon blood in my veins.

"Drinking blood, while appealing physically, is something I can do without on a psychological level." She shook her head. "Anyway, Pari sometimes gives me potions to try. Some have to be taken at intervals, which means they must be portable. And . . . actually, I'll just show you."

With that, she opened the door. No one was in the room. It reminded me a bit of a laboratory, just less high-tech, so I wondered what sort of experiments they ran in there.

Mauri seemed to know exactly what she was doing. Crossing the space, she opened a drawer, and pulled out a necklace with a circular pendant hanging from it.

"Not quite my style," I teased.

"It can hold blood. Perhaps enough to get you through a battle without having to slice yourself open. Or burn yourself."

Not a pendant then. A vial. Intrigued, I stepped closer to examine it.

"Yeah, I think this could work." She unscrewed the top. "If we made holes in the top, it would be accessible to your shadows, right? Do you think it's enough for a prolonged battle?"

I paused. Did I really want to go around wearing a vial of blood around my neck? One glance down at my hands, scarred from all the times I'd called my shadows, told me that this option was worth exploring. At the very least, it would make me feel slightly less of a monster.

No matter what the others said, I still had a tough time accepting my shadows, and I wondered if I truly ever would.

"This is worth a shot," I said with a nod. "Let's fill it up and see how long it will last the shadows."

CHAPTER TWENTY-TWO

LANA

It was early in the morning as we gathered in front of Castle Dalir to begin our march. I watched the army prepare, my gut tightening with worry that I hadn't felt before that moment.

"Are you ready to fly?" Pari came up beside me on Ra.

Her silver gryphon looked both majestic and fierce in his fancy helmet, like the one on Taima's head. The protective pieces reminded me of the war headdress horses used in the Middle Ages, but altered to fit a gryphon's head.

"As ready as I'll ever be," I assured the queen.

"Good," Pari confirmed. "We will go ahead with the rest of your siblings, my ladies, Garret, and Ebba. That way Armina can set up wards, and we can scout the area before the bulk of the army arrives. For them, it will be a full day of marching, and we will want them well rested every night."

Each time I spoke with her, it became clearer that her people were the most important thing to her. Even though she was marching to war, she was leaving most of her forces behind to protect Buyan and her people. Tau was among those staying, which gave me great relief. He was too good, too cheery to see war. He and Petal still needed to start dating, get married, and have little blue and pink-haired babies.

Though the extra numbers would have been nice, I really respected that Queen Pari put her subjects first, just as a queen should.

"Someone is meeting us today, right?" I asked, wanting to make sure I had the plan straight.

"Our allies from Strand claim they will meet us this evening. I can only hope they will make good time."

I pulled up the image of the map in my mind. "Got it. Or at least I think I do."

"You're doing well." The queen gave me a small smile. "Don't be afraid to ask me anything." She spurred into motion, calling her ladies over so we could get going.

I watched her, thankful for her help and the allies she'd wrangled. The responses Pari's envoys brought back from the allied kingdoms had been far less fruitful than the queen would have hoped. Only two of the five messengers returned with affirmative replies. From what she told me, the army that was supposed to meet us today had been a bit of a surprise to Queen Pari.

Strand was a small district in the Free Realm. They could only commit a force of fifty soldiers. Pari's strongest ally was Ys, Buyan's neighbor to the north. Their new queen, Crystal's bestie Mauri, and five hundred soldiers had joined us, bolstering Pari's hopes that no matter how large Oberon's army was, we could put up a good fight. The two other traditional allies were deep in their own skirmishes with neighbors, and the last one had flat out denied the queen's request.

Hearing that simple "no" had worried Queen Pari the most. Had Oberon swayed them? Would we meet them in battle? Or was there some other reason for their lack of aid? Whatever the case, we had to act. We were marching forth with just over a thousand fae at our backs. The army was small, but most of our plan centered around a secret infiltration, so we thought it would still work.

The sound of a bird call came from above us, catching my attention. Glancing up, I squinted. Naela was in the air, chasing after a bird that, judging by its colorful red and gold plumage, was certainly a species native to Buyan.

"Naela! Back off!" I yelled. She was such a dominant bird that sometimes she couldn't abide others in her space. Particularly, if they tried to dominate her.

Yet, Naela paid me no mind, just kept chasing after the bird, disappearing in the distance. I shook my head, hoping the creature got away, but with my familiar on their tail, I wasn't so sure that would be the case.

"Princess Lana!" Pari called out and motioned for me to come stand by her—a symbol that our kingdoms marched together.

"Go to your boyfriend, girl," I instructed Taima. "It's time to fly."

I joined the group going on ahead of the army, ignoring Armina's narrowed eyes on me as I slid in between Finn and Garret. She'd been prickly since the day my light sliced her open. Although the healers had done miraculous things, and she seemed recovered, I couldn't blame her. Still, I hated being looked at that way.

Together, we took off, heading south for Lyonesse. Once we were in the air, I tossed a glance behind me. The army marching south was already on the move, following us.

A pit opened in my stomach. This would be the first time I engaged in war, and there was a lot on the line. We'd practiced and planned, and gathered help, but now, all we could do was hope that all our planning would pay off. That soon we would divest my father of his crown.

Hours of long and uneventful flight later, Pari pointed to the ground. We'd made it over the hills that served as a rough demarcation line between Lyonesse and Buyan. About thirty minutes after we set out, Naela had joined us. I had not worried about her disappearance during the journey, knowing she could locate me. After all, she could find me in the center of Dublin, and I was much more conspicuous here.

Armina had the wards in place when the army arrived. With protections already up, the army could feed the horses, themselves, and even relax. Judging by the sweat and dirt on their faces, I was betting they wanted nothing more than to pass out and rest.

Queen Pari, my siblings, and I, however, had other plans for the after-dinner hours. The fifty soldiers from Strand had made excellent time, showing up before our own army. We planned on covering battle tactics and reviewing their magics after the rest of the troops rested.

Unlike in the Old Land, where guns, missiles, and other technologies were used in war, in Faerie you never knew what you were going to get. While most fae were elementals, there was always the hope we would get lucky and come across a fae with a power suited to our battle plan.

And we certainly had that with the soldiers from Strand.

Among them was a green-haired fae strongly gifted with earth, Alura. She was aces at sensing directionality based on the magnetism in Faerie, which Maria was learning to do too, but I was relieved to have someone more experienced along for the mission.

"Your powers will be perfect for infiltrating the castle from below," Queen Pari commented after speaking to the green-haired earth fae. "You will be with the rebel Fullfeather heirs in the tunnels."

"Thank you, Queen Pari. I hope to be of great help." Alura inclined her head. "I can also sense strong deposits of magic, which should radiate from the castle."

That got my attention. "Maybe, after we get to the castle someone can steal the thuribles the Feathered Fae bring back, and distribute the magic to anyone on the streets who might help us fight. You know, as a stretch goal."

"That will be secondary," Strand General Aketa agreed. "Giant tunnels can be unwieldy, so getting the subterranean team to the castle quickly is our priority. From there, the battle will dictate where our forces are most needed."

The giants helped build the castles and towns of Sinker Realm, the first realm of Faerie. Obviously, this meant that they had needed a place to live while building the kingdoms. Most fae found the look and smell of the giants offensive, so the royals decided the giants should live in tunnels under the cities.

Out of sight, out of mind, as they say.

I was sure that as long as Alura was in the tunnels, the underground team, which consisted of my siblings and a select group of other fae, would have no trouble getting to the castle. So, why then did I feel slightly unsettled as the queen and the general continued to talk, as if nothing could go wrong?

Was it just because I was unfamiliar with war? I glanced up into the dark sky, hoping that was the case, and when I rose the next day my jitters would be gone.

WHEN I WOKE THE NEXT MORNING, MY BOUT WITH unease had grown to a deep pit in my stomach. At my side, sleepy and oblivious to my discomfort, Garret snuggled closer.

"Morning, beautiful," he murmured. "Sleep, okay?"

"As good as could be expected." I didn't tell him about the weird feeling. It was just nerves. Or so I kept telling myself.

The camp woke early, hoping to cover a long stretch of desert. The march was a balancing act. We wanted to make good time, but not arrive in Lyonesse exhausted. Still, we had planned for the longest leg to be today, so we had to get moving.

We whipped up a breakfast of beans, bread, and fruit scavenged by the army as they walked through the jungles of Buyan the previous day. Once the camp was cleaned, I hefted myself onto Taima's back, and took off with the other advanced scouts.

The wind chilled my face while we soared over the black countryside. It was like I remembered it, barren, dead, and depressing as hell.

During our flight, I noticed Pari's normal loose riding style was different. She looked tense when we passed over the black lands—her expression pulled tightly and her mouth pressed into a thin line. It was only when Tamia wanted to visit her boyfriend, Ra, and we got closer, that I realized it was because Pari was crying.

Flecks of tears whipped across her high cheek-bones, disappearing into the air behind her, but the queen made no sound. Nor did she allow the anguish she clearly felt to settle on her face. I suspected it was the first time in many years that she'd seen Oberon's kingdom. She grieved for what had been.

My imagination conjured thriving farmlands, forests and lakes where craters of dirt now gathered. My hope was that soon the land would return to how it should be—lush, green and fertile. First, however, we had to defeat my father.

Hours passed in flight, and scouted for miles around where we'd make camp. The closer we got to Lyonesse, the more we needed to be absolutely sure we would not be ambushed. We all knew Oberon expected us—he would be an idiot not to—and while I could call him many names, 'idiot' was not one of them.

After we finished scouting, I landed and slipped off Taima's back. My legs wobbled when my boots hit the ground. Hell, I'd be sore tomorrow, but didn't have time to think about that now, knowing what needed to be done. The scouting team set to work unloading supplies, while Armina circled a wide perimeter to set as many wards as possible.

Faster than I would have thought possible with so many people, the army came into view, and we finalized preparations for the rush. Feeding the mares and stallions was an ordeal. So was the preparation of supper for over a thousand soldiers. Since the scouting team had ridden gryphons, rather than walked for hours, we ate last.

Maria joined me in the lineup to serve the soldiers, claiming her own pot of beans to stir. "It's hard to believe we didn't consider this before, isn't it?"

"You mean how our father is a manipulative maniac? Yeah, can't believe we didn't see that when he was being all charismatic and shit."

A playful punch landed on my shoulder. Though I was closer to the rumbler than before we left Lyonesse for our assassination attempt, the gesture held something new. It was the way real siblings acted toward one another. The past few days in Buyan had bonded me to Maria, Arlo and Himari even more tightly than our weeks in Lyonesse.

"You know what I mean." Maria stuck out her tongue at me. "How everyone in his castle is powerful, but no one else is. I feel so stupid for being blindfolded. And worried . . . we're marching on the heart of power. We are going to be the ones searching for him. Aren't you worried about what will happen when we get to Lyonesse?" Her playful tone dipped.

"I don't know what he has up his sleeve, so yeah, I've got a case of nerves," I admitted. I didn't think Maria was actually questioning if I was scared. She just wanted to know she wasn't alone. "Even though I held daily meetings with him, I have a feeling that father kept a hell of a lot hidden from me."

I tilted my head as a thought occurred. "Did you know he has a hidden chamber, beneath his study? Whenever we held meetings, he would always rise from the underground. Now I'm really wondering what's down there."

Maria rubbed her cheeks with her hand, pulling the skin down and opening her mouth in frustration. "I wanted a bit of excitement before my boyfriend proposed to me, because I lived the same boring life as everyone else in Mexico City. A job, marriage, kids in private school. The regular sort of mundane everyone wants. But I didn't bargain for any of this."

"None of us did." I patted her shoulder and gave my pot of beans one more good stir. "Now, what do you say you go tell the first group of soldiers their meals are ready? The sooner they eat, the sooner we can too. And I'm starving."

As an added bonus, maybe the food would fill the ever-growing pit of dread in my belly.

CHAPTER TWENTY-THREE

LANA

Later that night, after almost everyone turned in, I finally lay down on my bed mat. A soft groan left my lips, trying not to wake the others in my tent.

My inner thighs ached something fierce, and the gnawing worry in my core persisted. I wished it would go away, but also thought it natural to be uneasy. We were heading to war, so I suspected my body would not rebalance until after we fought and won.

Next to me, Finn snorted in his sleep, pulling a chuckle from me. He'd always been a noisy sleeper. Good thing I was so exhausted that I doubted it would matter.

Also sharing my tent for the night were Ebba and Garret. Who slept where in the camp was turning out to be pretty random, although Garret made it clear we wouldn't be parted. So far, he was the only one of my tent mates who hadn't made it to bed.

He'd gotten caught up with taking care of his gryphon while the rest of us walked to bed, and would be in momentarily. I pulled his mat closer to me.

Once the mat was situated, and I was about to lie back down, Ebba twitched so hard that I thought she might be having a seizure. Startled, I eyed her to make sure she was fine. She was, but something that had escaped my notice before caught my attention. Her mat lay close to Finn's, and their hands were inches from each other's.

My lips curled up slightly. Had they fallen asleep holding hands? When had that happened?

Another snore rang from Finn's lips, and though I was curious, I refrained from waking him to ask—I could ask in the morning, though.

The front flap of the tent rustled, and I smiled, hoping Garret would appear. A second later, Naela and Kane soared into the space. My familiar fluttered right over to me, while Kane nestled on the perch near Finn's head.

"Hey, Boss," I whispered. For the last two days our familiars flew alongside the gryphons and scouted the skies long after the advanced team landed to make camp. "Surprised you weren't already here. You should be knackered."

Naela released a soft sound and closed her eyes, as if to say *I am. No more talking*.

Snuggling beneath my blanket, I tried to get

comfortable. Somehow, probably because of my exhaustion, I dozed off quickly.

Vivid dreams of approaching Castle Phoenix filled my sleep. In one, Xerxes lit us all on fire before we breached the city gates. Then my father approached, his face furious, magic blazing from his fingers.

He stood over me and placed his hands around my neck. *"Such a disappointment. I—"*

A keening sound penetrated my dream, and I lurched up, gasping and clenching my heart. Tears rolled down my eyes, but I wiped them away quickly, hating that I cried over my father. Screw him!

Another wailing sound left Naela's beak, this one more urgent, and Kane echoed her. Shite, I'd forgotten she'd woken me, probably because I was making noise in my sleep, which I sometimes did when I had nightmares.

I turned to look at the hawks. "It's okay. I was dreaming. Sorry if I startled you."

My familiar's wings fluttered, and she launched off her perch to land on Garret's mat. I stiffened. Wait . . . where was Garret? He said he'd be right behind me. How long had I been asleep? I was groggy enough to think it had been a while.

Naela keened again, but it sounded like a low warning call.

Ice flew through my veins. Something was wrong. "What is it, Boss? Where's Garret?"

With the mention of his name, Naela lost it, releasing a shriek that woke Finn and Ebba. The latter shot up, her eyes alert.

"What's going on?" Finn asked, rising far more groggily to find Kane land on his lap, his wings frantically flapping.

Answering his question, both beaky faces pointed up toward the sky. The icky feeling pitting my stomach deepened. The sky. Something was up there.

"Get up, you two!"

"What the hell, Lan? What is it?" Finn protested, blinking heavily.

Ebba didn't hesitate. She leapt from where she lay, and grabbed her scabbard from the side of the tent. "Get up."

Finn jerked, but she seemed to get through to him when I couldn't, because he didn't question her, only struggled to stand and grabbed a weapon.

"Something's outside," I whispered, unsure if whatever it was had good hearing. "They sense something . . . in the sky."

"Feathered Fae?" Ebba asked.

"That or harpies, or . . . whatever else flies here." We'd seen harpies on the march to Buyan. They'd been disgusting, but I'd almost rather come across them than something else. Dragons existed in this world too, and that would be much worse. I swallowed the lump rising in my throat. "Garret should be here, but he never came to bed. I'm worried."

"Let's go find him." Ebba led the charge out of the tent.

No one roamed outside. The night was silent, except for our thundering heartbeats and the sound of our hawks' wings beating the air. Naela and Kane hovered around us, both glancing up at regular intervals. Though I saw no threat among the stars. It was too dark.

"Naela, come here." I lifted my arm, knowing I'd regret it later. Naela landed on my bare skin, her talons sinking into it. Though her grip was looser than normal because she was trying to be considerate, it hurt, and I winced. Finn did the same with Kane. Once the hawks were still, I caught a whisper of a noise in the wind. My eyebrows furrowed.

"Everyone stop moving," I instructed.

The second the two of them stopped, the sound grew. I recognized it—a faint flapping of wings. Squinting into the darkness, I almost facepalmed myself for my stupidity.

Thrusting both palms upward, I flooded the sky with light. My leg muscles immediately tightened, preparing me to run.

"Oh fuck," Finn whispered at the same time.

Boy was that an understatement.

Above us, a hoard of winged creatures swarmed. Half of them were birds of prey, but one stood out the most. I'd seen it's red and gold feathers the other day, and now I could slap myself. The bird Naela chased had been more than a bird! How did I forget the tropical-looking Feathered Fae!

Probably because he was never around. I could picture the fae who turned into a brilliantly colored bird, but I'd never learned his name. Nor spoken to him. He kept to himself.

The urge to scream for being such an idiot tickled my throat, but that would be a waste. I needed to pull myself together because it wasn't just birds swarming above us.

There were nearly an equal number of chimera coming for us. The creatures featured traits of other animals—like the gryphon did—but I would wager that those chimeras spoke and thought like a human. One even looked like the chimera I fought in the Successional.

Each wore a cruel smile on their face, but I was still trying to make sense of the mess of horns, hooves, wings, and tails swirling above when something else caught my eye. My stomach tensed and the pit that had plagued me, expanded tenfold. The birds and chimera each held tiny bags filled with luminescent liquid.

"What's in the sacks?" The words barely left Finn's lips when half of the bags rained from the sky.

Light exploded from me, turning night to day in an instant. In their tents, people yelled, awake. Naela and Kane broke out into a ruckus of screeching, and Finn shouted for everyone else to get up. Heads poked out of tents, but scowls quickly morphed into fear when others glimpsed at the sky.

While I didn't know what the bags held, I knew it couldn't be good for us, and our enemies had retained half of their weapons. We needed to drive them out before they could use them.

I broke into a sprint toward where the gryphons were tied. Thankfully, I found Taima quickly. She was awake, her eyes wide with fear as she scanned the skies. With trembling fingers, I untied her. "We need to get them out of here, girl."

Finn followed me, releasing his gryphon from the ties too. In my peripheral vision I saw Pari, Isis, Bellona, Ebba, Crystal, Arlo, and Maria all rush our way, ready to fight back.

Armina stayed where she was, just outside a tent, magic spewing from her. She was trying to put up some sort of shield before the traps hit the ground. Somehow our attackers had gotten past her wards though, which didn't give me hope. They were prepared for what Armina had to offer. My heart fluttered for a moment, wondering where Garret was, but as Taima pushed off the ground, my questions vanished.

I had one goal: drive our opponents away from the camp.

Her wings blasted us upward until we were leveled with our foes. They dispersed, trying to lose us, but we followed, breaking them apart again and again while they dive-bombed the camp. My light spread in front of me, hoping to catch sight of someone who I knew was a Feathered Fae, so we could capture it.

A golden eagle soared beside me, Arlo, his eyes flashing in the moonlight.

"Look for birds that aren't Naela and Kane. Attack them, if you can," I called to him. "And be careful with the chimera."

Letting out a screech, he disappeared into the night. With my brother ahead of us, I'd have to be more careful with my light magic. Hopefully, the others who had taken to the skies would recognize him too. Had Arlo considered that? My teeth dug into my bottom lip, but there was no going back. I had to trust that he'd considered the consequences. He was a smart guy, he must have.

I'd gone slightly astray, searching the skies for the Feathered Fae, when a wave of screams and bellows came from the ground. My breath caught in my chest and I turned Taima on a dime to face the camp.

Horror washed over me as I took in the scene in the distance.

Another round of bags had hit them, and it seemed that the combination transformed the luminous substance, or perhaps substances, into a vivid green gas. The gas crawled across the ground, collapsing soldiers in its wake.

Were they dead? It was impossible to tell from that far away. Another matter that worried me was the fact that some hadn't seemed to notice the gas. Their attention lingered in the sky, fighting off the occasional foe that darted out of the night while the vapors crept ever closer.

"We need to warn them to move further away!" I yelled, hopeful those who had taken to gryphons could hear me. We'd spread out a lot in an effort to disperse the attackers, so it wasn't a given. Taima and I plunged, trusting they would see me and join.

I was nearly back to the camp, when I spotted Himari in the crowd. Gas inched toward her. She tried to blow it away with her air magic, but it wasn't budging.

Guiding Taima toward my sister, I motioned for her to hop on behind me. She did, narrowly escaping the gas licking at her heels, and Taima launched back into the sky.

"You okay?" I asked, glancing over my shoulder.

"Hell no, I'm not okay! I'd stepped out to relieve myself and was running back to camp when others came running my way. I saw you guys flying but couldn't find my gryphon! What the heck is happening? Did anyone save Dawnrunner?"

I bit my lip. As I'd approached the camp, I'd been able to get a better glimpse of the destruction. I'd seen many downed gryphons.

"I'm not sure where he is," I replied, not about to jump to conclusions. Maybe someone else was flying her gryphon. "Did you see Garret anywhere?"

"No! I hope they're both okay," Himari breathed.

Not wanting to even entertain the idea that my guy wouldn't be fine, I nodded, and scanned the area. Finn must have heard my cries, because he'd returned to camp, and seemed to have gotten the word out to stay clear of the gas still creeping along the ground. Ebba and Pari were showing people to safety, and everyone had fanned out from the main area to stand on the edges. Some were trying to fight the gas back with mixed results. I wanted to help, but we had other urgent matters.

"You down for trying to catch those responsible for all this destruction?" I asked my sister.

"Do it." Himari gripped me tightly. Digging my heels into Taima's sides, we took off into the night to search.

We hunted amongst the stars for hours, and yet, we never found a single Feathered Fae or chimera. They had all escaped, which pissed me off to no end. Finally, when I could barely sit up straight any longer, I called it and we flew back to camp.

The closer we got, the more my anxiety rose. Hours had passed, but things had been bad when we left. Still, I tried to reassure myself that surely the gas would have dissipated by then. Or my side had figured out how to handle it. Everyone would be standing there, fine and safe.

When we arrived, we learned that the gas had been destroyed, eventually, but not before taking its toll. The poison left the camp absolutely decimated. People lay dead and injured in huge numbers. A lump rose in my throat with each new person I saw laying there, the color drained from their faces.

I milled among people trying to give solace to those who'd lost loved ones, and helped others trying to clean up the camp. All the while, I searched for one person—Garret. Except, no one seemed to know where he was. What had happened to him?

Once Isis completed the count, she declared that ninety-seven soldiers had died. The Strand army suffered the harshest losses. Their tents had been directly under the bulk of the swarm, and their part of the army was small. Pari's army suffered losses too, followed by that from Ys, Queen Mauri's kingdom. A couple dozen horses and three gryphons had also perished.

One person, my boyfriend, was still missing.

Dawn was upon us by the time we had all the bodies cleaned and prepared for the death rituals of their kingdoms and free state.

The gas the Feathered Fae and chimera had dropped was as wicked as it had looked. Skin bubbled off the corpses it left behind. Their eyes had sunk into their sockets, becoming a gooey mess. The green smoke had eaten the soft tissue first. Every time I looked at them, I couldn't help but wonder if the weapon had gotten Garret and somehow liquified him. Every time I considered it, I almost vomited.

Why was my imagination like that?

We dug graves, and every kingdom held its own service for those fallen. As Pari said the final words for the service of her fallen countrymen, my shoulders fell. In the distance, the sun rose. A few hours from now, we would have to march again, and my father knew we were coming. Arriving sooner, before he called in more allies like the chimera, was key.

Waiting would be foolish. Garret was either dead, or someone had taken him. How they kidnapped him, such a large, powerful man, I wasn't sure, but death was too hard to believe.

My father knew Garret meant a lot to me. He would use that against me.

My fists clenched. The battle had already begun, and we were losing.

LANA

We decided to save the surviving gryphons' strength and walk the rest of the way with the army. Arlo, Naela, and Kane would act as our eyes in the sky. I had to admit that I was relieved. While we'd make better time, the attack rattled me to the core. The gryphons too were spooked, and I didn't want to be on one's back when it flipped.

Although, after a few hours, the march became exhausting. The day stretched on, seemingly endless. I'd done this same march before, endured the long days, but I didn't remember it being as bone-weary. Probably because I hadn't been attacked, or stayed up half the previous night.

However, stopping for long stretches of time was not an option. The Feathered Fae would have informed the king of our location. My father expected us, and the less time we gave him to prepare, or worse, find more allies, the better.

Pari's ladies sidled up beside me, breaking me out of my marching trance.

"A word, illuminator?" Isis asked.

They rarely spoke to me. Never without Pari around, so what could they want?

"Sure?" I mumbled, my gaze flickering to Armina, and bouncing off of her. She still gave me the creeps.

"We've been discussing our plan of attack with the queen," Isis stated. "Queen Mauri and General Aketa were in on the talks too."

My lips pursed. "Why didn't anyone find me and ask my opinion?"

I wasn't a queen, but I *was* a princess general. If the general from Strand sat in on the talks, I should have been told about them too.

"It was an informal discussion, and why Her Grace is sending me to you now." Isis glared at me, as if daring me to fling another retort at her. I'd rather know what was said than make my point, so I nodded for her to continue. "As discussed when we left Buyan, we will maintain the three-pronged attack: air, land, and the giant tunnels, but the details have evolved somewhat."

"Okaaaaay. Like how?"

"You, Princess General Lana will be in the tunnels, as planned. They will need someone to light the way. Now Major Finn will split from you and lead the ground forces."

My gut clenched. "We were all supposed to be on the same team. We're supposed to advance on the castle as a united front."

My siblings and I did not want to separate. We wanted to infiltrate the castle and find Gio, Dak, Wik, and Victoria, and then confront our father together. He deserved to take on our collective rage.

"We can't be sure the Feathered Fae didn't take Garret," Isis replied. "If that's the case, your father might torture him for information."

I flinched. Though I'd considered that too, I hated hearing it out loud. In my hopeful mind, Garret sat in a cell, tired and maybe cold, but that was the worst of it.

"We need to change our tactics," Isis continued making her point. "That means breaking up the Fullfeather heirs and assigning capable soldiers to go with you and fill in the gaps in power your siblings would have provided. Alura, the fae from Strand will be your primary escort and guide."

"Where will I be?" Crystal asked, from where she'd been walking behind Armina.

Isis turned toward my sister. "You will lead the flight squad. The archers will go for the gryphons and those on their backs first. Any other wind worker or flying shifter will divert their arrows until the gryphons can land safely. As there are fewer of them now, we need every gryphon we can get to remain safe. I don't like to think of retreat, but in war that's always a possibility."

That meant Himari and Arlo would be in the skies too. My throat constricted. Was I going to be the only one of my siblings alone? Alura was fine and I trusted Pari's allies, but I wanted those closest to me there to help me stay strong. Only they truly knew what I was going through.

"The tunnel team will be the smallest," Isis focused on me once more. "For one, most giant tunnels are disaster zones. They've collapsed on themselves, and without someone to lead the way, it's almost always a suicide mission to traverse them. But that isn't the case for us. Princess General Lana will supply the light, and Alura will guide the way to the base of the castle. From there, you will find a way inside. All other earth workers will also be below with you, to assist moving any wreckage blocking the path."

My shoulders loosened. Maria would be with me then. My frustrations dimmed.

"The largest assaults will be on land. Queen Pari herself will lead this unit, along with the Queen of Ys." Isis' chest puffed out.

The intense pride that Pari's ladies in waiting took in their queen always amazed me. Although I wasn't sure why, it certainly was warranted.

Since I learned Pari was not a fraud, my respect

for the woman had skyrocketed. She'd proven herself time and time again. I'd never seen my father rush into battle, or even attempt to go see his fallen subjects after an assault. He didn't make a point to check on any of us when we'd been injured in training, or even after the Successional. However, Pari had done all those things.

"Everyone else is on land?" I asked, trying to make sure I understood.

"Precisely. The land assault will suffer the heartiest damages and serve as a distraction." Isis said, her tone clipped, all business. "We've chosen the strongest fire and water workers for the advance over land. We will need every advantage we can get, and these elements are well suited to blinding people with fear. Of course, your new talents are too, but we'd like to keep those under wraps until we get in the castle."

"Sounds like a plan," I muttered.

I still hated having to separate from most of my siblings, but the idea held merit. Not only would we have people watching our every step, but I suspected the land assault would be fantastical. It had to be, if they meant for it to divert attention from the tunnels. If all the Fullfeather heirs were out of sight in the tunnels, my father would sense something was happening. Yet, two of us, even me, might evade his notice—at least for a while.

Also, they were right to keep my new power hidden. If Casimir knew and was with our father, he would hunt me. I couldn't use ultraviolet light until the last moment, to bring my father to his knees.

"There's one more thing," said Bellona, who'd been stone quiet until now.

"What's that?"

"We're marching into the night."

I gaped. "You've got to be fecking kidding me."

"I'm with Lana on this one," Crystal piped up, the annoyance in her tone clear.

"Not one bit," Bellona smiled, as if she'd known what I'd say. "We'll make a few longer stops and rest along the way. Once we reach the forest outside of the castle, we'll take cover for another break, but none will be long. The woods won't hide us well, they're too barren, and timing is critical. We need to throw King Oberon off guard."

"Wonderful," I muttered. "Any more good news?"

I sounded like a sullen toddler, but I couldn't help it. The other leaders had made those choices without me, and my energy was depleted. How did they expect us to fight when we were so tired?

Adrenaline. The answer popped into my mind. How else did people sustain themselves through a battle? No one could really fight for hours on end without adrenaline pumping through them.

I glanced back at the army, all marching to fight. If they can do it, so can you, I told myself. Then I shut my mouth and continued marching toward Lyonesse.

WE TREKKED THE DAY AWAY, AND WELL INTO THE night, finally arriving at the forest of gnarled trees that surrounded the royal seat of Lyonesse. The darkness camouflaged the black bark, and because there was no greenery on the trees, or the ground, any small noise we made echoed through the barren woods. As a result, we spoke little and in hushed tones.

Throughout the miles we'd marched that day, we had stopped a grand total of three times to let our animals rest and take quick naps. It wasn't at all how I imagined going into war, but it was our reality. Pari, Mauri, and General Aketa had been right. We had no more time to waste. If we did not act soon, my father would make sure that we didn't even make it to Lyonesse.

At my side, Finn let out an exhausted breath. "Think it's about time for another kip?" His tone was soft and hopeful. Finn had always needed a full night of sleep. Until we came here, he was a pampered guy.

Then again, I wasn't any better. In the back of my mind, I wondered how long my body could produce adrenaline before I collapsed. Actually, I didn't want to think too hard about that option.

"We can ask." Queen Pari had called most of the

shots throughout the day, and after I got over my initial annoyance about the matter, I decided it was fine. She had far more experience than me in leading an army. Plus, we were marching with a contingent of mostly her people. For now, I was content to listen and learn from those who had been leading longer than I had.

I was about to call out to the Queen of Buyan, making her way to my right, when she stopped and lifted her hands. Everyone around the queen halted.

"We'll take a quick break." Queen Pari's normal volume traveled easily because the army was so quiet. "An hour tops. Then we continue our march to the castle."

"Brilliant," Finn breathed and gestured to our left. "I want to let my shadows out. They're annoying the shite out of me. I'll be back."

"Be quick," I urged, before moving toward the queen, wondering if she knew how much farther the city would be. When we marched out of Lyonesse we hadn't taken this route, so I was not sure of our exact location. The woods around our kingdom all looked the same to me here—broken, bleak, and dead.

"When will we get there if we continue at the same pace?" I asked once I was closer to Pari.

"Taking an hour of rest, we should arrive within two hours. Right before dawn. We might split after the break is over. I'd like to hear what General Aketa thinks on the matter."

A now-familiar hard ball formed in my stomach. The prospect of splitting up had distressed me the most. I wouldn't know where most of my siblings were as I fought my way toward the castle.

"I know you don't like the idea," Queen Pari admitted. "But now that our cover is blown, I truly think it's the smartest way to proceed."

"I see your point and I'm not going to argue," I replied, because that was what I'd decided, and I was sticking to it. "Let's rest."

She looked like she wanted to say more, but didn't, so I nodded my goodbye. Most people dropped where they stood, but I moved toward the far edge of the camp, where Finn had disappeared into the woods. It was a place where I would not be constrained by the bodies pressing around me. A cloud of the most horrific body odor hung over the army, which made it unpleasant to linger in the center when we weren't marching. Yet, the feel of so many people surrounding me was what set me on edge the most.

As I took a seat next to a tree on the outskirts of the army, I relished the solitude. If I lived through the battle, and we took Lyonesse, I would lock myself away from all other people for a week, and only Garret would come inside. I still clung to the hope that he sat in a dungeon, possibly battered, but alive. Considering anything else was unbearable.

Closing my eyes, I leaned my head back against

the tree. I was about to release everything troubling me and allow myself to take what rest I could snatch, when somewhere behind me a twig snapped.

Finn must be back already. That had been fast. I turned to wave him over, when a knife pressed against my throat.

"Funny meeting you here, little green general."

CHAPTER TWENTY-FIVE

FINN

I strayed far from the rest of the soldiers, before allowing myself some relief from the pressure inside me that had been growing for hours. It was nearly unbearable and although people claimed my shadows didn't scare them, I still didn't like unleashing them in front of others. No matter what came out of their mouths, people still stared, discomfort plain on their faces. If I was being honest, I felt the same discomfort, though less so by the day.

Of course, I wouldn't hesitate in unleashing my darkness during battle. Until then, I wanted a wee bit of privacy.

The leafless trees weren't much to hide my dark magic, but thankfully, the shadows blended in during the nighttime hours.

Small clinking sounds reached my ears, coming from

the vial pendant Queen Mauri had given me as it bounced off the metal and leather armor I wore. Usually, a soldier would tuck such wares out of view, but I wasn't risking it. I needed the blood handy to call my shadows, and I liked to keep the vial visible to make sure there was still blood available to them. If I ran out during the fight and had to resort to slicing myself open, then so be it.

Standing in the small clearing I'd found, I checked once more that no one was around and gripped the pendant.

"You can come out," I whispered.

The two shadows I normally produced appeared. There were more inside me, I could feel them, but I only ever seemed to call two at once. I was fine with that. Baby steps.

Immediately, a lightness overtook me. That was the weird thing about my shadows: they took up no room inside me, felt no emotions of their own, gave me no added weight, but I was always relieved to let them loose. It was like taking off a tie after a long dinner party.

"Fly about if you want," I said. "If you check on the camp, stay hidden. The next time I release you will be in battle. I need a bit of a breather."

The shadows soared off, hovering above the full moon for a moment before disappearing to do whatever shadows did for a laugh.

I closed my eyes. Finally, some alone—

A rock skittered on the blackened ground some-where behind me, not too far away.

"Lan?" I asked, since she was the only one who knew what I was doing. There was no answer, so I turned toward the sound just in time to see a man approach, a dagger glinting in his hand.

Fire blazed through my fingertips, and I hurled the flames at him, hitting him dead in the chest. A cry left his lips, but it fell silent when my shadows zipped back over and smothered him. He dropped to the ground, and I ran to him.

"Thanks, guys."

A blackened face stared back at me, disfigured. He was a spriggan, a cunning sort of fae with the face of a child and the body of an old man—at least in appearance. All the spriggans I'd met had been very agile, though they looked old.

The thing was, there were no spriggan in our army. The last time I'd seen them was when I went to Zatus and we'd spoken with Gory, who commanded an army of hired swords. My breath caught in my throat.

"We're not alone," I informed the shadows. "If you see the spriggans, kill them. Go."

They took off like a bullet, and I sprinted after them, back to where the army rested. No one was yelling or making noise that would indicate an attack, but most people had been trying to sneak in a kip before we marched on the city. Either the ambush party in the woods had not gotten to our camp, or they had, and they took advantage of the fact that the army dozed.

It was then I saw it. On the edge of our camp, a spriggan pressed a knife to Lana's neck. My eyes narrowed, and using my earth magic, I lifted a downed branch from the dry earth, and sent it hurling into the spriggan's back. It was pointed enough to spear him through the center.

A choked gasp left him, and he stumbled back. The moment he'd let up on Lana, she flung his hand away, and twirled to find me, eyes wide.

"It's Gory's men! They're in the woods!" she yelled.

"Shite!"

A scuffle broke out behind my friend. More attackers had slipped into the unaware army. "Come on Lan! Let's go!"

We leapt into the melee. Gory's troops had taken our force by surprise, but they had also arrived largely unprepared, whereas we were armed to the teeth. The hired swords might have actually been on their way to the castle to join my father in battle and gotten sidetracked when they came across us.

No doubt Gory saw Lana as a hearty payday, the bloody bastard. I was fairly sure this was not an attack my father had sanctioned. Not that he wouldn't do it, he absolutely would have done so. It was more that he wouldn't have been so sloppy about it. The King of Lyonesse was cunning and meticulous.

As we fought, the hired swords fell one by one, until they were all dead on the ground.

"How many?" The back of my hand wiped the blood spatter off of my face, while Pari's ladies swept the area, counting.

"Twelve here," Armina replied. "One of our own."

"Seven," Bellona added. "And two are from our camp."

"Five. None of ours, thank the Sinkers." Isis scanned the woods, her eyes blazing. "But there must be more hired swords in the forest."

I agreed with her, but if the swords for hire heard what happened, they wouldn't be itching to fight this army. Not now. I suspected that we greatly outnumbered them.

Gory and his men had seen an easy opening. He'd seen Lana perched on the edge of the camp, and the other guy had seen me—all alone. They recognized us as high-ranking Fullfeathers and had tested their luck at a chance to earn some gold.

Unfortunately for them, it had cost them their lives.

"There were more, undoubtedly," Queen Pari judged. "But they're probably running to the castle with their tails between their legs right now."

"Should we send trackers?" Lana asked.

"No," the Queen of Buyan answered confidently. "But this means our break is over. We don't even have time to bury the dead, for we must hurry. We need to run to the tunnels. From there, the land and arial squads will split."

Groans filled the air, but no one questioned it. Queen Pari was right. As soon as the surviving hired swords made it to Lyonesse, they would tell the king we were outside the city, hidden in the woods. We couldn't stay. We had to move.

"Shadows," I whispered. The next second they slammed into my chest, disappearing back inside me. I rubbed my chest. "Oww, that bloody smarts. Have some manners guys."

Isis approached, blue eyes glinting with fury over the armies' losses. "They killed a handful of people before we got to them. Your power is going to be a benefit to us in battle."

I didn't respond to the head lady in waiting, merely broke into a run toward the tunnels with the rest of the army. The battle was upon us and there wasn't a second to waste.

CHAPTER TWENTY-SIX

LANA

The tunnel yawned open, even more massive than I'd imagined. I stood a few meters from the entrance, but even with the distance, the dank scent of wet dirt filled my nostrils. As I studied it, I couldn't decide if traveling for miles through a wider or narrower tunnel would be better.

It would only take one explosion from above to cave in the ceiling. Even with a rumbler witch, and a handful of fae powerful with earth magic taking control of the rocks, traversing the underground of Lyonesse was a major risk.

No matter the size of the tunnel, in the end, they'd crush us just the same. My breath lodged in my chest. Trying to calm down, I turned away from the opening.

Maria stood behind me, understanding plain on her face. "Breathe. You'll be alright. We'll come out the other side, and think of all the people we'll be saving." She paused and nodded at my hands. "Don't forget, you're going to light the way, so it won't be as creepy as it looks."

She didn't reassure me about the weak ceilings. Or how she could control the tons of dirt around us, and yet, somehow her reassurances slowed my heart rate a touch.

My gaze traveled past her to the group. The land squad hadn't split from us yet, as had been the previous plan. Gory's attack had majorly thrown us off, and only now were Queen Pari, Mauri, and General Aketa regrouping.

Finn milled around with those who would approach the city from land—they'd attack soon after we dove into the earth. My heart hurt at the idea that he'd be in the thick of things, and I wouldn't be able to help him. When my best friend's gaze fell on me, his eyes widened, and he beelined for me.

Yeesh, I must look terrified.

"I'm going to round up the others," Maria added, breaking from me before Finn got there. She must have sensed that I wanted time alone with him.

"You alright, Lan?" Finn asked. "You've done this before. Remember Doolin?"

I snorted. "How could I forget?"

At the tender age of seventeen, Finn and I snuck into a cave on the Western coast of Ireland that boasted one of the largest stalactites in Europe. It had been a real laugh until we got deep into the cavern and our torch died.

Back then, I'd had very little confidence in my magic, but Finn still convinced me to proceed with our plan, even though I was bloody freaked, but we still snuck all the way into the cave and saw the stalactite with the flickering rays of my light.

He was reminding me I could do this. That even in the darkest, scariest places, light lived. And if light lived, I could use it. I'd guided us in and out of the Doolin cave safely, and I had the power to get us into Phoenix Castle too. With Alura's navigational help, and the earth fae to move any debris, our team should be unstoppable.

"Take care of Naela . . . and everyone else," I added.

There was no question in my mind that my hawk would not be accompanying me into the darkness. Naela was a creature of the sky and air. She would be much more helpful dive-bombing our opponents from above, and our side needed all the help we could get.

"Of course." Finn pulled me close for a hug.

We stayed that way for a long time, far longer than normal people would hug, but hell, we were heading into battle! Few people would deny a supportive squeeze when faced with that.

"Be safe," I whispered.

"You too, Lan."

Someone sniffed, and I peeked past my best

friend's broad shoulders to find the rest of my siblings —Himari, Arlo, and Crystal standing there. Crystal was shuffling her feet, tears clung to Himari's short, straight lashes, and Arlo appeared to be trying his best to remain strong—though the fidgeting of his fingers belied his anxiety.

A soft hand grazed my shoulder. "We have to be quick. Our group is ready, and Pari wants us to go first." Maria inclined her head to our siblings. "I've already said my goodbyes."

Behind her a small crowd of fae waited, with Alura at the front. The tunnel squad was ready to leave.

"Right." I squeezed my demon born brother one more time, before breaking away from our siblings.

Moving toward Crystal, my arms encircled her as if we'd never had an issue between us in all our lives. If there was ever a time to forgive and forget all that had ever happened, that time was now.

"I'll see you at the castle," she whispered, melting into me.

Saying goodbye to her, Himari, and Arlo wrecked me. Hopefully, in a few hours I would see them all again and we'd save the others.

"See you soon, Lan," Finn echoed once more. Naela fluttered around us, her sharp gaze throwing me woeful glances.

"See you soon. Naela, listen to Finn, and stick with Kane. I love you, Boss."

She keened, but remained close to my best friend. Tears pricked my eyes as I turned and left with Maria.

Our group entered the tunnel, and a few meters in, the darkness became all-encompassing. My magic sprang to life within me, begging me to use it, to resist the crushing darkness. I obeyed, letting light pour out of my palms, casting a new reality before us.

The tunnels were wide, the path nearly as smooth as a city sidewalk. Along the edges, lay detritus reminiscent of that found near construction sites in the Old Land. Except, here, instead of crisp bags and candy wrappers, it was the crumbling bones of small animals. A fox skull here, a large leg bone there. A massive line of vertebrae someone had taken the time to realign, stood out the most, but there were more mundane things too.

A wooden chair the size of a car, a long slender branch with a pointed tip that may have been used as a giant toothpick, a cradle big enough to fit ten soldiers.

Giant babies had been born down here, in the dark and the dank. How sad. Out of all the prejudices I'd witnessed in Faerie, it seemed to me the giants had it the worst. It was no wonder they were protective of their lands. Looking back, I found it miraculous that Skade, the giant chieftainess I'd convinced to fight for my father, didn't rip our heads off the minute she'd spotted us in the False Realm.

A flare shot up behind me, making me jump.

"Sorry," a fae muttered. "It was a little hard to see back here, but I'm not great with fire."

"Noted. Sorry, I won't slack again." I pushed my light out further, encompassing the entire squad. My light didn't extend too far ahead of us, but that was fine. We couldn't be sure my father wouldn't have soldiers down here, and wouldn't want the light to give us away. We only needed enough light to see where we were going and feel secure.

"Alura," I motioned for the earth fae to join me "Guide us."

Taking the point position, she led the group.

We'd been walking in almost absolute silence for thirty minutes when I heard the first signs of battle raging above us. An explosion, or perhaps a stampede of hooves shook the ceiling. Our army was closing the short distance from the deserted quarry outside Lyonesse to the city wall. Soon, others would fly overhead and take the brunt of the archers' arrows. So far, our strategy was proceeding as planned. Everything, that was, except that we'd now come to a fork in the tunnel.

"Which way?" I turned to Alura.

"Give me a second. I need to focus."

She closed her eyes, and a soft green glow, the same color as her hair, emanated from Alura as she searched for the magical reservoir that was Castle Phoenix. Her power drifted down both tunnels before disappearing.

After one heart-pounding, freakily long minute, Alura opened her eyes. "Right."

"You're sure?" We did not have time for mistakes, not as war raged on land.

"Absolutely."

We took the right path, traveling deeper into the tunnel network. Soon enough, alcoves that looked like communal spaces, and short tunnel offshoots that opened into what looked like single-family homes appeared.

Massive toys and rough-spun blankets littered the ground. Besides the single crib we'd seen and a few chairs, furniture was rare. We never saw a bed or table for a family to gather. It seemed we'd found where most of the giants lived, but none of the alcoves or dugout caves could be called homey.

A soft sniffle came from behind me as we entered an offshoot tunnel that led into one of the giant homes. I twisted and found Alura wiping her eyes.

"Are you okay?" So far, I had yet to come across a single Faerie-born fae who outwardly regretted having treated the giants terribly.

"It's a stain on this land." Alura gestured around blankets and toys. "Fae could've made their own castles. They sank entire islands from the human world to create this realm. What was stopping them from building castles out of easily-quarried marble besides needing to exert power?"

Though I'd sympathized with the giants many

times before, I never thought about it that way. What *had* stopped the fae?

"I don't know." I turned around to retreat out of the offshoot. "I agree with you. Let's make sure that type of treatment doesn't happen again, but this time with people in the Old Land."

"Absolutely," Alura confirmed. "This way."

A few minutes later we came across an intersection with eight off-shoots spread out from the tunnel we'd been traveling.

"What is this?" I whispered, noting how the offshoots resembled a giant star.

"Must be the boundary of the city," Alura considered. "I know the tunnels in Strand have offshoots like that. Plus, I feel a lot of magic pulsing from above. It has to be soldiers defending the walls."

"Can we assume there will be more tunnels the deeper we go?"

"That would be an excellent assumption." Vibrant green light flew from her again, soaring down all the tunnels, trying to pick the one that would be the most direct route to the castle.

Amazed, I nudged Maria. "You need to pick up some tips. Her powers are way more impressive than yours." I winked playfully.

"You mean if we survive tonight."

"Damn. So much for lightening the mood, Maria. Aren't you all about the fun?"

"Sorry. If I'd had a margarita before, I'd be way

more chill. Instead, the closer we get to the castle, the more freaked out I get." Her dark brown eyes flickered to the surface.

"It's this one," Alura called, saving me from having to respond as she gestured to the tunnel second from our left.

As a unit we pushed on, our speed increasing with each step. Above, the ceiling shook, and pebbles fell on our heads. Though I couldn't hear the battle, ghost screams filled my ears.

I was sure everyone was thinking the same thing. The land assault was underway. Perhaps they'd breached the city wall, or perhaps they were attacking it at this moment. The air strike would be assisting them. Once the city wall was broken down, we were the key to infiltrating the castle in secret. We had to get there, and fast.

The tunnel we careened down twisted and turned through the earth. Alura and I led the way, my light illuminating a few feet in front of us. We took a blind corner and suddenly, I put on the brakes. Maria bumped into my back, and behind her others yelped as they collided with those in front of them, but my attention was on the looming wall of rock in front of us.

"Damn," I muttered. We were totally blocked. Had Alura made the wrong decision? Or was this a tunnel we needed to go through, blocked up with who knew how much rock to get to the castle?

My attention shifted to Alura. "Are you sure this is the way?"

"Didn't Queen Pari say the giants closed off some tunnels before they evacuated? The royals asked it of them to protect the castles, right?" Maria countered my question with a question while her eyes locked on the wall of rock.

"They did," Alura agreed. "Pari herself admits to having only protected half the tunnels below her castle. It's too much effort to search for them all and ward them when the giants already did such a good job. There's no knowing if the giants did this at the behest of the king or if it fell naturally."

"Shite," I muttered. I was the leader here, and while Alura was the guide, ultimately, I had to decide what we did. So, did we stay and remove tons of rock, or turn around and explore the tunnels, hoping for easier passage that may never come?

"We needn't move it all." Maria continued assessing the situation. "Just enough so we can all slip through. That is, if it's not too deep of a blockage. We won't know until we try."

"Okay, give it a go." I commanded as Alura, who was saving her magic for navigational purposes, and I hung back. "I'll try my best to keep the lights on so you can work."

The earth fae's magic filled the tunnel and boulders the size of small cars flew past me, dotting the track we'd already tread. Progress was slow, and it wasn't until twenty excruciating minutes later, that someone let out a cry of victory. They'd made a hole. The other fae made sure they had the wall stabilized as Maria knelt in front of it and peered through it. To help, I pressed my light forward.

"What is it?" My stomach fluttered at Maria's wide brown eyes. Perhaps we were close. Did I dare hope, all the way to the castle already?

My sister turned to me, her lips tight. "It's just another giant home. This is a dead end."

"But how?" I looked at Alura.

She seemed confused too. "I don't know. I still sense magic coming from this way. Lots of it. Are you sure?"

"Positive," Maria replied.

Fecking hell.

"All right, let's get back to the intersection. It was the last time we made a choice, so maybe we need to reevaluate. You can rest there for a few minutes while we figure out what to do." Pissed and worried, we all headed back the way we'd come. I didn't understand what had happened, but I knew we could not waste more time standing around a dead end.

"It's like the giants tried to make it as confusing as possible to get through these tunnels," I muttered and shook my head. "And how would there still be magic in that home?"

Giants didn't even have magic! Besides their size,

the only magical property they could boast was that their skin was repellent of magic.

Alura frowned. "All I can think of is that the giants didn't want fae to come down here and find them. For years this was their only domain, and they protected it. I wonder if some ward makers came down here and charmed their homes for them? Maybe that charm has lasted a long time, and that's what I sensed."

"Maybe," I conceded because that was as good a theory as any. "All I know is that we have to make a fast decision when we get back to the intersection."

We continued to wind through the underground, and were nearly back at the intersection when a strange noise caught my attention.

Alura stiffened. "Are those footsteps?"

"Yeah . . . and they don't sound like they are coming from above," I assessed. "It sounds like—"

A hand yanked me into a side tunnel.

CHAPTER TWENTY-SEVEN

FINN

"Allow us to pass through the gates. If you do, there will be no blood spilled today! Not from my army!" Queen Pari proclaimed, her voice magically amplified to reach those standing on the wall.

Their arrows, aimed at us, didn't waver.

Normally, our poorly defensible position, coupled with the fact that my father was ready for our arrival, would worry me. Thankfully, our ward-maker had us covered.

Those on the walls didn't realize that though, and a second later a commander called an order and arrows flew. They pinged off the wards, falling harmlessly to the ground.

Pari raised her arms. "Again, I don't wish to hurt any of you. My only demands are that you let us through, and remove King Oberon from the throne."

Jeers and shouts came from the soldiers manning

the main wall of Lyonesse. Another round of arrows loosed, and annoyance rose inside me. Predictably, and frustratingly so, no one gave in to her demands. The sight of me next to the queen hadn't convinced anyone. If anything, it had riled up the opposing army even more.

Queen Pari turned to the army. "Armina." In the surrounding din, her tone was soft, reluctant. She didn't want to harm them, but the queen would ask no more.

It was time to take the city. My shadows bulged against my ribs, trying to escape my skin. Soon, I would have to let them out, but not now. Not yet.

A chorus of hisses flew in our direction the instant Armina stepped in front of the army, hinting that the soldiers recognized her. Armina's brows pinched together, forming the slightest of divots, but other than that small tell, she paid them no mind.

Her amethyst magic surged from her, slamming into a ward set up to protect the physical wall keeping us out of the city. The ward, previously invisible, lit up, crackling with electricity. Armina's hands twisted and turned, working through the defense. The way she moved reminded me a lot of Gio when he got into spinning a yarn about his wee fishing town, and the gossiping nonnas there.

My throat constricted. Fecking hell, I hoped he was okay. I hoped they all were. I wouldn't be able to forgive myself if something happened to them.

More arrows soared toward us, but Armina had kept her ward up while she attacked the one surrounding Lyonesse. Sweat dripped down her face, but none of the projectiles hurt our army as the famed wardmaker of Buyan continued to do her work.

A great *crack* sounded, followed by a *pop* in the air. Armina dropped her hands and turned, her long black hair flying behind her.

"The outer ward has fallen," Armina declared.

As one, Bellona and Isis took the point positions. "Rip down the wall!" Isis yelled.

Together, with other soldiers, she and Bellona began blasting the city wall. Armina retreated to position herself next to Pari.

Magic flew all around me, cracking the stone as I watched and waited. Huge chunks of wall fell to the ground, rolled toward us. Soldiers screamed, and dust billowed in the air, teasing my nostrils.

At that moment, I realized the peace of Lyonesse had only ever been an illusion. Had Queen Pari wished to attack the kingdom, she could have done so in a second. The relative lack of magic in the area made Lyonesse very vulnerable, and her army was strong. So strong she had left most of it at home to protect her people. She could have conquered Lyonesse *easily*.

Yet, she hadn't. She didn't wish violence upon the fae there. She desired a substitute for our father, a person she trusted. Someone who cared about the kingdom and would help build it back. She had that in Lana.

I hoped she trusted me too, but I was fine with not being on the throne. Power had never been my driving factor. Learning, living in the moment, and being with those I loved, were my reasons for living.

I wasn't so sure how Lana felt about being in charge. That remained to be seen. First, we needed to win the battle.

One thing at a time, I thought as another section of the great rock wall crumbled, and the fae standing atop it fell with the rubble. A few who had air power caught themselves before they landed with a *splat*, but our forces were quick to attack the survivors, disarm them, and offer that they surrender quietly. Those who refused, fell again. Others were shackled.

"The way is clear," Queen Pari announced. "Forward."

Our army surged through an opening wide enough for ten people to walk side-by-side. I waited until the queen marched, knowing my place was beside her. The people of Lyonesse needed to understand we stood with the queen. It had to be as clear as the daylight bursting over the horizon that we fought with her willingly—not as captives, forced.

I hoped seeing us here, with Queen Pari, would be a sign that something was wrong. I hoped they would question it and listen. The soldiers had not, but perhaps the civilians would. Soon, their world would explode open as we told them of the atrocities my father had committed.

My teeth ground together as my shadows swirled in my belly. "Knock it off."

"You should release them."

I glanced over my shoulder to find Armina's dark eyes boring through me.

"You and Lana are both terrified," the wardmaker continued.

"We're inciting a war," I shot back, annoyed. "Who wouldn't be scared?"

"Not about that. You fear how strong you'll become if you embrace the full breadth of your power. Why is that?"

"Armina . . ." Queen Pari warned as we breached the city wall, and the army plowed forward around us. "Now is not the time."

"It's fine," I told the queen. At least the question took my mind off what was happening.

"Lana has always been careful with her magic," I answered Armina. "Most don't consider light a deadly tool, but she always has. It scared her, and probably stifled her magic." My best friend had never said as much, but I just knew it to be the case. Armina should understand somewhat, seeing as she'd been a recipient of Lana's recent attacks.

"Any magic can be deadly. Whether your magic is good or bad depends on how you use it." Armina hissed, when someone who had probably fallen with the wall tried to attack her. Her sword ran through them.

"Wards?" I prompted, taking everything in, needing the distraction. Wards protected those behind them, within them. That was the only way I had seen one used.

"Watch." Armina nodded in front of us.

A wall of soldiers rushed forward down a city street, stomping through the rubble. All around, citizens of Lyonesse scattered from the streets, but the foreign army did nothing to them—as the queens and General Aketa commanded. The fae of our kingdom were innocent, and most of them were also weak. The only fair fight would be with the soldiers.

"Eye on the middle." Armina lifted her hands above her head, and as if she were throwing a ball, flung them forward. The soldier in the front wave of opposition stopped as if he'd hit a wall.

"That's not that deadly."

"Not done," Armina muttered. Her fingers splayed open wide, and as she squeezed them tighter, the soldier trembled and curled it on himself. He seemed to be trapped in a glass jar, one that grew ever smaller.

"Wards are protective, but get caught in something too small for you, play it too safe, and you'll stagnate. That's as good as death, and exactly why you need to let yourself free." Her dark eyes leveled on me, a story in their depths.

A cry diverted my attention back to the man caught in her ward, crumpling, dying. I swallowed. The lesson was brutal, but maybe that was what I needed. People knew about my shadows, but I was still hesitant to use them. With an army running toward us, one larger and more supplied than our own, hesitation was no longer a luxury we could afford. I gripped the blood vial.

"Release." Against my skin the vial heated ever so slightly, telling me the shadows accepted the blood. "If you see Ryker or Sai, don't touch them. Ronan either."

They were the soldiers I knew and loved. The ones I did not want to see hurt. Even if Ronan had no idea what was happening and fought against us, my shadows would not cut him down.

"Incapacitate the rest. Kill only if you must."

Two shadows thrust forward to battle the front line. Civilian fae screamed and ran down the street, slamming doors behind them. The armies moved like wolves circling around one another and striking at the most opportune moments. Fire spread as more fae used the element to take on their foes. It did not take long for me to lose track of my shadows, but that was fine with me. I'd seen them in action many times. They did not need me to babysit them.

A soldier approached me, sword aloft, fire blazing

from one of his hands. Without hesitation, I blasted him back with a gust of wind, and he hurtled through the air, crashing into a storefront behind him. His body slammed against the wall, and he slid to the ground.

"Traitorous scum!" A voice I recognized shrieked. The tone sent chills down my spine.

Whirling about, I searched for Master Meegra, and found her battling Ebba tooth and nail. My heart stopped for a moment, before I leapt into motion, sprinting toward her. I pushed through the battle, arms flicking from side to side, forcing waves of attackers back.

Opposing soldiers attacked me by the second, each trying to cut down the major first order, the Fullfeather prince who had betrayed his city. I fought each one efficiently, with all I'd been taught. As they fell, I hoped I had not done irreversible damage. I wanted to take the throne from my father, but not kill his subjects.

A gryphon screech filled my ears. I looked up to find the aerial front had joined in. They were fighting for us, but they too had problems. The Feathered Fae fought on both the ground and in the air, and yet, they weren't our only opponents in the skies.

Chimeras, hundreds more than the night they ambushed us, filled the sky. Most of their riders were armed with bows and arrows. As I watched, an arrow plunged into Crystal's gryphon's flank. The beast reared back and spun, threatening to throw my sister off it. My heart raced a mile a minute. I needed to help! From the corner of my eyes, a flash of darkness passed over a blazing fire. My shadows!

"Shadows!" I boomed. "Aerial attack!"

Immediately, they soared upward and clashed against the enemy.

"Help!"

Ebba's scream cut through the melee, and my eyes snapped over to her. The breath stuck in my throat.

Somehow, Meegra had forced her flat on her back, and whatever magic the Master Feathered Fae performed, she now possessed the upper hand. Her power pressed down on Ebba, her delicate face turning blue. Meegra was suffocating her.

"Nooo!"

Air magic gusted out of me, blowing a new surge of opponents back onto their arses as I sprinted to Ebba. When I finally got close enough, her face was as blue as the sky at noon, and Meegra had a blade pressed to her neck.

"Let her go!" I demanded, fire blazing in my hands.

Meegra's cold eyes lifted to meet mine. All around her soldiers gave her a wide berth as they fought, leaving us in an odd vacuum amidst the raging battle. "Was wondering which of you I'd see first. Where is the illuminator witch?"

I swallowed. There was no way in hell I was giving Lana up, but I could not watch Ebba die either.

"Tell me, or your little girlfriend here won't last long," Meegra cooed, knowing what to say to cut me. "She's here, isn't she? But where?"

So, they didn't know about the tunnels yet.

"Did you hear me, demon?" Meegra hissed, losing patience. "Tell me where Lana is, or this one dies." A bead of blood appeared on Ebba's skin, the threat intensifying.

Stalling, I inhaled. "She's not here."

"What do you mean she's not here!" Meegra sneered. "We know she's turned traitor. Clearly, she convinced you too. Otherwise, you would not be fighting with that foreign whore."

"She hasn't turned traitor. We've learned the truth. We learned why everyone here is ill and weak. How can you live with yourself?"

Ebba squirmed on the ground, and I wondered why she hadn't used her powers. When I saw Oren, the Lyonesse wardmaker not far away, I realized why. I remembered Armina disabling the soldier with her ward, and was sure that Oren had done the same to Ebba. Somehow, he'd pinned her down so Meegra could take her revenge.

"Live with myself? You idiot." Meegra's green eyes narrowed. "What His Majesty has planned will help all faekind. He—"

A bolt of gold dove from the skies, snagging my

attention upward. Arlo! Talon's extended, Arlo rushed Meegra. At the last second, she saw him too, but instead of attacking with magic, she lifted the blade from Ebba's neck.

Ebba gasped in a breath, but did not rise, confirming my belief that Oren had trapped her. Hands pressing against something invisible, her eyes met mine with fear.

Meegra slashed at the golden eagle, who darted away, successfully evading her attack.

"Shadows," I called, now sure Meegra would not pierce Ebba's throat. In an instant they materialized out of the jumble of bodies above us. I pointed to Oren and Meegra "Attack!".

My shadows shot toward them, and Meegra's eyes widened as she darted backward. The next thing I knew, both Feathered Fae transformed into birds, soaring into the battle above to hide—my shadows on their heels.

I ran over to Ebba. "Are you okay?"

"Fine. But I can't get up. I—"

Someone rushed to our side, and I nearly attacked but stopped just in time for Armina to press her hand against the invisible barrier. She snorted. "This is the best their wardmaker can do? What an amateur."

A cracking sound filled my ears when she destroyed the ward Oren had made. Ebba lurched up and wrapped her arms around me.

"Thank you! But they'll be back," Ebba assured,

pulling away, eyes serious. "Unless your shadows get them. But if they don't . . ."

"We're screwed." I glanced up. All it would take was for Meegra to dive out of the sky and plunge her talons into my exposed back. "We need to get to the castle. We have—"

The sight of something in the distance stole my words. Something that made my blood freeze.

In the direction of the castle, a blast of fire blazed like a geyser out of the ground. With a shaky finger, I pointed. "Ebba, what the bloody hell is that?"

CHAPTER TWENTY-EIGHT

LANA

"So, the Princess General decided she wanted to run around in the slums, eh?" A hot breath washed over the back of my neck, its raspy whisper filling my ear.

"Stay back or she dies!" another voice, that one female, called out, sounding closer to the opening of the alcove my squad was rushing past when I was snatched.

I tensed when a dagger dug into the soft flesh of my throat. My teeth ground harshly. Having a knife pressed to my throat was becoming far too common for my liking.

I inhaled, trying to calm down, and immediately gagged. Whoever had a hold of me was definitely not a castle guard. He smelled sour, as if he hadn't bathed in months. No soldier in King Oberon's court would be allowed to go around smelling like that. Still, if he wasn't a soldier, who was he? My eyes flashed across the dark tunnel, to discover a dirty female clutched Alura from behind too.

"Who are you?" I asked.

"What's it to you, little princess?" My captor snorted. "Why not return above ground and enjoy your posh life? No need to worry about the rest of us. Your father certainly doesn't." The man spat on the ground.

"You're his subjects." These people had to be rebels of some sort. The same people that Posy had mentioned they protected.

The blade dug into my throat.

"The citizens of Lyonesse he'd rather not remember," I corrected myself, and the blade let up ever so slightly. "I'm no longer loyal to my father. We're here to stop him."

The ratty-haired fae woman gasped.

"Heard you spent some time in Buyan," the man said. "The queen there opened your eyes, did she?"

"Yes," I squeaked, and the man released me.

I whirled around to face him. He was tall, bone thin, and looked as dirty as he smelled.

"Yes, she did." My tone became stronger. "Why are you down here? Why didn't you leave Lyonesse once you became disenchanted with your king?"

Knowing what I knew of my father, it made sense that there had been subjects abandoned. Those who received no rations and were not strong enough, without the influence of a bonegate, to hold on to magic.

A roar of laughter left the man. "Leave? Leave, she says!" He looked at the group as if expecting us to join him. "You think it's as simple as walking across the wasteland of a desert your father created? Simply traipse over the sand and hope you find enough water and food to last you for days? No offense, princess, but even someone from the Old Land should know better."

"The king and his Feathered Fae watch the expanse between Lyonesse and Buyan," the woman added. "Only the desperate try to leave Lyonesse without help. And the Queen of Buyan can only send help once or twice a year."

"The desert is too harsh to travel through?" I wouldn't blame them if it were. The road from Lyonesse to Buyan was long, dry, and bleak.

"Difficulty doesn't faze us. But if the Feathered Fae happened upon us, which they usually do, they know we are easy targets. Largely defenseless."

An image of Naela diving for a rabbit came to mind, but in their case the rabbit was . . . Horrified, I sucked in a breath. "You can't be serious."

"I am, princess," the woman answered. "My son wanted to go to Buyan before Queen Pari sent envoys to help. I didn't want him to, but there was no controlling him. Said he'd send word when he got there. Thank the Sinkers he didn't make it far before the Master Feathered Fae herself swooped down on him. He managed to fall into one of the side tunnels and make his way back home. Others haven't been so lucky."

My stomach churned. "What are your names?"

"I'm Deema." The woman stuck a thumb out to the man who'd grabbed me. "And that fool is Regin."

"Good to meet you." Another question filled my mind. Actually, a million did, but that one seemed the most pressing. "If you can't leave, how do you get food and water?"

"Palace guards, two in particular. They are part of the rebel faction, and help feed our settlement."

My brow lifted. "Do you mean Sai and Ryker?"

"Sounds like you know them." Deema's mouth split in a grin.

"If not for them, we would have starved long ago," Regin admitted.

Sai and Ryker knew of these people too. How many others did? Did Pari know? Or did Ryker and Sai keep that quiet to protect those here? My eyes widened. "How many of you live down here?"

Deema shrugged. "Around fifty. More come weekly, but some pass on. It's a hard life."

Fifty fae, all living in hiding right beneath my father's feet. An entire neighborhood being fed by scraps from the castle. Fae who hated him. Behind me, Alura cleared her throat, and I knew what she was thinking. We were delayed. Who knew how many of our own soldiers could be dead already? We had to move, but before we did, I wanted to offer those who lived down here an alternative—a way to change their fate.

"We are here to overthrow my father. I invite you to fight with us. If you don't want to, that's fine, but we'd appreciate it if you showed us the most direct route to the castle. We need to get there quickly."

"Seriously?" Deema's eyes grew wide.

"Absolutely. It's time things change in Lyonesse."

The other two stared at me for a moment, slack-jawed, before Regin snapped out of it.

"Never thought I'd agree with a Fullfeather, let alone fight alongside one, but I guess there's a first time for everything. We'll stop by the camp to see if others want to join first. Then to the palace. Follow me."

Our squad fell in line behind Regin as he ran down the same tunnel we'd been rushing through earlier. When we got to where eight paths shot off from the main thoroughfare, Regin and Deema veered to the far left. There was no doubt in my mind they knew where they were going, I just hoped their route was fast and we could get to the castle promptly. Our friends and family were fighting above while others were in a castle under attack.

Like Garret . . .

Stop, I told myself. Thinking about where he

might be and in what condition hurt too much. Just follow Regin and Deema.

It didn't take long until Deema and Regin led us to another grouping of what were once giant homes. Except, these were not unoccupied. Instead, the fae made use of the underground dwellings. Someone had even carved what looked to be a small school into the walls of the vast tunnels. It was pretty miraculous what they'd done with so little. If we had more time, I would have loved to look at everything.

However, time was not on our side.

Regin ran down the side tunnels, yelling for help and collecting more soldiers. Fae heeded his call as if they'd been waiting for it, striding out of their alcoves already armed to the teeth with swords, daggers, and chisels. I assumed the weapons were used in case guards found their way into the tunnels to search for them. Many wasted no time crying out insults against the king, their desire for revenge on my father motivating them.

Their anger was perhaps the best weapon of all.

"This is crazy," Maria whispered.

"It's kind of like Petra," I agreed as we followed Regin to his own home, so he could pick up his weapon. "And these people . . . I don't even know what to say."

"How does our father not know where all the missing people went?" Maria reasoned. "Wouldn't the Feathered Fae tell him if someone went missing, and they didn't catch him in the expanse between Lyonesse and Buyan? Or is there no way of identifying people in the city?"

My eyes narrowed at my sister's shrewdness. The thought hadn't even crossed my mind, but Deema sidled up next to us before I could find an answer.

"The king lives in a fantasy land of his own making. Part of him believes his people love him unfailingly. Mostly, that's true because they're brainwashed. But another part of the king knows the truth, and that part shows no mercy to those who speak against him. If you do not fall into those camps, and you disappear, it's as if you don't exist. Personally, I think it's better this way."

I'd seen that sort of compartmentalization of the king's emotions first-hand. During the Successional, our father had claimed it was a ritual for fae kings and queens to ignore their children before the tournament. However, I later learned from Pari that while the royals frowned upon showing favor to one child over another, they did not simply ignore their children. His doing so was simply a way for our father to compartmentalize his emotions. He pretended we weren't his children until the danger passed, and then he could build a relationship—albeit a manipulative one—with the ones who lived through the Successional.

He was so fucked up.

Don't think about it, I told myself and searched

for a distraction. It appeared right away, in the form of a woman walking toward me with a shovel. My eyes widened. I'd seen that fae before.

The woman never stopped staring at me as she moved closer and closer, finally stopping when we were face to face. Her daughter, the green-skinned girl who'd seized my attention the day of the parade, was the spitting image of her. The last time I'd seen the woman, her blue eyes had been dull and tired, now they twinkled with amusement.

"I see you've learned the truth." The woman winked, a smile twitching her lips. "My girl saw it long ago. She had a vision that you'd be the one to free us —or die trying. The one to bring our magic back. Are you here to make your promise to my daughter come true?"

My mouth dried up with her statement. The girl had wanted to pledge herself to me, not my father. Me. Now it turned out that she'd seen this in the future? Or the possibility of it? Was she a prophet, or was the future certain? Trying to find her, I peered around the woman.

"This is no place for a child," she answered knowingly. "And her visions are not set in stone. You must make your choice and pursue it with all you have. Only then will it be most likely to come true." She cocked her head to the side. "But she will wish to hear from you."

Determination grew inside me, and fists clenching

at my sides, I met the woman's stare. "Then tell her I have come to make good on my promise. Today, my father's rule ends, and a new season for Lyonesse begins."

It felt too bold to say I would lead, although that's what everyone was thinking. I still didn't really want to, but there would be time to discuss that later. Staying alive during the war took priority.

"Very good. We wish you the best of luck, Princess Lana." The woman bowed and left.

Regin, Deema, and a fresh retinue of about twelve additional fae appeared a moment later.

"Are you ready?" Deema asked.

"Let's move," I replied.

We set off together, but those who lived in the tunnels led the way. Ten minutes later we approached what looked like a dead end. That was, until Regin and Alura step forward, both examining the rock face with amusement.

Regin placed his hand on a stone, and it shifted inward ever so slightly. I blinked, stunned. It was a door—one far too small for a giant—carved for the forgotten of Lyonesse, those who lived in the tunnel.

"This hidden door will lead us straight into a storage closet off the main hallway, which funnels into the castle kitchens."

Regin cracked the door open a bit more, but it didn't make even the slightest of sounds. Someone had enchanted it to be that way, probably to protect those who used it. I suspected the door was the only way those in the castle got food to them.

"If you wouldn't mind, Princess General?" Regin gestured forward. "Usually, Ryker or Sai come through the opposite way—when there is no one around. Once we're with them, no one questions our presence. They assume we're being taken to work in the kitchens. Without one of the cousins we need a cover, or we'll attract too much attention before we can take hold."

I understood. Any soldier who saw this band of miscreants pop through the tunnel would slay them on sight. We needed an illusion to get us all into the hallway. From there, we'd split strategically.

Since coming to Faerie, I'd worked remarkable magic. Magic that I never dreamed of, but I'd never hidden such a large group. Still, if we wanted to keep everyone safe for as long as possible, there wasn't really another option. Taking a steadying breath, I began pulling light in front of me. It came quickly, almost like I was working someone else's magic.

Once the illusion felt right, I maneuvered to the front of the group. There was no way in hell I was letting anyone else go first.

"Time to save the kingdom," I declared as I slipped inside Castle Phoenix.

CHAPTER TWENTY-NINE

LANA

The others tiptoed to where I waited in the hallway, my illusion cloaking the area. Down the hall, pots clanged in the kitchen. Voices rang, and strangely, one sort of sounded like someone was giving a speech. Booming and assertive. But why? Were they rallying fighters and setting out to defend themselves with pots and pans? My teeth dug into my bottom lip.

"The kitchen is that way," I spoke in a low tone as the last person joined us in the hall. "I think we should check it out first, see who's there. We might need to subdue them, but we can manage that. Fae with weaker powers work in the kitchens." Or at least that was what I'd been told. I'd never been in the kitchens. Never even got near them.

"I don't want to harm them since they're doing their job, but we need to quiet them because they might sound the alarm. Everyone okay with that?" It wasn't just that I was being careful. The voice coming from the kitchens was familiar, but they were too far away for me to be sure.

The dirt covering Regin's face sank into smile lines as he grinned. "I'm never one to turn down a trip to a kitchen."

"Okay. Everyone stays close. I can cover us with the illusion, but my reach is only so large." I extended the mirage rendering us invisible as far as I could, so it would hide the squad. We neared the kitchen door when I heard the booming voice again. Sinkers, it sounded so familiar, but I couldn't be sure who the voice belonged to through the thick wood. I pressed my ear to the door.

"What the hell is going on down here?" a female voice growled. "You better explain yourself quickly. Why are these people here?" A real growl emanated from her, and the image of a wolf popped into my mind. My heart leapt.

Wikolia! My sister was behind the door! Did that mean they were alive, safe, and not even in a cell?

"Maria, come with me!" Pushing open the door, I walked past the boundaries of my illusion, and a half dozen pairs of eyes swung in my direction. I smiled, taking in the familiar faces, but got sidetracked a second later. A group I didn't recognize huddled in the corner. They were dressed in rags and glaze eyed. Were they kitchen workers? I'd certainly never seen them in the hallways. My eyebrows furrowed. Wait . . . did I *recognize* one?

"Lana! Maria!" Ryker rushed forward to hug us. "We have not received a message from Queen Pari, but when the first aerial wave breached the city walls, I hoped she would use the tunnels too."

"That's where we were," I confirmed.

Ryker exhaled. "I'm relieved the king didn't think to send troops down there, and you made it here safely."

"We're fine. I have others with me. Is it safe to drop my illusion?"

Ryker's gaze flitted to the people in the corner. "They won't do anything."

The urge to ask why they were in the castle kitchens in the first place was strong, but my sister stepped forward before I could ask.

"What's he talking about? Tunnels? Aerial attacks?" Wikolia growled, her eyes already shifting to the intense amber tone they became in her wolf form. "What in the world is going on? The castle is being attacked, and there are humans down here! And who the hell are those dirty people with you, Lana?! I demand answers!"

Humans?

"Wik, calm yourself," Gio came up behind her, his dark eyes full of questions. "Lana, what's going on? Why are you here with the opposing army? Or are you using their attack as a distraction?"

"We just got down here," Sai called from where she stood next to a surly looking Victoria. Dak was there too, but as always, he was sitting back and taking it all in quietly. "Your father has kept them in their rooms since Finn and the others left. Only Feathered Fae were allowed to speak to them. We have not had time to explain the truth."

"Right." My stomach knotted up. "Garret?"

"Under the king's command. Brainwashed," Ryker shook his head and his curly mane swayed.

"What?" My heart thumped so hard it hurt. "How?"

"Your father has a potion he's employed in the past," Garret's best friend explained. "It's dangerous to the person who takes it. Dangerous to the king too since he has to take it to create a bond with the person. Because of the risks, His Majesty uses it sparingly. When someone takes the elixir, it is noticeable they are not in their right mind. They're completely under the king's control. When Garret returned, they forced him to take it."

"How do you know?"

"We saw him brought in," Sai replied. "Since then, we've only seen him outside the king's private chambers once. He didn't even look at us."

My throat tightened. "Can we reverse it?"

"With an antidote… Or a powerful emotion." Sai pressed her lips together.

I wanted to twirl around and burst out of the

kitchens to rescue Garret, but couldn't. Not yet. Plus, if he was with my father, he was in less danger than most. At least, until we got to him. First we needed my siblings to understand what had happened. Also, what was that about humans?

"Take a seat," I urged.

My diviner brother did so, without question, but the white wolf's chin jutted out stubbornly. Wik crossed her arms over her chest. "What the hell is going on?"

A burdened sigh left my lungs. We'd lost so much time in the tunnels, I had to make this quick. It took only a few minutes to tell them what had happened after Queen Pari captured me, and everything since. Only when I got to the part about speaking with Posy, did I pause.

"She's our grandmother." Ryker outed himself. "Our family has been spies for years."

Sai swept toward me, joining the group of soldiers and tunnel dwellers. "We help those whom the crown punishes for wanting a better life, or even talking about it. Those who see the truth of what's happening. Sometimes, when we can, we move people from the tunnels to Buyan."

Dak's mouth fell open, and the others looked similarly gob smacked.

"Why didn't you say anything before?" Victoria asked, sounding strangely small, not at all like the diva she liked to portray. My vila-elf sister appeared calmer than Wik, but I hadn't convinced them all yet either. Hesitation shone clearly on their faces.

Dammit, why wasn't Finn here? The moment his name popped into my head, pain shot through my heart. I hoped he was okay. Hoped they all were. Finn oozed charisma. He'd have said the right thing to convince them of the truth, and get them motivated to fight. If he were here, we'd already be in the midst of fighting.

"What would you have done?" Ryker asked. "You met your father after years of not knowing him. You were new royals and dedicated to the crown. He made sure only those who *wanted* to see him arrived here. Those who would go through the steps and follow the clues. Others, and there *were* others, probably threw the invitation in the bin."

Ryker's truth cut me to the core. Father had selected only the children who would go to great lengths to meet him. He'd been smart to do so. I'd broken into a bloody cathedral to get to Faerie!

"Manipulative bastard," Regin muttered, even though I doubted he knew about the clues that led us to the bonekeys.

Gio opened his mouth, clearly about to ask something, when a roar from outside shook the pans hanging on the wall. Plates shimmied off shelves, shattering.

Victoria let out a shriek, and Maria, still standing behind me, grabbed my wrist.

"What in the world?" I breathed, heart racing.

"The dragon . . ." Sai looked pained. "Those who live and work at the castle are forbidden to speak of it. Enchanted not to."

"Why? We've seen the beast. It's not like it's a secret."

"Because it's the Crown Prince's familiar," Ryker confessed.

"What the hell?!" Maria exclaimed.

"Uh, why are you just telling us now?" I asked, not understanding.

"We couldn't risk it. The king has castle workers enchanted to say nothing about it, and while our grandmother gave us the antidote to that potion, we couldn't risk you knowing. What if one of you said something to the wrong person? It would endanger our family." Sai shrugged. "And honestly, it wasn't that important before. The dragon has been chained for years."

It made so much sense. Why else would they keep a dragon, a dangerous creature if there ever was one, on the castle grounds? She didn't even try to get out of her enclosure, at least not as often as one would think.

The Fullfeathers always had had a proclivity for winged beasts. Leave it to Casimir to surpass even a phoenix.

"If the dragon is loose, then the battle is well underway," Sai admitted to her cousin.

"We have to hurry," Maria's voice came out raspy with urgency.

"Lana, where's Crystal?" Victoria asked. "Where are the others?"

"She's here. Outside. On a gryphon." Saying that out loud made ice trickle through me. Crystal rode on a gryphon when a freaking dragon soared through the skies!

The others seemed to realize that we needed to get moving at the same time, because Gio, Dak, and Victoria stood at once.

"We're in," Gio announced. "Let's confront him."

"And stop the war!" Victoria looked petrified but also resolute. She was far more resilient than her Barbie exterior would lead one to believe.

"Wik?" I asked, uncertain, but saw her nod.

"I always thought there was something off about the dude. I hoped I was wrong, but . . . I'm not surprised."

"What should we do about them?" My gaze strayed to the people huddled in the corner. Aside from when the dragon roared and they pressed closer together in fear, they'd barely moved an inch.

"They won't go anywhere," Ryker assured. "They're human slaves. They live just off the kitchen and are enchanted not to leave."

"What?!" I shrieked.

Wik threw up her hands. "This place is so fucked up!"

"The king takes slaves," Sai said. "They're humans who accidentally wander into Faerie. Or sometimes he has his Feathered Fae lure the pretty ones over and . . . they stay."

My throat closed up with dread. How many other secrets did our father have? My gaze found the man who looked familiar, and I studied him finally deciding that, yes, I had seen him before. A castle worker told me he was ill, and I'd bought it. My gut twisted. He wasn't ill, just human, and trapped.

"People can't talk about them," Sai explained knowingly. "For the same reason they can't talk about the dragon, they're enchanted not to. The potion maker is talented, and in the king's pocket."

Another roar shook the pots and pans lining the walls. "There's more, isn't there? More we don't know?"

"Mountains of it," Sai's violet eyes locked on me. "I'll tell you after we win this thing."

Taking a steeling breath, I stepped forward. "I'll lead."

We filed out of the kitchen, down the hallway, and up the stairs. When we reached the entrance to the castle, split wide open to display the grounds, I saw blood and bodies littering the ground. Either the air or ground forces had already made it inside the palace, or tried to and failed.

Heart racing, I faced the group. "My family, Ryker and Sai, come with me. The rest of you, fight as you will." I was going to the most dangerous part of the battle, and as much as Deema and Regin vowed they wanted revenge on the king, there was no way I was leading them straight to his chambers. He'd annihilate them.

"Are you sure?" Alura asked, stepping forward. The foreign soldiers had been silent since we entered the castle. They were happy to let me lead, but I understood why she questioned my choice.

My father was powerful. Vengeful and cruel. He would not be merciful, particularly not to foreign soldiers who sided with Pari.

"Positive. Help our side. Take the castle." I pointed left.

The others ran off in the direction I indicated. Once they vanished, I hung right. Footsteps followed, telling me that my siblings, Ryker, and Sai were with me. My breath heaved in and out of my chest as we sprinted down the hallways, each suspiciously deserted. Judging by the courtyard, I would have thought there were more people in here. Had Oberon ordered everyone outside to fight, or had we just not come across them yet?

Sinkers, I hoped that Queen Pari would end the battle fast. If Casimir had a dragon, who knew what else the king and the prince had to throw at us? Memories of the murderous spriggans, naga, chimera, and giantess from the Successional flooded my mind. Aside from using the power of his own prodigious army, I had no doubt my father would unleash whatever heinous creatures he had at his disposal.

A flash of motion caught my eye as I crossed an intersection of hallways. I shot a glance over my shoulder and saw, to my horror, that a guard had seen us. His response was not that of a soldier confronting his commanding Princess General. Unbridled hate blazed in his eyes.

I whirled around. "Separate!"

My siblings, Ryker, and Sai threw themselves to the side seconds before I blasted light down the hallway.

The guard flung himself out of the direction of my attack, avoiding what would surely have been a horrific burn. Unfortunately for me, he was a soldier through and through, trained to stay calm under stress. The moment the wave of light passed he was on his feet again.

Another round of infrared light shot from my hands, but I missed again. He kept running, his hands lifted, prepared to strike.

Gio joined my assault, sending a tsunami of water down the hall. My heart lurched. The water might knock the guy out, and that would be fine, but I didn't want to kill anyone who was enchanted with freaking potions! I would defend myself, my friends, and family, but I would also try to avoid killing anyone until they knew the truth about their king.

The guard's eyes widened as the water rushed toward him. He turned to run, but a hurricane-force wind coming from a cross corridor blew him off balance. It also forced the water to the side, out an open window. The guard, still on the ground, smiled as he hauled himself up.

A moment later, cold laughter rippled down the corridor, and Meegra stepped into view.

Ryker and Sai moved, but the Master Feathered Fae was faster. With a flick of her hands, two blocks of marble slipped out of the sides of the hallways, crashing straight into their heads.

The cousins fell.

Shite, she'd wiped out our strongest elementals in one go!

"Princess General," Meegra gave me a chilling smile. "His Grace will be so pleased that I found his traitorous daughter."

The guard we'd nearly washed away sneered as if I was the lowest of trash.

"What are our orders, Ash?" Meegra continued, and three more Feathered Fae stepped forward, Ash being one of them.

Someone had cut him across the face with a blade, but he didn't look scared, worried, or even perturbed. His dark eyes locked on us like we were prey.

No one in my group moved. We'd all been on the

receiving end of Meegra's power before. Ash was nearly as strong, and twice as vicious.

"We're to find the illuminator and bring her to King Oberon. Use any force necessary."

"Did King Oberon specify the state the traitor should be in?" Meegra prompted.

"Alive, unfortunately."

I withheld my growl. My father, no matter how much he distrusted me, had some use for me first. I could play on that. If I wanted to keep my life, I had to do it.

"Bloodied is fine, though. She need only be able to talk," Ash continued. "As for the other half-bloods, King Oberon wants only the captains. The rest are dispensable. We're to show them that Lyonesse does not take kindly to a bastard rebellion."

My blood froze, and I stiffened. The mercy King Oberon would show Finn, Crystal, and me would not extend to any of my siblings. What had I done asking them to join me?! I spun to tell them to run, but it was too late. Their faces were blue. One of the Feathered Fae was employing a tactic I'd seen Himari use, ripping the air from someone's lungs.

"No," I whispered, horrified. I should have sent them with the other fae! Should have sent them far away from me! "What have you done! What—"

I whirled around in time to see a stone soaring at my face. Then everything went black.

CHAPTER THIRTY

FINN

Ebba and I raced toward the castle. Though the battle still raged, somehow the only thing I could hear were two words chanted over and over in my mind.

The dragon. The dragon. The dragon.

They were releasing the dragon!

Ebba claimed that was the only thing that could have produced so many flames. It only took me a moment to be certain that she was right. A fire-worker couldn't do that—I knew that firsthand. Yet, the few times I'd seen the dragon kept at the castle she was sickly, on the verge of death. The idea that she produced all that fire was astounding. And apparently very real.

I glanced up, glad my shadows and Kane were with us. I'd tried to call Naela, but she'd refused and stayed with Crystal, fighting in the air. Hopefully, Lana wouldn't be too pissed that I left her. The bloody bird was as stubborn as they came.

We were nearly to the castle gate—which I planned to barrel my way through with sheer force of will—when Ebba reached out, grabbing my wrist. She stopped me before we were within sight of the guards who patrolled the gate.

"We'll enter through the servant's quarters."

With a nod, I fell into step beside her. Although I would have done it alone, I was glad Ebba was at my side. Glad she was fighting with me while we searched for Lana and the tunnel team.

My muscles burned, but I only pressed on, harder and faster. We had already rounded half of the castle, when something stopped me dead in my tracks. The wind whipped up into a storm so strong that we couldn't take another step forward.

"Kane!"

He joined us, latching on to my arm to take cover. Shielding him, Ebba and I pressed our bodies against the building, hiding in the shadow for protection. Barely a second passed, before a massive black beast soared above.

"The dragon!" I gasped, unable to believe I was seeing her fly. She had been bound by wards for months! "Wait a minute . . . is Casimir riding her?"

An image of Casimir calming the dragon a few

days ago came rushing back. He knew the beast well, but how?

Ebba blinked. "Yeah, he is. But why?"

I had no response. For once, I was speechless as we waited for the dragon to pass over on her way to the battle. As soon as I realized that's what they were doing, conflict rippled through me like a wave. The crown prince, a very strong lightworker, was going to join the battle on the back of a dragon . . . and he'd be fighting against us.

My heart screamed we should go back and help them, but my mind knew we couldn't. All of our hopes rested on unseating my father, on exposing him for what he was, and he was inside Castle Phoenix.

"I didn't know he could ride it," Ebba continued, still stuck on the dragon.

A strange inflection in her voice called my attention, and I cocked my head, regarding her. It sounded strained, like she knew Casimir could ride it, but couldn't say otherwise. Why would that be? "Are you sure?"

Her eyebrows pinched together. "Of course, I'm sure. We're wasting time. Let's go."

She led the rest of the way around the castle, and we slipped inside using an innocuous door nearly hidden by chopped wood and supplies. Immediately, the blood, chaos, and fire reigning outside disappeared, leaving only cool, white marble. It was eerily quiet too, the sound of battle barely penetrating the stark walls.

I looked around, not recognizing where we were. My time in the castle had not been spent in the servant's quarters.

"Follow me." Ebba gestured right. "We have to be careful. Most of the troops are outside, but there will still be guards in the castle."

Again, I let her lead, Kane at my side, while my shadows remained at our backs—unfaltering. As far as I knew, not even a dragon could destroy them. That gave me solace, because Casimir riding on the dragon had been one hell of a surprise.

Though, I was sure my father had many, many more to come.

We wound our way through the corridors, and we were almost to the tower where my father took his meetings—the place I was sure he would be hiding safely—when footsteps hit my ear.

A laugh, high and cold followed. My fists clenched. Meegra.

I shoved Ebba into a nearby alcove. Kane followed, perching above.

"Shadows!" I hissed, tapping my heart space. I couldn't risk Meegra seeing them. Not when she had evaded them before, and we were so close to where we needed to be. The sensation of them entering me momentarily knocked the wind from me.

We waited as Meegra's laughter waned. No matter how much I wanted to take her on, I wanted to find my father more. No more distractions. A minute later, their footsteps completely faded, and I exhaled. "We should—"

"What have we here?" A fae soldier, light-footed as anyone who ever lived, walked right in front of us. He extended his arms, fire blazing at the tips of his fingers. Ebba pulled her sword and slashed the fae in half.

"Damn, woman, that is savage," I whispered, impressed by her yet again.

Her weapon slid back into its sheath. "We learned early in our training not to rely only on our magic. It can be taken away by potions, wards, or bindings, but if we have a weapon, even just our fists, we can still survive."

"Point made." I agreed with her.

Of course, I had learned to fight with steel and fists too, but she was right. It was easy to become reliant on my magic and the shadows. I glanced down at the vial.

It had only taken Queen Mauri and me a few training sessions to learn that the shadows' strength was directly correlated to how much blood they used. In the battle they had used a lot of energy, more than usual, so the blood in the vial was disappearing faster than it ever had.

Depending on how long the fighting lasted, I would have to cut myself open and give them fresh blood, or rely on my power, my steel, and fists, like Ebba said.

"By the way, we're even now." Ebba's hand wiped the sweat from her brow.

"What do you mean?" Slipping out of the alcove, I joined her in the hall. We didn't run, but walked quickly. We were getting closer to my father's tower, and had to take greater care to be quiet.

"You saved me from Meegra in the fight. I just saved you. The both of us actually."

A smirk tilted my lips. "We're not quite even. Remember I saved you from that frog in the garden? The one you threw yourself into my arms over?"

Her mouth dropped open. "You can't be serious."

"Shooed it right away." I worked hard to keep my tone leveled. "I protected you like a true gentleman."

Her eyes narrowed and a thrill ran through me. Getting Ebba a little riled up was my favorite thing, because then she got feisty and that was hot.

Halting, she grabbed my shoulders.

"Don't you think we need to—"

Ebba's lips pressed to mine.

The kiss sizzled all the way through my body, from my lips to my toes. It felt as if I were aflame, consumed with the feel of her. When she pulled away, she gasped for breath, her eyes wide. My breaths ran deeply too, and I couldn't take my gaze off her. She was the most beautiful woman I'd ever seen.

"Are we even now?" Ebba asked, her tone light, and dare I say, flirtatious?

"Damn straight we are," I grinned. "Now, quit trying to seduce me, Captain. We have to find my father." I winked, which made her snort.

More than anything, I wanted to kiss her again, but we both knew time was short, we were exposed here, and we were close to our goal, so we got on with it.

Hurrying down the hallway, we turned down the one that would lead us straight into his private tower, but immediately skidded to a stop. Bodies lay on the ground. People I recognized.

"Ryker! Sai!" I gasped as my gaze landed on Maria too. She had been with Lana. The rest of our siblings, the ones we'd been unable to take with us were there too, all splayed out on the ground like rags.

One by one I called their names, but no one stirred. They were out cold. Clearly Maria and Lana had gone through the tunnels and found the others with Ryker and Sai. After that, I had no idea what had happened.

"We have to wake them," I urged. "We can't leave them here."

Ebba went straight to Sai, her bestie, while I dropped next to Gio. Shaking him gently, I hoped he would wake. There were no visible injuries on any of their bodies, so I wasn't sure what had knocked them unconscious.

After a full minute whispering their names and checking on each person, I returned to Gio in time to watch his dark brown eyes fly open. He gasped so loudly that I jerked back.

"Hey," I called softly, not wanting to add to his distress. "Are you okay?"

His brown eyes landed on me. "Been better. Where have you been?"

"What happened to you?" I asked at the same time.

"Answer me." His gaze shifted to Ebba, his eyes widening impossibly further. "And don't tell me that in my absence he has seduced you. A man's heart can only take so much, mi bella."

A laugh choked out of me. No matter how dire the situation, Gio always managed a joke.

"There's a battle outside," I reminded. "They released the dragon. We were coming to find you guys and Lana, but found you here."

Another strained breath lodged in my brother's throat, as if he'd remembered something. "Yes! The dragon! It's Casimir's familiar."

Ebba and I exchanged a shocked glance.

"Surely Ebba would have tol—"

"The guards can't say anything," Gio explained. "They are given a potion, or something, that makes them keep royal secrets. They know the dragon exists but can't say anything about its connection to our brother. Ryker and Sai got the antidote from their grandmother so they can talk, but never told us. There wasn't a point before."

"Posy gave them an antidote . . ." Recalling Ebba's strained tone when she spoke of the dragon, I turned to her. "You really didn't know."

She seemed to be listening, but struggling to comprehend.

"It doesn't make sense," she confessed. "I feel like I *should* know that the dragon is attached to Casimir, but . . . No. I didn't know."

"It's not your fault, bella," Gio encouraged, throwing her a flirtatious smile. "All that matters is she's gone, which means our brother is gone. That's good, because Meegra grabbed Lana."

My stomach dropped, but at that moment, the others stirred. I kept myself in check, watching their eyes open one by one.

"What did they do to you guys?" I asked once I was sure they were all awake.

"Pulled the air from our lungs," Victoria coughed. "They did it well too. I feel like I've been out for a year."

"Can you run?" I asked.

"They damn well better be able to," another voice called.

My head whirled to find Crystal rounding the

corner. Arlo, still in eagle aspect, soared next to her, and Naela flew right behind him.

"Crystal?" The relief in my voice was evident. The more people we had, the better. "Where's Himari?"

"Still fighting," Crystal replied. "I saw you run into the castle. It was really hard to get past the chimera and find you, but I knew what was happening and that I needed to be here. The aerial attack needed Himari more. Her air magic is the strongest, and now they're taking on the dragon."

My mouth dried up. We had to win this, and fast.

"I'll be honest," Dak spoke, trying to sit up. "I don't think I can run. I don't even think I can move." His voice sounded wheezy, not deep and low as normal.

"They may have collapsed one of your lungs. Maybe just a partial collapse," Crystal considered. "Strong air workers can do it, and if that's the case, he can't come. You'll probably heal fast cause you're a shifter, but don't push it and make the injury worse. Especially because if we lose, you'll need to run. Save your lungs for that." Crystal's face was somber. "What about the rest of you?"

Gio, Ryker, and Sai were fine, but Victoria, Maria, and Wik were nearly as bad off as Dak. We couldn't make them join us.

"You guys have to stay here," I concluded, looking at them. "Hide in one of these side rooms."

"We don't want you to fight without us!" Victoria seethed, and then began coughing so hard she could no longer speak.

"We don't want to either," Crystal shot back. "But you'll be more of a liability than you will be a strength. And if our father runs, which he might if we can get the jump on him, someone needs to be out here to stop him." She leveled Victoria with her gaze. "Use your song. That will stop him."

"Fine," Victoria spat. It was clear that was the last thing she wanted to do, but she saw the wisdom in Crystal's reasoning.

My eyes ran over those who would stay. They were lucky to be alive, and although I wished they could help us, I was relieved that at the very least, they'd be here to help one another.

A faint keening noise escaped Kane's beak. He wanted to come too, but I didn't want that at all. Our father had Xerxes and while Kane, Naela, and Arlo were birds of prey, none were a magical phoenix.

"Kane and Naela, can you stick with Arlo and be on the lookout for the dragon?" My father would surely have some way of warning Casimir if he needed help. So if he did that, the dragon would return too.

Understanding my reasoning, Arlo nodded. Kane, however, gave me a forlorn look before agreeing like Arlo had. Naela glared, which I expected.

"Naela, Lana said to listen to me."

She looked away, but I knew she'd do what I said, what Lana wished.

"Alright then, we have to go," I announced. "But you lot should take off."

The birds left, and Ebba, Crystal and I helped the others into a side room. Once they were situated, my group continued to my father's tower. We rounded the final corner, and it came as no surprise to anyone that the door to my father's private chambers were closed.

"How are we going to get in?" Crystal asked. "We can't knock."

"My shadows can get us in."

"Damn. Those are handy." She couldn't hide the envy in her voice.

Though I wanted to deny that they were, I could no longer say such a thing. They were scary, but also very handy.

As we got closer to the door engraved with a massive feather, we slowed our pace. Though King Oberon would be an idiot not to expect us, we needed to preserve as much of the element of surprise as possible. Glancing down, I gripped the vial. The blood was nearly gone but I didn't want to wait. Couldn't bear to do so. After this, I'd have to slice my palm to use the shadows. If it helped us win, I'd do far worse.

"We need you," I whispered.

My shadows emerged smoothly to stand before me like inky soldiers.

"Let us inside," I instructed, "and protect us as we enter."

They dissipated into smoke. I watched as their forms pooled at the floor and pressed against the door. Suddenly, they froze, and a high pitched wail filled my ears.

Everyone gripped the sides of their heads.

"What the hell?" I hissed. "Guys, what's—"

My shadows disappeared, and so did the sound. The thumping of my heart stopped. Where had they gone? They weren't inside me. Nor could I see them.

"What happened?" Crystal whispered. "Are they inside the tower?"

"That sounded like the devil," Gio added, and crossed himself in the way only he and Maria ever did.

"Not the devil," a voice we all knew boomed as the door to the chamber swung open on its own accord. "But close enough. Demon magic is the only foolproof way to battle a demon born, and keep out Finn's tagalongs."

"Demon magic?" There were no demons in Faerie. I possessed demon blood and powers, but I was no demon. There were barely any in the human world. "How—?"

The words died in my throat as the door opened all the way. My father stood near the firlon. The battle happening in the streets of Lyonesse was on full display through the flames, while Meegra and the other Feathered Fae waited at his back. Garret, too, was among our enemies, holding a tormented looking Lana bound and gagged.

Next to her, a slight form sagged, held up by two servants.

Another demon born witch—my mother.

CHAPTER THIRTY-ONE

LANA

My heart pounded so hard I thought it might crack my ribs.

Behind me, Garret grabbed my wrists tighter, as though worried that I'd burst out of the rope binding me and rush over to Finn. I wanted to scream. To make Garret listen, but even if I could speak through the gag, it wouldn't matter.

One look and I knew he wasn't really there.

Pari had mentioned the king employed a master potion maker, perhaps the Sinker Divine, who I had yet to meet. However, Ryker and Sai confirmed the king used elixirs and potions to control others. In Garret's case, it had worked. Whatever potion my father forced Garret to drink had stripped the man I loved of his soul.

When I managed to pull myself out of the depths of unconsciousness, the king had seemed happy to give the command for Garret to bind my hands and gag my mouth. I had expected his glee if this happened. Far worse was the fact that Garret had followed the orders without question.

I wasn't sure the man I loved even recognized me. At the thought, pain shot through my core. The expression on Finn's face when he took in his mother, sagging between two servants, compounded my agony.

When I first saw Mrs. Fairchild, I'd been shocked too, but I made sense of it with terrifying rapidity. I'd watched the crow swoop through the bonegate when I dropped off Mam, felt the slap of its wing against my cheek. I'd glimpsed the flash of white in his black beak. Felt the horrid question of why a Feathered Fae would be going to the Old Land burn in my gut.

Now I knew what the crow had been tasked to do. He hadn't been going for Mam, as I feared afterward, but after Finn's mother. How completely shortsighted and vain of me. Sure, a lightworker was valuable, but Finn was proving to be even more of a novelty.

Finn was the only one of us who possessed magic the King of Lyonesse didn't fully understand. I suspected my father wanted to use Finn's demon gift for his own vile purposes.

"What did you do to her?!" Finn roared, plowing into the expansive tower suite on his own, a mistake that Crystal, Ryker, and Sai rectified by dashing forward and joining him. Gio and Ebba hung back, sealing the door and standing guard. I wondered where the rest were, if they were okay.

"She's alive," the king replied in a lazy drawl. He didn't move an inch from where he stood in the center of the room, revealing a sense of dominance. "And if you behave, she'll continue to breathe," our father assured. "I hadn't realized how useful your dark power could be, Son. Not until you broke into my chambers. It's how you survived that night in Buyan, isn't it? How you got the others out."

Finn's face paled. He had to be reliving what his shadows had done that horrible night when we'd tried to assassinate an innocent woman.

"That's answer enough." Oberon smirked. "If your shadows can do that, they can annihilate the guards at my bonegate." His golden gaze dragged back toward us, to land on Mrs. Fairchild. "I will keep your mother here until I can be sure the bonegate is mine."

My brother's fists clenched. "Like hell, you will. Release her. And Lana."

"Insolent scum!" Meegra hissed, her green eyes enraged. "How dare you demand your king to release a traitor! How dare you speak to him—"

"Silence." The king held up his hand, his face like stone, and Meegra fell silent. "My son seems to believe he has the right to command me. I have to say, that's a first."

Even through the thick tension in the room, our

father's tone was smooth, charismatic. Not rushed or even irritated that war loomed outside his castle. I'd never again fall under the spell of his voice, but I could see how people had for years.

That I'd been so taken in still made me ill.

"Your Majesty, surely you will not allow his impertinence? Let me handle him." Meegra narrowed her eyes, ready to make a move should her king want it.

Behind her, four other Feathered Fae were also at the ready. I knew only Ash and Ellette, though I'd seen the other two male warriors around, I wondered about their skills. Depending on how this progressed, I might be discovering them firsthand. Would the others be strong enough to take them on?

"Stand down," Oberon quipped, as if Meegra was nothing but an annoying ferret running around his heels.

The king swept to the side, his long white hair billowing behind him while he maneuvered into a position that allowed him to take in the entire room, rather than the front of it. Meegra made a move to stand with him, to guard him, but he shook his head, gold eyes locking on me momentarily. Whatever he was about to say, wouldn't be good.

"I'll release your mother, Finn. But you understand I must keep a hostage. Lana will do, yet you must make a choice."

I inhaled sharply. My attention swung toward Finn, and I shook my head. I wanted to scream, *don't choose me!* I tried to speak through the gag, to tell him I could deal with this. I was strong enough, but from the look on his face, Finn would not cast me aside so easily.

The loyal idiot. He needed to get his mam out of here safely! The king had used her blood to shield his chambers from Finn's shadows while I was unconscious, but I very much doubted Mrs. Fairchild realized she had magic, let alone how to use it. She was more at risk. I'd get out of here . . . somehow.

"Well? What do you say, Son?"

Finn's lips pressed into a tight line. "No deal." Fire burst throughout the room.

Our father's smile widened, as if he'd expected such an outburst. "Have it your way." The king clapped, the sound echoing in the space. "Kill the guards. Keep my children alive. Take the hostages below."

The king stepped forward, arms flung wide, and a tidal wave washed through the chambers. The water put out Finn's flames, but also caught my friends unaware, bowling them over to the floor.

As my friends struggled to stand against the rush of water, the servants holding Mrs. Fairchild dragged her, rounding the firlon, en route to the hole in the ground I'd seen my father appear from many times.

Garret pulled me toward it too, following orders. Yet, as Crystal, Gio, Ryker, Ebba, Sai, and Finn met the Feathered Fae and the king head on, I could no longer stand by and hope my man would come to his senses. I had to do what I could to help. Jerking, I struggled against the binds around my wrists.

"Stop resisting." Garret pulled me closer to the entrance to the mysterious room below. "I have ord—"

It took all my strength, but I ripped away from him. Ready to defend myself, I whirled around in time to find Garret lunging at me, his gray eyes wild. Already regretting what I'd do next, I called white light and blasted it in his eyes.

Garret fell back, a roar erupting from his lips, as he stumbled into the alcove that housed a tapestry of the Sinker of Lyonesse. He flailed trying to stay on his feet. In his effort, he gripped the tapestry and ripped it from the wall.

Taking advantage of the fact that no one else controlled my movements, I called ultraviolet from the air and brought it dangerously close to my face. The searing light burned through the rag gagging me. Once the last thread melted away, I spit it out and shook my head. The heat evaporated, leaving only the lingering sensation.

Unfortunately, in the seconds used to liberate my mouth, Garret had recovered. He reached for me, once again, and I directed another beam of visible light toward his eyes. That time, I pushed into the alcove with him.

He wasn't coming to his senses, and helping, so I

would have to do this hands-free. Directing light from the air wasn't my favorite way to fight, I preferred to call the light and use my body as a conduit, because it was far more precise. But at this range, washing his face with light and blinding him was easy and wouldn't cause lasting harm. Plus, for the time being, the alcove kept us safe from other attacks. I had to take advantage of that and break the hold the potion had over him.

"Stop resisting!" Garret growled yet again, rubbing his eyes when I let up momentarily.

"Then listen," I hissed. "Just listen and keep your eyes closed. Or I'll do that again."

His jaw tightened, but he didn't open his eyes. I suspected I had seconds before he tried once again to act on his orders. I needed to tap into a deep emotion, like Sai mentioned.

"Garret, I know you're in there," I urged. "The guy who has a mother he loves. The man who believed in a girl who was shite at magic. The guy who would do anything for his friends." My gaze flickered back to Ryker and Sai. "And they'd do anything for him."

He cringed. Did that mean I was getting to him?

"Garret," I whispered. "Do you know who I am?"

"Princess Lana Fullfeather."

"No. *Just Lana.*" Memories of our first days

together and my guard's insistence that he call me 'my lady' filtered through my mind.

My moment of hesitation was too long. His arm rose and his eyes opened, the potion overriding what I was trying to do. Another beam of light left me, flooding his eyes, and he yelped, stumbling backward into the wall.

At that same moment a boom pulsed behind me. It flung me forward, closer to Garret. I tripped on the downed tapestry and barely caught myself as rubble flew through the tower. Once I was stable, I whirled about and peeked into the main room.

A gasp escaped me. Someone had blown a hole the size of a bus into the wall. I could see the kingdom beyond, as well as the fighting that still raged in the streets. The dragon flew in the skies. My throat dried up, but when Garret groaned worries over the dragon were vanquished to the back of my mind.

I twisted to find him picking himself up, shielding his eyes with his hand.

"Sorry," I offered, feeling bad that he was in pain. "But I warned you." Then, determined to get through to him, I pushed forward. "Garret, I'm Lana. Your girlfriend."

The word sounded so weak compared to how I felt for him. Wrong. I needed to be honest with myself, go deeper.

"And I love you, Garret. I love you and I need you to come back to me. To be with me. I love you."

Unsure if touching him was the right thing to do, but needing him on our side, I closed the distance between us and pressed my lips to his.

His mouth felt warm, soft, right.

Garret's body trembled for a moment before a seizure ripped through him. He pulled away, a painful sound working its way out of his throat and he fell to the floor.

"Lana!" He clutched his heart.

I froze, not sure if that was a reaction brought on by the potion or what. When his eyes flew open and locked with mine, I knew it had worked. His eyes were clear, bright. My words—my truth—had gotten through to him.

"Lana," he rasped as if there wasn't enough air in the room to fill his lungs. "I'm so sorry."

"Nothing to be sorry about. You were forced."

"I listened to *him*. I tried to hold you captive . . ."

"You weren't in your right mind, but you are now. Untie me. We have to help the others."

He quickly did as I asked, and once I had use of my hands, we turned to take in the room. My heart beat faster by the second.

Somehow, no one had fallen dead, but they had torn the room to shreds. The hole in the wall loomed, smoke pouring out of it as fire spread, forcing those engaged in battle to dance among the flames. Tapestries went up in smoke and the long table and chairs in the back of the large space were demolished or tossed about the floor. Only the firlon remained untouched.

My frantic gaze couldn't find Mrs. Fairchild.

"Finn's Mam . . ." I trailed off, unsure of what to do. Check on the woman who shouldn't be here at all? Or . . .

My father and Finn fought with all their might. Next to them, Ryker and Sai fought Meegra, who held both of them off and sniped at Finn every chance she got. The rest battled further away. My fists balled up.

Like hell would I let anyone hurt those I loved. I had to believe that if Mrs. Fairchild was taken below, she would be safe. At least for the time being.

"Come on!" I yanked Garret's hand, and we ran into the fray.

CHAPTER THIRTY-TWO

LANA

Wind swept through the gaping hole in the tower's wall. With each slash of a sword and thrust of power the battle grew more vicious. I wanted to rush around and help everyone, but knew that'd be idiotic. One person in the room mattered more than the others. One person could bring the battle to an end with a word.

Finn and our father fought closest, so I veered right to fight at my best friend's side. Garret split left to assist Ryker and Sai against Meegra.

I came up alongside Finn just as he deflected an attack from our father. "Nice work getting through to him."

"Thanks." I launched a beam of bright light in the king's eyes. Unfortunately, he was ready for my assault. His hands shielded his eyes, and a tornado expanded from floor to ceiling to whirl around him.

"Air and water," Finn quipped.

"No fire?"

We already knew our father was proficient with earth. He'd created the jungle in which we'd fought the Successional, but I'd rarely seen him use his fire. Was that because it was a weak element? Or did he like to keep it in his back pocket? If it was the latter, I hoped it would never emerge. The king's private chambers were large, but fire was hard to control. That Finn had used it earlier had been purely emotional.

"Not sure," Finn gasped, using his own air magic to push back the wind funnel encroaching on us, trying to sweep us off our feet. "I—"

Crack! The ceiling above us caved in.

Adrenaline spiking, I yanked Finn out of the way. We stumbled a few meters to the side, closer to the door.

"Three is enough anyhow!" I yelled over the fall of rubble and the shouts of others. I could no longer see them with all the dust in the air. We needed to seal the deal, and fast. Then I could make sure the others were okay. I eyed the tornado still spinning around my father, wondering how to break through it. "Finn, do you think—"

"You *fools,*" an icy voice hissed, cutting off my question.

I whirled around to find Meegra. How she had gotten there was a mystery. At least, that was the case until I glanced toward where my friends had been fighting her. The breath lodged in my throat. Garret, Ryker, and Sai were all laid flat on the ground. How!? They were the best fighters of the bunch!

My blood froze when the realization of how outnumbered we were dashed through me. That left only Crystal, Gio, and Ebba still battling with us. The flames and smoke brought on by someone's magic hid them from my eyes, but I hoped they were winning against whichever Feathered Fae they fought.

"How dare you attack the king?!" Meegra raged, snapping my attention back to her.

My eyes narrowed. She questioned why I'd attack the man who'd been using me? Who'd put me in death's path. I'd show her.

"How dare—argh!" Pain shot through me, hot and stinging. I looked down and freaked. Fire consumed my feet, and was inching its way up my calves. The sight of it was enough to terrify me, even though in the back of my mind I knew it couldn't be true. Pure fire, not true. If it were, my skin would be bubbling.

Still, it did hurt like hell, produced vile smoke, and was hot, so it was real enough. I tried to fling it off, but the flames stuck to me like glue.

"Bloody hell!" Finn screamed, his face contorting and he lost his balance.

A low, unamused chuckle rang around us. "My

children abandoned me, but Master Meegra has always stood by my side. My best soldier."

Pride gleamed in my father's eyes, making my teeth grind. Although I thought I'd seen him look upon me with pride before, that had been a lie. He'd never looked at me that way, with genuine pride and love, the kind a father and daughter with an actual relationship would share.

Oberon was even worse than I'd given him credit for, and since I learned the truth, I'd given him *plenty* of credit. I wanted to retort, to fling an insult in his face. His dismissal pissed me off, but more than that, it cut deep. He was a liar, and the worst kind of person, but that little girl who still lived inside of me couldn't help but want the attention and affection I never got from my father.

"Why would we trust you?!" Finn growled between gritted teeth. As he spoke, water sprayed from his hands, some of it landing on me.

Mist flew upward. It smelled sour, unnatural like the blaze, but it dulled my pain somewhat.

Unfortunately, all Meegra had to do was flick her hands, and the flames surged up, higher, hotter.

"You never gave us a chance to get to know the real you," Finn snarled through the agony I knew was rolling through him. "You hid your true motives."

"It was none of your business," Meegra spat. "A king answers to no one. Least of all to bastards from another realm."

Lifting her hands higher, the flames rose to our hips.

A scream ripped from my throat, and my knees buckled before I caught myself from falling into the fire. I tried to call light to our aid, but found I couldn't. I couldn't even think, let alone use magic.

Our father positioned himself right in front of us. His golden eyes took us in, unflinching at our pain. "It's a pity though, isn't it? The waste? I hoped you'd share the Fullfeather values. But you don't desire the greatness that allowed our house to rise from the slums. All of you are average, nothing special."

"Go to hell!" Finn roared as the fire inched upward, devouring us.

Suddenly, a projectile, no, *two* projectiles soared in through the open wall and slammed into Meegra's face.

She screamed and her concentration broke, alleviating the fire as she flailed. The fire gone, my senses came rushing back, and I saw the projectiles were actually Naela and Kane.

"Familiars!" my father growled and clapped his moon white hands together.

Xerxes appeared in a blaze to hover over my father's shoulder. At the sight of the phoenix, my stomach sank.

The king's moonwhite fingers pointed at Naela and Kane, both still terrorizing Meegra. "*Kill.*"

"No!" Yanking light from my surroundings to

coalesce into a sword, I leapt forward and brought it down on my father.

He had not been expecting the assault, so my light blade cut through him. A laceration gaped along his chest, and his mouth fell open as he collapsed to his knees in front of me.

"My Grace!" Meegra wailed when the hawks detached themselves from her face to flee Xerxes, who went after them as his master commanded. They soared out the hole in the wall.

I glanced back at Finn in time to see a stone statue flying for his head.

"Finn!" I pointed behind him while the statue hurled closer, mere feet away.

It nearly collided with his skull when the statue hit an invisible wall, and fell with a *thunk* to the ground. My heart leapt, and I darted back toward Finn, scanning the room as I went. It didn't take long to locate our saviors.

Queen Pari and Armina stood by the door. Armina's hand was extended as she controlled the ward that saved Finn's life.

"It's over, Oberon," Pari proclaimed, looking regal despite the blood drenching her white attire, splattering her face. "Give up now. Your soldiers are dying in the streets."

My father staggered to his feet, seething, golden eyes narrowed. "*You.* You caused all of this trouble."

"I believe that honor goes to you and you only,

Oberon." Pari tilted her chin to the ceiling. "Surrender."

A flicker of some unnamable emotion crossed the king's face, and for a moment, I thought he would do as she said. For a moment, my heart stopped. For a moment, it seemed so simple.

Then a roar shattered the king's silence, the horrible sound far too close to the tower. The flapping of wings and whipping of the wind followed. Gulping, I forced myself to turn and face what I already knew must be coming.

With the tower side blown open wide, Casimir and his dragon—which looked much healthier than before—were on full display. He aimed straight for us.

The king, seeing that the others were distracted, sprinted away, Meegra right behind him. Together, they made their way toward the dragon. Pari and Armina snapped out of it first and began hurling attacks, but I knew better. Once the dragon got here, we were screwed. We needed to get the feck out.

"Grab the fallen and get out!" I yelled, hoping the others could hear me, even though they were all in their own fights.

Finn leapt into action, and we both darted to our friends who were passed out on the ground. I wrestled Sai on to my shoulder, while he hauled Garret.

"Help! Someone help!" I screamed because no

one else had appeared yet, and I really needed them to hear me. "We need help with Ryker!"

"I'm fine," Ryker groaned, finally waking up from whatever magic Meegra had used on him.

"Like hell you are." Crystal appeared out of nowhere, ash and blood streaking her face. A bleeding wound graced her chest. "Ebba!"

The other woman was at her side in an instant. Together they hefted Ryker, and we ran for the door, but not before a flash of gold caught my eyes.

I twisted to see Arlo soaring into the tower, cutting off the dragon as it came ever closer. A second later, Arlo was at my side, a shriek ripping from his beak.

"We know! The dragon! Run!"

Pari and Armina, who had continued hurling attacks at Meegra and Oberon while they retreated, twirled to race to safety.

"Where's Gio?" Finn shouted when we were nearly to the door

My heart sank. Oh no! Where was Gio? I hadn't seen him since the fighting started. I was about to search, but the dragon was closer now. Too close. I'd never be able to find Gio and make it back. As if to confirm that thought, the dragon belted out a ferocious roar.

We made it through the door, and a few meters into the relative calm of the white hallway, before the floor shook with the dragon's landing. It shrieked its displeasure, and a rotten stench, tinged with smoke, filled the air.

Knowing we'd have to defend ourselves, we set down Sai and Garret, pushing them right against the wall. They didn't stir and that worried me. My father had given Meegra license to kill them. Had she? There wasn't time to check Sai for a pulse as we sprinted from the hall.

The door to the king's chambers was still wide open, allowing us to see inside. My father stood at the dragon's side, Meegra next to him, working her magic. My brows pinched together before what she was doing became crystal clear. Mrs. Fairchild came into view, levitating on a gust of air wielded by Meegra.

"No!" I hurled a stream of light at the king, knowing an attack on him would stop Meegra in her tracks.

My light soared and hit the king. He screamed, and I swallowed painfully. What had I done?!

Without thinking, without trying, I'd accessed ultraviolet light, and attacked him again. When he toppled over, I knew that I'd done serious damage. Meegra screamed, her face the picture of anguish as her attention trained between the levitating hostage she was trying to steal, and her downed king.

Casimir leapt off the dragon with murder in his eyes. He rushed over to our father, his gaze locked on me. Then a blast of light flashed from him, hurtling toward us. Time seemed to stop because even from that far away, I knew he did not intend us to survive that flash.

"Hit the ground!" I yelled.

Everyone dropped and a wave of heat, even more energetic and deadly than ultraviolet, rippled over us. My skin crawled, taking in the orange light. Casimir had done it. He'd accessed gamma radiation, becoming a full lightworker, capable of controlling every sliver of the spectrum.

My eyes squeezed closed as I tried to keep my shit together.

Only when the ripple of energy washing over me waned, did I dare to look up. I half expected to see Casimir marching toward us, prepared to take the lives of anyone who lived through his onslaught. Instead, I caught Meegra shoving a limp Mrs. Fairchild onto the dragon's back, just as Casimir mounted the beast once more.

"Mum!" Finn leapt, racing down the hall toward the open door.

"Finn!" I knew his pain, wanted to end it, but what on earth was he thinking?! None of us could take on a dragon!

Casimir cast one more glare, and for a moment, I thought he would launch off the beast and come for Finn. Instead, the crown prince leaned forward and spoke in the dragon's ear. I couldn't hear the words, but there was no need. The dragon opened its maw, and a furnace gleamed red hot inside.

"Finn!" I shrieked. "Stop!"

Fire bloomed from the dragon's maw, enveloping the tower, and funneling toward us. A sob lodged in my throat. I pressed my face into the cold marble again, waiting for death, hoping my friend had sought cover.

Death didn't come. The heat came. The fear. The dread. Yet, no dragon fire rained down on us. Lifting my head, I peeked, wondering what stopped it and gasped.

Everyone else remained on the ground, but Armina stood, a ward filling the space where the door to the king's private chambers would be, had it not been disintegrated by flames. Against it, fire slammed, trying to break down the ward. And just behind the ward stood Finn, his face pressed against the magical barrier, his expression pained.

"Hold fast, Armina!" Pari commanded, her tone confident in her ward-maker.

Sweat poured down Armina's face, and a muscle in her jaw fluttered wildly with the effort while the fire pounded harder—seemingly never ending. Yet, the ward-maker held firm against the blaze of dragon fire. Finally, after what seemed like a ridiculously long time, the blast of assault died.

Armina gasped for breath, but her queen was

there, helping keep her on her feet. "Keep it up. The dragon might try again."

The breath stalled in my chest, and only when the sound of beating wings filled my ears, did I inhale again. The dragon was flying away.

"Careful," Pari warned. "It might be a trap."

It might have been, but Gio was in a room alive with fire. I stood, wobbled only a bit, and ran toward Finn, who remained rooted in place, watching the crown prince take his mother. I didn't even check on my best friend before I sprinted through where the ward had been, telling me Armina had either let me through or dissolved it completely.

"Lan! Wait for me!" Finn called after me.

I couldn't wait. We'd left a man behind in the tower, and I had to find him. Frantically, I scoured the room, my gut churning when I found Gio laying in a far corner, his skin burnt, his chest fluttering with shallow, staccato breaths.

My hand flew to my mouth. "No! Gio!" I fell to my knees, wincing when my skin hit the hot stone floor. Tears pricked my eyes. A moment later, Finn was there, his hand on my shoulder.

"He's alive," Finn whispered. "I can see him breathing."

Barely. What were we going to do?

A roar sounded from outside, and I pulled in a horrified breath.

"They are leaving," Queen Pari assured me.

Glancing behind me, I found that everyone except Sai and Garret had followed us. Those with water magic were putting out the flames. Together, Crystal and Pari took up position at the gaping hole in the tower wall. They gazed out over the city.

"Are you sure?" I asked, my attention oscillating between Gio and the queen. If the dragon returned, I wouldn't even have a chance to look for a healer for my brother. We'd all be dead.

"They're heading north." The queen's lips pressed together.

Buyan was north of Lyonesse. I gulped. "Are you—"

"Buyan will be fine. I left an army there, in case this happened. And while Armina is here, there are other wardmakers who can protect the kingdom from a dragon," Pari assured, as if trying to reassure herself. "If I know your father, he will seek allies in the Beast Realm. Refuge. But this won't be the end." She turned, her eyes landing on Gio, her head shaking. "Let's get him to the healers' wing. Then we need to sweep the streets to see to the injured and dead."

CHAPTER THIRTY-THREE

FINN

I strode down the palace hallway, ignoring the rubble strewn about the floors. It would get taken care of in due time, but first, we needed to care for the injured and the people of Lyonesse.

The battle ended soon after Oberon fled the scene. His soldiers surrendered, though not willingly. Most did not believe our side of the story, and because of that, the dungeons were overflowing. It wasn't a great outcome, but we all agreed we couldn't risk a rebellion from the inside.

Although we'd done the right thing, my throat closed up as I remembered the soldiers in the cells. How they spat at us and called us bastards while we locked the doors. Even some of those we'd pulled out of the dungeons, the wrongfully accused, didn't trust us.

Thankfully, some did. Alvina, Garret's mother,

was one of those who stood with us. She'd hobbled out of the darkness, proclaiming that soon everyone would see the truth. Her look of relief when she gazed upon her son had shattered me.

King Oberon still held my mother hostage.

Tucked inside, my shadows surged, and intense sadness washed through me anew. They were commiserating with me.

"Not your fault," I muttered to the shadows. "Who knew that my mother's own blood possessed the power to keep you at bay? Certainly not me."

I hated thinking about that. Not because I'd grown to love the shadows, I was still learning to live with them, but they were useful. They were my one true advantage over a powerful, full elemental fae. Without them, I was on par with the bulk of the soldiers in the Lyonesse army. Yet, there were people who were far more skilled than your average soldier.

Armina. Prince Casimir. Queen Mauri.

I cringed. According to Lana, our lightworker brother now had power over the full spectrum. He wielded all four elements too. Casimir was a force of nature and I didn't know if anyone could take that from him, not like the king had rendered my shadows useless.

Reaching my destination, I eased open the door to the healers' wing. Gio lay in a bed, surrounded by Dak and Victoria.

"How is he?" I approached his bedside.

It was a miracle our brother had not died when the dragon fire washed over him. He hadn't spoken yet, but we had a theory as to how he survived. Crystal had posed the idea that his water magic surrounded him in a bubble of water, shielding him from the flames.

If she was right, his water magic hadn't been quite enough, as he'd still been injured, but it had kept him alive long enough for us to get him help. If he'd survived any other way, I was curious to learn how. We might need to use the tactic later.

"Not much difference." Dak's shoulders slumped. "Any word on the Sinker Divine's whereabouts?"

"None. He seems to have disappeared from the kingdom."

Those who believed us, those who weren't whispering about the Bastard Rebellion with ire, were helping to search for the Sinker Divine—the fae who could produce potions to lift veils of illusion cast by our father. It was thought that the Sinker Divine could also help bring the humans our father trapped here back to their senses.

As it stood, none of the healers knew what to do with them, and Ryker and Sai's grandmother could only do so much to reverse potions others had taken. Her ingredients were limited, but the Sinker Divine, wherever he was, had to be better stocked.

We just had to find the bloody snake.

"The king might have sent him into hiding as we marched south," I said.

Victoria exhaled a soft, resigned sigh. "What about the city? How's the rebuilding going? We've been on Gio duty for hours and you're the first to visit." Fear brimmed in her eyes, fear of hearing the truth, which was understandable.

Having Queen Pari here was helpful. She smoothed over many matters pertaining to the kingdom and rebuilding. However, her presence was also harmful, in the sense that most of the citizens of Lyonesse still mistrusted her.

Even after the battle stopped, scuffles broke out among the fae of Lyonesse. Neighbor fought against neighbor. Friend against friend. Family against family.

"I haven't heard of anything for a couple hours." I looked out the window above Gio's bed, and caught sight of the torn-apart city beyond it. "Lana will make a speech soon. She wants us all present for support." Needed us there was more like it. My best friend was terrified of giving a speech, knowing no matter what she said, most would view her as a usurper rather than who she was—someone who wanted to free the fae of Lyonesse from tyranny.

Victoria's dark blue eyes traveled to Gio, locking on his burnt skin for a moment before trailing back to me. "Someone will watch him?"

"Alvina will be by. I just wanted you two to know, and to check on him for myself. But I have a few things to do before the gathering. See you later, okay?"

With that, I left the healing wing, more relieved than I wanted to admit by being on the move. Gio had been the worst injured, and I hated seeing my fun, vivacious brother like that.

His poor state also made me wonder how much worse it was going to get. Our brother had a dragon for a familiar and we hadn't known. What other secrets was our father keeping? How many other allies did they have?

How horrible would his retaliation be?

It didn't matter, I supposed. Late last night Lana, Crystal, Queen Pari, and I had come to an agreement. Once everyone healed, once we had convinced the army to fight with us, we would find King Oberon and force him to bend the knee. We would officially dethrone him, because he couldn't be trusted.

I hoped we would do so before he did anything to my mother.

When I found Lana, she was alone in our father's private chambers. In truth, I hadn't even known I was heading there, or that she would be there, but something told me to look there. We'd been friends long enough that I knew how her mind worked.

My steps took me deeper into the chamber, and I glanced around at the tower. Everything was burnt to a crisp. Well, everything but the firlon. There was some type of magic in that object that allowed it to sustain the dragon flames blasting over the stone.

"What are you doing?" I leaned against the enchanted object. At the far side of the room, Naela and Kane perched at the edge of the hole blasted open by magic. They gazed out on to the city, equally blackened and chaotic as the room where we stood.

"Still trying to get into the subterranean chamber." Lana scowled at the circle on the floor that resembled an overly-large manhole, but made of stone. "I've seen him rise from it countless times. It seemed a simple mechanism, and yet, I can't open it. What in the world is he hiding in there?"

The muscles in my jaw locked. King Oberon had kept my mother there, and he hadn't opened it for the servants who escorted her. So how had they done it? "Did you find the servants who took Mum down there?"

Lana's head slowly shook. "I didn't even see them after the battle. They might still be in there." She didn't say that she doubted they were alive, but it was in her tone.

I agreed. Meegra levitated my mum out of the chamber, but she hadn't helped the servants out, and it wouldn't have been difficult for her to kill the servants with magic. She was, after all, the Master Feathered Fae. A killer, and a skilled one at that.

"I would try with my shadows, but they still can't emerge in this tower." Whatever our father had done with my mother's blood seemed permanent. At least it was in this space. I'd tried to access them a half dozen times so they could help us into the subchamber, but they stayed put, deep inside me.

Lana loosed a long breath. "I figured. I don't know if there will be answers down there, but there has to be a reason he wouldn't let anyone enter it."

"He might have let Meegra in his little hidey hole," I said. "Her magic got my mother out after you struck our father."

An unnamable expression fluttered across Lana's face. I sensed she felt bad for injuring our father. Lan possessed a good heart, and didn't like to cause pain, no matter how much someone deserved it.

"You did what you had to do," I assured her.

Her golden eyes lifted from the floor to meet mine. "And there's still so much more to be done."

"That there is," I agreed. "We'll get it done together. We'll establish new leadership in this king-dom, *fair and good* leadership, bring back magic, and make the fae happy. We'll change lives for the better, Lan."

"Yeah," she murmured with a soft smile. "And save your mother. Looks like we have a lot on our plate."

Walking to my best friend's side, I wrapped her in my arms. We hadn't touched often since we learned we shared blood, for a while it had been much too awkward, but all that was behind us now. We had so many important things to deal with, and a deeper understanding of each other than we ever had.

"Together, we can do anything," I vowed.

"The light and the shadow." Lana chuckled, squeezing me back and resting her head on my shoulder. "If I've learned anything since being here, it's that there's room for both, time for both. I'm so glad you came to Faerie with me."

Incredibly conflicted about that notion, I inhaled deeply, but could not deny my gut reaction. "So am I, Lan. So am I."

If you enjoyed this book, please make sure to leave a review. They motivate me to write the next book and give me a way to gauge reader interest in my series.

The Bonegate Series was born after I visited Ireland, the homeland of Lana and Finn. I went to Trinity, their university, flew a hawk, and journeyed the west country (even the Doolin cave Lana and Finn got stuck in!). All the while, these characters and their siblings and love interests were in my mind, forming, coming to life. I hope you love the as much as I do!

There is more to this world. If you have not read The Fanged Fae Series, a sister series to The Bonegates Series, it's available and complete now. The Fanged Fae Series features, Queen Mauri of Ys.

All the magic,

Ashley McLeo

<u>Spellcasters Spy Academy Series (Magic of Arcana Universe)</u>

A Legacy Witch: Year One

A Rebel Witch: Year Two

A Crucible Witch: Year Three

An Academy Witch: Prequel

The Complete Spellcasters Spy Academy Boxset

<u>The Wonderland Court Series (Magic of Arcana Universe)</u>

Alice the Dagger

Alice the Torch

<u>Standalone Novel</u>

Stealing Maid Marian's Heart (Magic of Arcana Universe)

<u>Fanged Fae Series - A Bonegates sister series</u>

Blood Moon Magic

Faerie Blood

<u>The Bonegates Series - A Fanged Fae sister series</u>

Hawk Witch

Assassin Witch

Traitor Witch

Illuminator Witch

<u>**The Royal Quest Series**</u>

Dragon Prince

Dragon Magic

Dragon Mate

Dragon Betrayal

Dragon Crown

Dragon War

<u>**The Starseed Universe - An Irish Witch Urban Fantasy**</u>

Prophecy of Three

Souls of Three

Rising of Three

The Starseed Universe (five-book boxset)

ABOUT THE AUTHOR

Ashley lives in Portland with her husband, Kurt, their dog, Flicka, and the house ghost that sometimes makes appearances in her charming, old home.

When she's not writing urban fantasy and portal fantasy novels she enjoys traveling the world, reading, kicking butt at board games (she recommends Splendor and Dominion), and frequenting taquerias.

For all the latest releases and updates, subscribe to Ashley's newsletter, The Coven.

As a Coven member you will receive a weekly update from Ashley and exclusive teasers, information about giveaways, and sneak peeks into her author life. You can also find her Faccbook group, Ashley's Reader Coven and join in on the fun there!